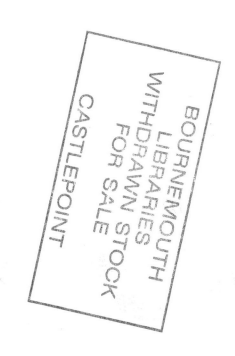

Old Bones
Buried Under

By the same author

Loose Cannon
The Meddlers

Old Bones
Buried Under

June Drummond

ROBERT HALE · LONDON

ISBN-10: 0-7090-8100-6
ISBN-13: 978-0-7090-8100-5

Robert Hale Limited
Clerkenwell House
Clerkenwell Green
London EC1R 0HT

2 4 6 8 10 9 7 5 3 1

Typeset in 11/16pt Sabon
by Derek Doyle & Associates, Shaw Heath
Printed in Great Britain by St Edmundsbury Press
Bury St Edmunds, Suffolk
Bound by Woolnough Bookbinding Limited

Old Bones
Buried Under

Prologue

On April Fool's Day of 2005, Chief Detective Inspector Fergus Lowry of Abbotsfell was informed by the assistant chief constable of his area that he had been promoted to the rank of superintendent, with effect from 1 May.

The ACC also announced that Superintendent Burne, the present Abbotsfell incumbent, who was due to retire in May, had been drafted to a task force dealing with urgent anti-terrorist measures, and would for the last month of his service reside and work in Buckingham.

Which meant that Fergus would be in charge of the understaffed Abbotsfell station for the next few weeks.

The ACC's parting remark was that nothing much could go wrong in a month, which caused Fergus to reflect that the ACC's opinions were infallible. He was always wrong.

I

The storm was a killer.

It sprang from the pack ice of Hudson Bay, sank a coaster off Newfoundland, and ravened eastwards to maul the belly of England. The lash of its tail brought torrential rains that flooded rivers and drowned flatlands. By the time it reached Abbotsfell in the Chilterns, it had claimed fourteen lives.

In its last throes it found the landfill on Abbots Mount, and clawed a long wound from which welled a thick sludge of mud, builders' rubble and household junk, The mess surged down the hillside and engulfed the road that linked Abbotsfell with the free-way to Watford.

The tremor of the landslide was felt by the occupants of the house 400 yards away. John Thorneycroft, about to lift his tankard from the table at his side, turned to stare at his host.

'What in hell was that?'

Fergus Lowry was already on his feet, hurrying to throw open a window. The rain had ceased, but icy gusts still swept across the valley and whined through the distant woods.

'It has to be the tip,' Fergus said, and crossed the room to the telephone.

'What tip? Tip of what?' Thorneycroft was aggrieved. April was supposed to be springtime. Fergus had promised sunshine and trout fishing, not tempest and earthquake.

Fergus ignored him, speaking urgently into the phone. After some minutes he came back to the fireside. 'There's an old sand pit on the Mount,' he said. 'Five years ago the council decided to fill it in. People were allowed to dump anything except toxic or perishable waste. I kept telling them the land was unstable, but no one took a blind bit of notice. They only stopped the dumping last year. Thank God Tess and the kids aren't here.' He reached for the keys of his car. 'I have to go and check the damage.'

Thorneycroft stood up. 'I'll go with you.'

'No need, mate. Sergeant Barry's bringing up the cavalry.'

'Nevertheless.'

'Good then.' Fergus looked pleased. 'I'll find you some gear.'

He rummaged in the cloakroom for oilskins and boots. Thorneycroft reflected that many men would have sent subordinates to deal with a rubbish dump, but Fergus was over-conscientious. They'd served five years together in the SAS, and ended up in the same orthopaedic ward, Fergus because he'd never learned to run from trouble, and Thorneycroft because he tended to leap before he looked. Now Fergus was a country cop, and Thorneycroft a forensic psychiatrist. Plodder and chancer; nothing had changed,

Outside, the ditches overflowed, and the one-time trout stream to their right roared and tore at its banks. Fergus edged the 4x4 along until its headlamps shone full on the landslide. It looked menacing, standing ten feet high across the road, held in precarious check by a scrawny stand of pine and blackthorn. Its sides drooled glaucous mud.

The two men climbed out of the Jeep and Fergus handed Thorneycroft a torch. 'I'm going up the Mount,' he said. 'There may be more to come down. You keep an eye on this lot.'

He moved away up the slope. Thorneycroft studied the debris. It scared him. The mass sucked and muttered as if alive. Fed by a gush of water from the hillside, it swelled as he watched.

His eyes focused on an object that was surfing the crest of the pile. It spun sluggishly on a slick of mud, toppled, and shot down to the tarmac at his feet. It was a kit-bag such as sportsmen use, and it stank like a wet dog. He bent to examine it. Its heavy plastic zipper seemed intact. Thorneycroft tugged at it and the bag opened, exposing a perspex box furred with mildew. He scrubbed it clean with his handkerchief and shone the torch on its surface. What he saw caused him to let out a yell for Fergus.

A skull leered up at them from the shadows of the box. It was as toothless as a Halloween pumpkin, and some trick of refracted light made its empty eye sockets glint with unholy malice.

They studied it in silence. Then Fergus said, 'Maybe it's plastic. A theatre prop, or a throw-out from some medical school.'

Thorneycroft reached to touch it. 'Nope. It's bone. What's more, the teeth have been knocked out, a crude hammer and chisel job, you can see the cuts in the jaw bone. Could be someone wanted to prevent identification by dental records.'

Fergus straightened. 'Are you trying to say this is a crime scene? You know what that means? It means I can't move anything until the medical officer's made his examination. I'm supposed to take photographs and measurements and secure the area of the crime.' He swept an arm at the crumbling hillside, the spreading dump. 'How do I secure this? Umh? When those trees collapse, which they bloody soon will, this whole heap will roll down into the river, and God knows where it will end.'

'You can secure the human remains,' Thorneycroft suggested. 'Leave them here and you can kiss them goodbye.'

'Too right.' Fergus stooped to lift one end of the kit-bag. 'Take that end, and keep it level. I don't want anything damaged.'

They carried the bundle to the Jeep, wrapped it in a groundsheet, and locked it in the back. As they did so, three vehicles arrived from the town. A police car delivered Sergeant Barry, built like a lock forward, and a Detective Sergeant Kelly, whip thin with knowing eyes. There followed a truck piled high with sandbags, and a van from the Public Works Department, both of which pulled up at the foot of the Mount.

All the newcomers went into immediate conference with Fergus. Left to himself, Thorneycroft headed up the hill. He found a sheep-track and climbed it until he was confronted with a chain-link fence. Beyond that lay a dirt-track that must once have given access to the landfill. Now it was obviously disused, clogged by nettles and brambles. A second fence protected its upper side. Thorneycroft guessed that somewhere along it lay a locked gate.

He started back down the hill. On the far side of the landslip he could see the headlights of two more trucks. A detachment from Watford, perhaps?

Fergus was waiting for him on the road.

'I have to get back to the nick,' he said. 'I must talk to the top brass. This road's going to be closed for some time. We have to search the muck in case there are other body parts. We're short-handed at the moment, with Voysey in hospital. I'm going to need reinforcements. I'll take Kelly with me now, and Barry will stay to see to things here.'

'What about the bag?'

'We'll drop it at the morgue. Dr Taft – our pathologist – will meet us there, and Kelly can stay to see to unpacking and photographs and the rest. Taft will do the pm tomorrow. I'd be very grateful if you'd attend that, John, and we'll need a statement from you, about finding the skull.'

'I'll make it tonight, if you like.'

'Tomorrow will do. I'm sorry about all this. It's a lousy way for you to start your leave.'

'Forget it. What can I do to help?'

Fergus hesitated. 'Will you go back to the house and phone Tess? she's in Auckland with her parents right now. The number's in the book on my desk. Tell her about the landslide, tell her no one's hurt, the house is safe, and she's to stay in New Zealand.

Don't let her freak. I'll call her tomorrow.' He gave the house keys to Thorneycroft. 'And field any incoming calls, will you? Tell 'em about the landslip, not about the bag.'

A man from the PWD interrupted them. 'Chief Inspector, we ought to sandbag the lower side of the road; keep the stuff from shifting.'

'It's too late for that,' Fergus said. 'The roots of the trees are already lifting. I can't risk having men buried alive.'

'I know my job.' The man was affronted, and Fergus dropped an arm round his shoulders. 'I know you do, Jimmy. Put the sandbags along the lower edge of the tip, stop any more muck coming down. That's the best we can do.'

Thorneycroft left them to it and headed back to the house. In Fergus's study he checked his watch – 8.15, breakfast time in New Zealand. He made the call to Tess. It took him some time to convince her that Fergus, the house, and the residents of Abbotsfell were unharmed, and she mustn't think of returning to England.

'I hate being away,' she said tearfully, 'but Dad's so frail, he loves having the boys here, and there may not be another chance.'

Soothed at last, she ended the call. Thorneycroft shed his oilskins and boots, raided the kitchen for bread, salami, cheese and pickles, and poured himself a Scotch on the rocks. He settled in a chair by the telephone, and redirected the occasional calls to the police station.

At ten, Fergus rang. 'We took the bag to Taft,' he said. 'He had a quick look at the skull.'

'And?'

'It's real, not plastic. There's a hole in the back of the cranium. Taft says the old blunt instrument. I told the assistant chief constable what Taft said, and he didn't buy it. He thinks the skull's probably a student's prank.'

'What sort of prankster bashes out a skull's teeth and chucks it on a rubbish dump?'

'Friends of the ACC, maybe. It doesn't look as if we'll get much help from outside. Everyone's understaffed, and worried about possible terror attacks. Did you speak to Tess?'

Thorneycroft reported the conversation, and Fergus thanked him and went back to work.

It was about an hour later that Thorneycroft was drawn to the window by a creaking, rumbling noise. He saw lights moving rapidly away from the Mount. The barrier of trees below the road had collapsed, and the debris was rolling over and around the wreckage, sliding towards the river.

He was tempted to return to the scene of action, but mindful of Fergus's wishes, he watched from a distance.

By midnight the phone calls had petered out. He lay down on the sofa and went to sleep.

He was woken at six by the sound of a loudhailer. He rolled off the sofa and went to the window. The wind had dropped and the scene was as busy as a Brueghel.

On the Mount, workmen were building a makeshift retaining wall across the bottom of the tip. Most of the debris that had blocked the road had transferred itself to the river-meadow, damming the water and creating a shallow lake in the field beyond.

Labourers were shovelling what was left of the dump into drums, which they then loaded into a large cartage van. Sieving that lot for pieces of skeleton would be a mammoth task. Labour intensive. Tell that to the commissioner.

He bathed, shaved, dressed in jeans and sweater and made for the kitchen. The Esse stove provided welcome heat. He brewed coffee and made toast, and was settled at the table when he heard the Jeep come up the drive. Fergus walked into the hall, spotted Thorneycroft, and came to join him.

'Coffee's fresh,' Thorneycroft said, but Fergus waved the offer away.

'I had something at the station. I'm only here to clean up a bit and phone Tess. And sort things out with you.'

'What's to sort?'

'I can't take leave as I planned, and I can't leave you here, with no one to cook or entertain you.'

Thorneycroft buttered toast. 'Last night you asked me to attend the post mortem. Does the request still stand?'

'Yes, of course. I'd be glad of your advice. I only wish I could appoint you to the case.'

'Why don't you? Won't the powers that be accept me?'

'Of course they will, but . . . well . . . we couldn't afford your fee.'

'Bugger the fee, I'll do it pro bono. I'm an approved consultant to the Metropolitan Police – arrange for them to second me to you for the duration of my leave.' As Fergus still hesitated, Thorneycroft smiled. 'I want to be part of this investigation, Fergus. I found the skull. I'm involved.' The smile broadened. 'And Claudia Hibberd lives near Harpenden.'

Fergus brightened. 'Oh? I didn't know you were still chasing after her.'

'Faint but pursuing,' Thorneycroft said. 'What time does Taft want us?'

'Ten. Are you sure you want to be part of this?'

'Mm.'

Fergus went off to make his call to Tessa. Thorneycroft poured himself a second cup of coffee and drank it slowly, eyes closed. He was trying to conjure up Claudia's face, but the image of the skull intruded, blocking her out.

Thorneycroft scowled at it.

'I'll see you at the morgue,' he said.

II

Walking to the mortuary next morning, Thorneycroft asked Fergus how he rated Dr Taft.

'He's good at his job,' Fergus said.

'So was Genghis Khan.'

Fergus didn't reply. He was scanning the High Street, which had borne the full blast of the storm. Shop windows were shattered, tiles littered the pavement, and the pin oak by the war memorial lay with its roots in the air.

Thorneycroft said mildly, 'If I'm on this case, I have to know how to handle your resident pathologist.'

Fergus grunted. 'Nobody can handle Taft. He's efficient, in court he's brilliant – he can reduce expert witnesses to pulp but he's the devil to work with. He's arrogant, rude, he hates to co-operate. You'll just have to roll with the punches.'

They reached the mortuary. It formed the central area of a face-brick complex bestowed on Abbotsfell by a tobacco tycoon. To its right was the courthouse, and beyond that, the police station.

Inside the building they passed the reception desk, computer rooms, X-ray and laboratory facilities worthy of a major city. The Abbotsfell dead, thought Thorneycroft, did it in style.

In a changing room they donned sterile suits, theatre caps, masks, boots and gloves. Taft, Fergus said, was obsessive about such things. A uniformed assistant conducted them to the morgue and autopsy sector. As they passed through the steel entrance doors they met the smell of formaldehyde, carbolic and deodorant that couldn't quite vanquish the odour of pickled death.

Taft was in the main autopsy theatre, watching a man in green overalls position two metal gurneys under a hanging microphone. Whatever was on the gurneys was covered by sterile cloths.

Taft did not greet the newcomers, but held up a hand, warning them to remain by the door.

He was a small man, and his surgeon's suit looked too large for his thin frame. His face in profile was parrot-like, a short curved beak couched between puffy cheeks.

Thorneycroft studied his surroundings. The theatre was well lit and well equipped. A mobile camera on a stand stood against one wall. The dissection tables were empty, and no one was working at the machines and instrument tables.

Taft dismissed his attendant, and signed to Fergus and Thorneycroft to approach him. He ignored Fergus's polite greeting, and fixed Thorneycroft with a round-eyed stare.

'The chief inspector tells me you're to be drafted into this enquiry,' he said.

'I hope so.'

The round eyes switched to Fergus. 'Has the appointment been condoned?'

'Confirmed', Fergus corrected.

Taft sniffed. 'So, Doctor, I understand you are described as a forensic psychiatrist? A profiler, is that the word?'

'Only on American TV,' Thorneycroft said.

'Huh! Frankly, I don't consider yours to be an exact science. It is mere guesswork, incapable of being scientifically proven.'

'A great deal of what is termed science is in fact guesswork. We theorize about black holes and the Big Bang, don't we, but we can't test our theories in a laboratory.'

17

Taft said tartly, 'I believe in what can be proven. I don't believe in fairy tales. Now I suggest we get on with our work.'

He turned to lift the cloth from the first gurney. Arranged on its steel surface were the trophies from the landslip – the kit-bag, the perspex box (now split in two) and the skull. Thorneycroft started to lift the mask to his face but Taft flapped a hand at him. 'No need for that. All these items have been massively contaminated, on the tip and elsewhere. Your puny breath won't affect the evidence.'

He reached up and switched on the overhead microphone, intoned the date, the time and the names of his companions, and launched into his recital.

'Last night, Chief Inspector, you delivered certain items into my care. They have been correctly handled, labelled and stored so as to ensure that the chain of evidence is not broken.

'This morning my deputy, Dr Levine, and I made a preliminary examination of the material. We recorded our findings on tape. A copy of the tape awaits you at the reception desk. Also copies of the back-up photographs taken by Levine on polaroid camera during out work. We have taken numerous samples, which are now being tested in our laboratory. These preliminaries being done, we cleaned the articles in order to try to discern their prove-nance. Sergeant Kelly was present during all these operations.'

Taft, plainly, had conducted the post mortem without Thorneycroft. A warning to keep off his turf.

Fergus looked displeased. 'Were there fingerprints?'

'None that we could discover. The kit-bag was soaked with effluent from the tip. The box had been wiped clean of prints, inside and out. As you know, we have sophisticated means of detecting prints. We found none.'

Fergus nodded. Taft moved closer to the gurney and adopted the lecturer's stance.

'Now. The outermost covering of your bundle of tricks was the kit-bag. It's made of heavy plastic, dark purplish blue, with the maker's logo, 'Wimbourne Sports', on its side. The firm is well known. It manufactures medium-priced sports goods of all kinds. I imagine that over the past two years, many thousands of this type of bag have been sold in the UK and abroad. Our people will make a full assessment of the item; they will try to determine where, when and how it was manufactured and sold, but that will take time.

'As you can see, the bag is badly stained. We will try to establish whether the marks on its outer and inner surfaces came from the tip, or from other sources.

'My own examination was necessarily superficial, but I did not find bloodstains or other human emissions on the bag. We'll run further tests. After such long exposure to the elements of earth and sky, there's little chance we'll find trace material such as skin, hair or fibres, but we'll do our best.'

Thorneycroft intervened. 'You speak of "two years", and "long exposure", Dr Taft. Are you saying that the skull has been on the landfill for two years?'

'No. I'm saying that over the past two years many thousands of kit-bags of this make must have been sold, and the task of identifying the last owner of this one will be very difficult. I am also saying that the bag has been exposed to the elements for some time. The tip was closed to the public over a year ago.'

'The kit-bag could have been dumped on the landfill more recently, by anyone nimble enough to climb the gate or fence.'

Taft shrugged. 'Time will show what is fact and what mere conjecture.' He moved towards the perspex box. 'Inside the kit-bag was this box, made of very tough perspex. We had to cut the lid free. It had been sealed with strong glue, which we will analyze.'

'Any identifying marks on the box?' Fergus asked.

'A serial number.' Taft lifted the base of the box and turned it so that they could see the number embossed on the perspex. 'There's no maker's name. Possibly there was some kind of label. London may be able to help us there.'

'Try Merrifield and Todd,' Thorneycroft said. 'Wholesalers. They make glassware, and their goods are despatched from their factories in this sort of box. I have one at home.'

Fergus was already scribbling in his notebook. 'If this is one of their products,' he said, 'there's a chance they can tell us the area of sale, or even the name of the first buyer.'

Taft wasn't listening. He had lifted the skull in his gloved hands, and swivelled it round to face Thorneycroft.

'We come to our chief exhibit,' he said. 'The late Mr Joe Soap, orphan of the storm. Luckily, his box was cushioned by bubble plastic, which saved him from damage on the landfill. There were no prints on the sheeting, or the inside of the box. No trace elements.' He ran a fingertip over the skull's surface.

'Joe Soap himself is remarkably clean. There is no skin, flesh or ligament attached to the bone. No brain matter. No hair. No teeth. Clean as a whistle. It's my opinion he was carefully washed.' Taft flashed a yellow smile. 'He may even have been boiled.'

'Boiled?' Fergus grimaced.

'As in, "Go boil your head".' Taft broke into giggles. 'Cheer up, Chief, he was dead at the time.' Taft raised the skull to display its underside. 'Note the foramen magnum, the hole through which the spinal cord would have been connected to the brain. There's no sign of damage in that area. The skull was probably detached from the rest of the body a considerable time after death, when decomposition was well advanced, or complete, and violence was not required.'

'How long ago would that be?' Fergus demanded.

Taft puffed out his cheeks. 'It would probably take a year for the body to become totally skeletonized. Circumstances vary, of course. I don't think Joe was exposed to the elements. I think he was buried and left to return to dust in nature's way. Maggots and burrowing predators could have helped things along. Then at some point after the bones began to disarticulate, the head was dug up, cleaned, and the teeth were removed, in an attempt to prevent identification of the victim.'

Thorneycroft said, 'Why do you say the body was buried?'

Taft did not answer directly. He turned the skull, revealing the back. Near its base was a hole, surrounded by a network of fracture lines.

'Blunt instrument,' Fergus said.

'Yes. Someone or something struck him a crushing blow. I'd say it was a right-handed attacker, who stood slightly to the side of the victim and delivered a swinging blow. The fracture lines form a star, you see, and there's a piece of bone missing from the middle of the star. We searched the box and wrappings but we couldn't find the missing piece.'

'What sort of weapon, do you think?'

'Mmm . . . it could be a stick with a knobbed head, or any piece of metal or wood that had that shape. Which is speculation, not fact, you understand.'

'Was the blow fatal?'

'Potentially. It would have rendered the victim unconscious, and damaged the brain, but it might not have been the immediate cause of death. Somebody could have cut Joe's throat, or shot him in the heart, after he was knocked out.'

Fergus frowned. 'That crack on the head . . . How can you be sure it didn't happen while he was underground, or on the land-fill?'

Taft touched a finger to the fracture lines. 'Here, at the centre, round the hole, you see how the bone's bent inwards? The injury was inflicted on a living person. Live bone . . . green bone . . . bends. Dead bone doesn't.'

Thorneycroft repeated his earlier question. 'Why do you say he was buried?'

Taft beckoned him closer. Pointing, he said, 'There were grains of sand trapped in the fracture lines, inside the skull. We retrieved samples. Dr Levine is an expert in such matters. He says it's not chalk soil, which we have in this district, but soil from a sand-and-loam area like south-eastern England. It's likely the victim was buried in that sort of soil, and left there long enough for disartic-ulation of the skeleton to take place. Then something decided the killer to disinter the head, forcibly remove the teeth, and transfer the skull to our landfill.'

'Why go to all that trouble?' said Fergus. 'Why not just chuck it in the Thames, or smash it to pieces?'

'Why indeed? Happily I don't have to answer such questions. I leave riddles to the profilers of the world.' Taft offered the skull to Thorneycroft. 'Well, Doctor, what's your opinion?'

Thorneycroft examined it in silence. At last he said, 'The bone is strong, the cranium large. Large mastoids and a well-defined brow ridge. The wisdom teeth had erupted. I can't swear to the sex without seeing the pelvic bones, but I'd say the victim was Homo sapiens, Caucasian, a mature male. We'll learn more from the labo-ratory tests.' He looked at Fergus. 'You'll arrange for a reconstruction of the face?'

'Yes, as soon as possible.'

Taft said harshly, 'Then I hope you find someone better at the job than that idiot Dempsey. The last model he made looked like the queen of the fairies.'

Thorneycroft was startled by the rancour in Taft's voice. He was glowering at Fergus like a child deprived of a toy. Could it be he resented not having a reconstruction expert on his staff?

Fergus ignored the scowl. 'Why was the kit-bag so heavy?' he said.

At once, Taft's mood changed. He smiled seraphically, and with the air of a conjuror presenting his best trick, he stepped to the second gurney and whisked away its covering cloth.

Alone on the polished steel stood a second skull.

'Oh, Grandmother,' said Thorneycroft softly, 'what big teeth you have.'

'All the better to eat you with,' Taft answered, and for the second time that morning, he broke into delighted giggles.

III

Fergus moved first. Striding past Taft, he picked up the second skull and hefted it in his hands. 'This isn't real, it's a plaster cast. Where and when did you find it?'

Taft looked complacent. 'First thing this morning. Your man Kelly watched me unpack it from the bag. Didn't he tell you?'

Fergus compressed his lips. There'd been no chance to talk to Kelly. There were bones to be picked with Taft, but not now, in public. Taft seemed disappointed at the lack of response.

'I imagine it was placed in the bag as ballast,' he said, 'to make sure Joe Soap sank to the bottom of the landfill.'

Fergus eyed him. 'Why use a thing like this for ballast, when an ordinary brick would do?'

Taft spread his hands. 'Frankly, if I had to jettison that monstrosity or a brick, I'd save the brick every time.'

Thorneycroft stepped forward. 'May I see it?'

Fergus handed it over.

It was smaller than the real skull, and the plaster had been coated with a paint or fixative that gave it a copper-brown sheen. It was, he thought, the model of an apeman, but not like any he'd seen in museums or on TV. This face was flatter, the brow ridge less heavy, and the jaws didn't project in a snout. The nose was quite narrow and sharp. The teeth, though large, were not the

24

formidable fangs of an ape.

Glancing up, Thorneycroft saw that both Fergus and Taft were watching him intently. He said slowly, 'I'm no palaeontologist, but this could have been made from a genuine fossil ... a recent species of hominid. Not Homo sapiens, but something very close. It's gracile, not robust.' He caught Ferqus's mystified look, and smiled. 'Gracile species are lighter-boned than robust types.'

'Why make a cast?' Fergus asked. 'I thought fossils were hard, like rocks.'

'They're more fragile than they look,' Thorneycroft answered. 'Some of them are worth big money. Owners keep them under lock and key, but a cast can be made for display in a museum, or for a lecturer who doesn't want to lug a valuable fossil around the world.'

'So this one probably belonged to someone in that line? A fossil collector, or a lecturer?'

'Seems likely. It's not the sort of thing you find on the average mantelpiece.'

Thorneycroft turned to hand the cast back to Taft, and saw that he was staring fixedly at the items on the first gurney. His face was twisted in an expression of concern, even fear, and Thorneycroft said quickly, 'Is there a problem?'

For a moment Taft stared at him blankly, then he erupted in fury. 'I don't want that damn junk,' he yelled, 'and I don't want your fancy opinions, either. You're talking poppycock. You don't have a shred of proof that it's the cast of a genuine fossil. There's no signature on it, no date, no place of origin. Any palaeoanthropologist worthy of the name takes care to establish the provenance of his finds. That thing's a fake, concocted from a child's picture book, or the brain of some crackpot. It probably came from the sort of shop that sells kitsch to tourists.'

He snatched the cast and slammed it down on the second gurney, then tossed a cloth over it. Wheeling to face Fergus, he said, 'I've wasted enough time on your guessing games. You'll have my report, with the X-rays and lab-test results, as soon as possible. Satisfied?'

'There's the question of DNA,' Fergus began, but Taft cut him short.

'I told you, we've taken all the necessary samples. DNA's not my job. Talk to Michaelson in Watford, or one of the London gurus.'

He made as if to walk away, but Fergus blocked his path. 'A moment, Doctor. The inquest's set down for Tuesday, but it's bound to be adjourned. There are so many uncertainties.'

'What uncertainties? I have none. The man was murdered. You'll get a verdict of murder by person or persons unknown.'

'Not from old Dr Smythe. He'll want a lot more clarity than we can supply right now. We can't even be sure it's murder. The man could have been a victim of culpable homicide, or even of accident.'

'And no doubt after he died he packed his head in a box and carted it across country to our landfill. Grow up, man!'

Fergus reddened. 'It might not have been the killer who tried to conceal the skull. Innocent people, confronted with a dead body, sometimes lose their heads.'

'Like he lost his,' Taft quffawed.

Fergus said sharply, 'People get scared and confused and they lie to the police. They're a pain in the arse, but they're not killers. The point is, we've a lot of work to do before we start looking for verdicts. We have to finish searching the tip, the river, and the surrounding ground for body parts. We have to try to establish the identity of the victim.'

'Small chance.'

'I mean to have a bloody good try.' Fergus was now as angry as Taft 'I shall be seeking expert opinion about that cast. It raises questions. I want answers.'

Taft whiffled his lips and glanced at his watch. Fergus moved close to him.

'This case could drag on for months, or it could break wide open tomorrow. When it breaks it will receive a lot of publicity, and that will play hell with my job, and yours. I do not want information leaked to the media, or to any unauthorized person. Apart from yourself, how many people know what was in that bag?'

Taft glared. 'Three. Your man, Kelly, Dr Levine, who is assistant pathologist, and Donald Monk, who's in charge of the storage facilities here. None of the three is likely to leak information. The laboratory technicians will be told only as much as they need to enable them to carry out their tasks. They will not be fed the lurid tales so dear to the heart of the press and the public. Good day, gentlemen.'

Taft marched to the main doors of the theatre, pressed a button to open them, and stood with bent head while Fergus and Thorneycroft walked past him.

They returned to the changing room, shed their green robes, washed away the clinging smell of the morgue, and put on their own clothes. As they passed the reception desk, Fergus collected the cassette Taft had promised them, and a bulky manilla envelope marked 'PHOTOGRAPHS DO NOT BEND'.

It was a relief to be back in the world of the living. The sullen skies of early morning had given way to washy sunshine, and the High Street looked tidier than it had done two hours ago, but at its far end a small crowd milled and chanted, watched by a uniformed policeman.

'Momple', said Fergus disgustedly, and at Thorneycroft's look of enquiry, said, 'Tyrone Momple, the town nitpicker. He's a stringer for several newspapers, and in his spare time he organizes protests. I hope to God he's not aiming to camp on our doorstep.'

It seemed, however, that Momple had had his say, and when they reached the entrance to the police station, they were met only by Kelly, who fell into step with them and gave Fergus a rapid summary of events.

'The road past the Mount's about cleared,' he said. 'They're sifting the muck that came down from the tip. Seventeen sets of false teeth so far, but no more human remains. The divers from River Patrol are fetching up junk; again, no bones. Reckon we won't find any more.'

'We have to complete the search. Where's Barry?'

'Inside, sir. He left Talmage to look after the road problem. We've been checking our own list of missing persons, and there's yards more coming in from the national computer bank. The lists are on your desk. And DI Voysey wants to see you – says can you call at the hospital this evening?'

Fergus nodded. 'What was Momple on about?'

Kelly rolled his eyes. 'Everything. "The road block deprives citizens of their rights. The tip's a health hazard. It's the job of the police to protect farmers' property, sources of potable water, and riverine rabbits." He wanted to know why we closed the road. I told him, because there could be another landslide. He said why were we sifting the muck and I told him we have reason to believe it contains material relating to a crime. He said what crime, so I changed the subject. I asked him was he playing hooker for the Rovers Saturday, because our front line was looking forward to settling old scores.'

Fergus grinned. 'So then he went home?'

'Yeah, he did. But earlier today, I saw him nipping out of the *Herald* building. Needling them to have a go at us, I shouldn't wonder.'

In the charge office they found turmoil. A policewoman was trying to calm a group of shopkeepers who were threatening to shoot looters. A drunk on his way to the cells was kicking the water dispenser and shouting obscenities.

Fergus button-holed a secretary and yelled above the din, 'I want a briefing called, two o'clock sharp, all personnel. See to it, please.'

Sergeant Barry emerged from the communications room and handed Fergus a bunch of message slips. Fergus glanced through them and groaned. 'Momple's been busy. Half of these are from the local authorities, the rest are from national newspapers, three of them Sundays. The shit's about to hit the fan. I'll have to issue a statement about the skull.'

He signed to his companions to follow him to his office, closed the door after them and waved them to chairs. Opening the envelope from the mortuary, he drew out a wad of A5 sheets, print-outs of the polaroid photos taken by Levine that morning. Thorneycroft noticed that the topmost sheet carried Levine's signature, and a telephone number. Fergus spread the sheets on his desk, slotted Taft's tape into the JVC player at his elbow, and pressed the play button.

The voices of Taft and Levine, clinically neutral, described their examination of the kit-bag and its contents. At times Fergus stopped the tape to link it to the photographs. The recording ended with the discovery of the plaster cast.

They heard Levine say sharply, 'There's something wrapped up in the plastic.' Moments later he reverted to his former monotone. 'The bag contains not only a human skull but a life-sized plaster cast of what appears to be a hominid.'

Taft made no comment on the discovery, except to note that the examination was concluded at 9.17 a.m. There followed details of the samples taken from the various exhibits, for laboratory testing.

When the tape hissed to a close, Sergeant Barry said, 'This cast. The hominid. Is there a picture?'

Fergus pointed to the last line of Levine's polaroids. 'A plaster cast of one of our ancestors. But Taft thinks it's a fake.'

Barry tapped the photograph with a thick forefinger. 'Fake or real, what's it doing in that bag along with a human skull?'

'Taft thinks the owner of the skull was killed by a heavy blow to the base of the skull. The body was then buried in sandy soil, not

29

here in the chalk area.'

'How long ago?'

'Two years, or less. Some time after the burial, when the flesh had decomposed and the bones were no longer joined, the head was dug up. The teeth were knocked out, presumably to prevent identification of the victim. The skull was then packed in a box, put in a kit-bag along with the plaster cast, and transported to Abbotsfell tip. Taft thinks it was dumped before access to the land-fill was barred – in other words about thirteen months ago. He says no fingerprints were found on the material. They'll carry out the routine tests, under our supervision.'

Fergus paused, then continued. 'There are some strange contra-dictions. The destruction of the teeth and the lack of prints suggest that whoever dumped the bag knew something about routine methods of detection. That much information is available to anyone who reads crime reports, or watches TV. On the other hand, he apparently doesn't know about DNA testing, or that we can reconstruct the victim's face from the skull bones.

'The question arises, why didn't he destroy the skull completely? Why was it disinterred from its first burial place? Why, how and when was it brought to this town?'

Barry rubbed his nose. 'Maybe he thought this was a good place to be rid of it. If it hadn't been for the storm, the bag would still be safely buried.'

'Which raises another point,' Fergus said. 'The perpetrator knew about the landfill. He knew how to reach it. He had local knowledge. It's possible he lives here.'

Kelly shifted in his chair. 'Could be a local man who's moved to live elsewhere.'

'Could be.' Fergus looked at Thorneycroft. 'What's your opin-ion, John?'

Thorneycroft said slowly, 'You don't have to live in a town to learn things about it. Perhaps the perp worked here for a while, or came here on holiday. There's also the possibility that more than one person was involved in the crime.

'Let's say the killer lives elsewhere. He's strong enough to deal a crushing blow, bury the body, dig it up again to retrieve the head. He cleans the head and knocks out the teeth. He's muscular, cold-blooded and single-minded to the point of obsession, a dangerous person to cross. He's also pretty clueless about modern methods of identifying a corpse.

'The packing of the skull and the transporting of it to the land-fill seems to be the work of a different sort of character. The skull wasn't destroyed; it was carefully boxed in a way that would protect it from damage. Likewise the cast. There's something weird about all that. It was almost . . . a ritual burial.'

'So who was the undertaker?' asked Kelly.

'Someone whose motives differed from the killer's. Someone who acted not in rage, or passion, or fear, but in a calm, method-ical way.'

'So what was his motive?'

'Powerful self-interest. Love. Money.' Thorneycroft spread his hands. 'Taft's right – speculation is a waste of time. We need facts, and the first priority is to identify the victim.' He turned to Fergus. 'This man Dempsey. Is he as incompetent as Taft says?'

'He's not much good,' Fergus admitted, 'but he's available, and affordable. That counts, to a small-town force.' He hesitated. 'Doesn't Claudia do reconstructions?'

Thorneycroft frowned. 'Not of murder victims. She helps plas-tic surgeons correct cranio-facial abnormalities in children. She sticks pins into a model skull, joins them up with strands of wire, and a computer does the sums about how much has to be done to each area of the face. The advantage over using the old clay method is she can make allowances for age, state of health and so on.'

'Would she take on this job?'

'Maybe. That's her call, not mine.'

Fergus nodded. He glanced at his watch.

'We have a briefing in twenty minutes,' he said. 'Because the landslip was unstable, we had to start searching for human remains last night. We had to use civilian workers, which means that by now half Abbotsfell is spreading wild rumours. I'll set the official line this afternoion, and call for a press conference for 9 a.m. tomorrow, at which I'll state the following:

' "On Wednesday night, a human skull was discovered among the debris washed down from the tip. It may be a discard from a museum or medical school, but we are conducting an investigation into its history. The coroner has called for a preliminary enquiry on next Monday, at 10 a.m. Dr William Taft who is the resident pathologist for Abbotsfell, will describe the findings he made at the post-mortem examination.

' "The police authorities are checking lists of missing persons, local and from further afield. Every effort is being made to establish the identity of the deceased. Anyone able to supply relevant information should get in touch with Abbotsfell Central Police Station, et cetera." Any other suggestions?'

Kelly spoke. 'Will you mention the plaster head, sir?'

'No, I won't. I want an expert to tell me what it is before I chat to the Press about it. That story stays within these four walls.'

Barry and Kelly left the office. Fergus gathered up the sheets of photographs and looked thoughtfully at the number Levine had written there. He pulled a telephone towards him and tried the number but after a while shook his head.

'It's his afternoon off,' he said. 'I'll try again later.'

IV

The briefing and the questions that followed took nearly an hour, after which Thorneycroft left Abbotsfell's finest to restore order in its precincts, and went on a drive of exploration.

From being a small village at the foot of the Mount, the town had developed westwards and southwards, covering low foothills and water-meadows. The roads that connected it with the larger cities were modern and wide, except for the link road to Watford.

The industrial area to the north was also on flat, newly developed land. The Mount was the highest point in this stretch of the country, and Thorneycroft wondered if it had provided a fortress for the villagers in time past. He made a circuit, and found a narrow track that led up the back of the peak. Parking the car, he walked up to the crest, and found he could see the remains of the tip and the debris strewn across the road. The dam in the river had been breached and the water was flowing normally, but he thought regretfully that there'd be no trout fishing in it for some time.

It would have been possible, he decided, for someone to bring the kit-bag up this way, climb the fence and throw the bag on to the landfill. The question wasn't how but why the thing was done.

He noticed that there was more rain about. Small, puggy clouds were piling up to the west, and the sky was taking on a nasty yellowish tinge. He returned to his car and to the police station, and at six o'clock went with Fergus to visit Detective Inspector Ronald Voysey.

'What happened to him?' Thorneycroft asked, as they drove through the streets to the hospital. Fergus grinned. 'He went on a milk-free diet, and then was knocked down by an ice-cream cart. It's not funny, really – he has a broken arm, three cracked ribs, and his neck's in a brace. The doctors say he's out for another week, but Voysey's mad keen to get back. He sees this case as the way to promotion. He could be right.'

They found the DI in an evil temper, ready to complain about the doctors, the nurses and the hospital food, but as soon as Fergus mentioned the kit-bag, he was all attention. Fergus gave him a full account of the events of the past twenty-four hours, including the interview with Taft.

'Taft was on the blower to me this afternoon,' Voysey said. 'Wanting to know where I was.' He shot a sidelong look at Thorneycroft. 'Said he didn't like intruders on his patch.'

'In a murder case,' Fergus said firmly, 'there's no such thing as a patch. You use anyone, do whatever it takes, to find the killer and put him away. Taft knows that as well as we do.'

Voysey watched him. 'Was it murder?'

'Taft thinks so. We don't even know who the victim is, yet. We need a reconstruction of the face so we can publicize it. John knows someone who can do the job.'

'Oh? Who?'

'Dr Claudia Hibberd. She's a computernik.'

'Anyone's better than Dempsey.' Voysey moved, wincing, and Fergus said, 'When will you be out of here?'

'That fool doctor says a week. I told him I have work to do.'

'Do what he tells you. I'll see you get daily reports on the case. You can call me if you need.'

As they left the hospital, Thorneycroft said, 'You know, if my presence causes problems, say the word and I'll quit.'

'Don't worry about Voysey. He lacks imagination, but he's a good cop.'

'Actually, I was thinking about Taft.'

'Don't. You're officially employed. I fixed it this afternoon. If Taft doesn't like it he can lump it.'

When they reached the house, Fergus said he must phone Tessa, and went off to his study. Thorneycroft sought the kitchen, examined Tessa's deep freeze, and by the time Fergus returned from a lengthy conversation, had a gargantuan meal on the go.

They ate hungrily and without much talk, each busy with his own thoughts. Dinner over, they left the washing up for tomorrow's Mrs Mop, and took their coffee to the living room. Settling into a chair, Thorneycroft said, 'Why does Taft dislike you?'

Fergus yawned widely. 'It's a long story.'

'Condense it.'

'Well . . . When Tess and I came here, we'd been married six weeks. It was a case of new wife, new job, and we didn't know a soul in Abbotsfell. Taft's wife Maisie was kind to us; introduced us to people, helped us find a small flat, you know the sort of thing.

'She was a fluffy little woman, but not a fool. It didn't take us long to see that she was lonely and unhappy, and that the cause was her husband. Taft wasn't physically abusive, but he criticized her all the time, in front of other people. Told her she was useless, stupid. For two years we watched her falling to pieces. She began to drink a bit too much, and that gave him another reason to belittle her.

'The second year we were here, after Matt was born, we bought this house. Maisie came here a lot. Taft didn't like that, but he couldn't prevent it.

'That Christmas, we invited both of them to join us for Christmas dinner. Taft refused, and apparently that was the last straw for Maisie. She went shopping in our biggest store and nicked a teddy bear. She was caught and accused of shop-lifting. Taft stormed into the shop and slated the manager; the manager lost his cool and insisted on pressing charges.

'I tried to get him to change his mind but it looked as if Maisie would be dragged into court. Then Tess took over. She got hold of Maisie's brother in Birmingham and told him that no way did Maisie need or want a teddy bear; what she needed was shelter from Taft's treatment. The brother followed through, and the result was that when the case came up, everyone including the magistrate saw Maisie as the victim, and Taft as a right bastard. Maisie didn't even get a slap on the wrist. She left Taft and went to live with her brother and his family. The divorce went through the next year.'

'And Taft blamed you?'

'Yup. Said I put Tess up to it. The man's a mess. He's arrogant, aggressive, full of childish resentments—'

'And scared.'

'Scared? Taft? No way! He's a cock on a dunghill.'

'That was my first impression of him, yes. When we walked into the autopsy room, he started as he meant to go on – he didn't greet you, he tried to rubbish me and my opinions. Once he began to make his report, he calmed down. He became confident, authoritative and totally truthful. That's his code, scientific accuracy, the pursuit of truth. Yet at the end he broke that code. He told a deliberate lie. He insisted the plaster cast was a fake.'

'Maybe it is.'

'Maybe. But Taft doesn't think it is. Remember what happened on the tape. At the point where the cast was unpacked, Levine was startled, interested and vocal. Taft made no comment; he didn't think it worthy of comment. Likewise, when he showed it to us, he acted like some sort of conjuror. "Hey presto, look what I found!" It was a joke to him.

'But a short time later, when I said it was the cast of a fossil, a

36

hominid, he froze. Then he started to yell; his hands shook. He tried to convince us the cast was a fake but his body language said he was lying. Taft was – is – terrified we'll investigate the cast.'

'Why, in Heaven's name?'

'I think that, quite suddenly, he remembered something, realized something that links the cast not only to the dead man, but to someone else, perhaps the killer. Taft doesn't want us to focus on the cast, Fergus, he wants us to ignore it. He wants early closure on this case, an open verdict on Monday, and after that just a file gathering dust in some basement. I want to know why Taft lied. It's important.'

'Everything's important,' said Fergus wearily. 'I've said I'll try to get expert opinion on the cast but God knows if I'll succeed. I'm about to be swamped by routine enquiries. I'll be up to my eyes in lists of missing persons, interviews, the media. I'll be expected to check if anyone in the UK, or abroad for that matter, has a head-less skeleton to match with my skull. I'll have to try to trace the history of the kit-bag, the box, the plastic wrapping . . . all dull, routine jobs, but they're what solve most murder cases.'

'I know. I have two suggestions. First, let Claudia reconstruct the skull. Publicize the result. If someone comes forward to iden-tify it, apply for early X-rays of the person named, from hospitals and radiologists. Compare those X-rays with the ones Taft took of the skull. Look particularly at the frontal sinuses. If the old and the new X-rays match exactly, you'll have positive identification of the victim. Then you can try to obtain material to run DNA tests.'

'Right. And your second suggestion?'

'Get good photographs of the plaster cast. Show them to an expert in the fossil field. Get an opinion on what the cast repre-sents.'

'I don't want the cast made public.'

'Get a promise of secrecy, in writing.'

Fergus, looking unconvinced, changed the subject.

'When will you talk to Claudia?'

'I'll drive over to see her tomorrow.'

'You'll miss the press conference.'

'All to the good, if you want to keep things low-key.'

'True.' Fergus got to his feet. 'I'm dead beat. I'm for my bed.' He started for the door, then turned back. 'By the way, I called Levine this evening. He says that Taft didn't take any photos of the cast with the sharp-focus camera. Levine took several, without telling Taft. He's had copies made. We can have them any time we like.'

'Great. I'll get hold of them tomorrow and show them to Claudia.'

'You do that. 'Night, John. See you tomorrow.'

Fergus drifted away like a sleepwalker.

Thorneycroft tried to call Claudia but she was out. He left a message on her recording machine, reflecting as he did so that he was seeking to involve her in a homicide investigation without first consulting her. Crazy. He wondered why she, of all the women he'd ever known, could most easily reduce him to idiocy.

Upstairs, he saw from his bedroom window that the road was nearly clear of debris, but blue police tapes still closed off sections of the surrounding countryside.

No lights showed on the far side of the river, and mist curdled the eastern end of the valley.

Somewhere a dog howled. The sound rose and fell, unutterably mournful. There came to Thorneycroft's mind a picture of the skull, its toothless mouth agape in a wavering howl for justice.

V

By nine the next morning, Thorneycroft was skirting Hemel Hempstead, bound for Harpenden. In a folder in his briefcase lay copies of Taft's photographs of the skull, and also Sam Levine's sharp-focus pictures of the plaster cast.

Levine had insisted that Thorneycroft must come to his home to collect the folder. 'Taft'll go ballistic if he finds out I've given stuff to you,' he said.

'Why have you?'

Levine's lips protruded mulishly. 'The cast was in the box with the skull, wasn't it. Taft says the man was murdered, which means the cast is material to the case. Taft's trying to suppress material evidence. It's my duty to see the police get what they need to secure a conviction.' His eyes narrowed. 'Show Taft he's not God Almighty.'

Ironic, thought Thorneycroft, that Taft by his bloody-mindedness was fixing attention on the very thing he wanted to conceal.

The photographs were technically excellent, taken from several angles and supplying far more detail than the polaroid snapshots they'd viewed the day before. Levine had labelled the folder 'Photographs of the plaster cast of hominid head, species unknown'. Below that he'd added his signature and the date. Each picture bore the Abbotsfell Mortuary stamp, and Levine's signature. He'd nailed his colours to the mast. Interesting.

Green cornfields gave way to woodland, and then to smallhold-ings and scattered bungalows. Claudia's house was larger. It had stood in open country when she married Vin Hibberd, but devel-opment had encroached and the area was now peri-urban.

Thorneycroft didn't believe that it was memories of Vin that kept Claudia at Witanwold. Their marriage hadn't been all that happy. Vin was a spectacularly successful soldier, marked for high rank and fame, but there'd been no room in his life for domestic-ity. When he was killed by a sniper in Kuwait, the general view was that Claudia would sell the property and move, either to further her career in London, or to go back to her family roots in Devon.

She did neither. She made alterations to the house, turning the ground floor into her workplace, with computer room, studio, laboratory and X-ray facilities, and in the basement a dark room and records room.

The top floor was where she lived, and the granny flat at the end of the garden was let to a retired couple.

As a close friend of Vin, and a member of his team, it had fallen to Thorneycroft to tell Claudia of his death. He had helped her with business matters and dropped in occasionally to see how she was doing, but nobody was more surprised than he when he fell in love with her. His taste had always run to tall, racy, fashionable women. Claudia was small and rounded, and bought her clothes at chainstores.

She had an old-fashioned sort of face, very smooth-skinned, with large grey eyes and a curling pink mouth. Her hair was glossy as polished bronze, but she often tied it back with a shoelace.

She was studious, devout and conventional, not his cup of tea, and he couldn't get her out of his mind. Over the two years he'd danced attendance on her, she'd made it plain she didn't want a close relationship with him, proper or improper. She seemed to enjoy his company, she was happy to spend most of her leisure time with him, on occasion she worked with him, but that was as far as it went.

Thorneycroft was unused to such treatment. Conquest had been the pattern of his life, in and out of the army. Yet this woman, whom he wanted above all others, saw him as life's booby prize.

He'd thought at first that she kept him at arm's length because he was divorced; but when he taxed her with it, she said that wasn't the reason.

'Then what is?' he demanded.

'You have no faith,' she answered.

'I'm a Christian. I go to church.'

'You go to weddings, baptisms and funerals. You go for your friends' sakes, not your own.'

Disconcerted, he said, 'I have faith in us. I believe we're good together. We could make a marriage work.'

She smiled at him, a little sadly. 'That's not enough, John. Not for me.'

Repeated rejection, he found, was not only painful but corrosive. It destroyed his confidence, made him behave like a lunatic. He bought her expensive presents she wouldn't accept. He tried to impress her by taking flamboyant risks, he argued with her, he stayed away from her for what seemed a very long time. Nothing helped.

Yet he was sure she was close to loving him. On his last case she'd helped him to track down a serial killer. The man had set a trap for him, and nearly succeeded in killing him. Claudia had found him dying, as she thought, and had cradled him in her arms and crooned 'Don't die, don't die' in a very satisfactory manner; and if the nurses in the hospital were to be believed, she'd haunted the intensive care unit for two days and nights, 'Praying like a ruddy mantis.'

But as soon as he started to mend, it was back to best friends and no bloody nonsense.

Thorneycroft sighed.

The storm had left its mark on Hertfordshire. There were trees down everywhere, and the lane that led to Claudia's property was a mudslide. A length of yew hedge had collapsed, taking her front gate with it.

Claudia met him at the front door and he kissed her on both cheeks.

'Thanks for letting me come. I hope I haven't interrupted your work.'

She shook her head. 'Yours. I've been surfing for palaeoanthropology. There's reams of it, you wouldn't believe. We can talk upstairs.'

He followed her up the stairway to the living-room. This occupied the sunny side of the upper storey, and a large part of its east wall was double-glazed, affording a long view of the garden, a copse, and undulating fields.

The furniture was modern Swedish, light wood sleekly contoured. The easy chairs were upholstered in natural leather with bright linen cushions, and the ornaments were sparse – a peacock-green bowl, an African mask, a vase of tiger lilies. A Seago landscape dominated the south wall, and a portrait of Vin stood on an easel. The portrait was unfinished, cut short like his life.

Claudia brought tea and muffins, poured for Thorneycroft and herself, and leaned back in her chair.

'The line was iffy this morning. Did I hear you say you'd found a skull?'

Thorneycroft launched into the story. She listened quietly, stopping him when she wanted a point clarified. He gave her Taft's and Levine's photographs and she studied them carefully, paying particular attention to the pictures that showed the injuries to the base of the skull and the jaw.

Finally she raised her head. 'If the body was decomposed by the time the head was dug up, it shouldn't have been difficult to extract the teeth. So why these savage cuts?' She pointed to the scars round the empty sockets. 'Was the killer some kind of maniac?'

'He may have been. It's also possible he tried to extract the teeth before the body was buried, found it too difficult, and only completed the job when the head was disinterred.'

'It's weird. The whole thing's weird.' She laid the photos aside. 'Why are you getting into this, John? You're supposed to be on leave.'

'I owe Fergus.' Seeing her look of disbelief, he said earnestly, 'He saved my life once. We were trapped on this exposed hillside. Heavily outnumbered, no cover, withering fire. Did I mention it was snowing at the time?'

She gave an involuntary giggle and suppressed it. 'Answer my question.'

He frowned, searching his own mind. 'I'm interested. The situation is unusual, you must admit. I really do want to help Fergus. Also it gives me a chance to be near you.'

'John . . .'

'You asked, I'm telling you. Will you marry me?'

'No, for the umpteenth time.'

'Only the twenty-second. I'm an excellent prospect, you know. I'm clean around the house, honest to a fault, I know my two times table and I can recite most of "The Boy Stood On The Burning Deck". May I have another muffin?'

She gave it to him. As he took it, he said, 'Fergus needs a reconstruction of the skull. I mentioned your name. I wish I hadn't.'

'Why?'

'I don't want you mixed up in another murder case.'

'That's my decision, isn't it?'

He nodded unhappily, and she smiled. 'I enjoyed working with you last time. I guess I'll enjoy it this time. Tell me something. This

Dr Taft . . . you don't like him, do you?'

'No.'

'Why? Do you think he's the killer?'

'No. At least, the thought did cross my mind, but not for long. Taft's far too canny to drop that kit-bag on his own home ground. But he knows something he's not telling, something connected with the plaster cast. I want you to make a reconstruction of that, too. It may give us a lead to the identity of the victim. It's also important to find out if the thing's a genuine copy of a prehistoric cranium, or just a modern fake. I plan to locate a guru in the old bones field, who can tell me what species, if any, the cast represents.'

'How about Max Slocombe?'

Thorneycroft blinked. 'Slocombe wouldn't give me the time of day.'

'He might. He's my godfather. I can give him a call and see if he's prepared to meet you.'

'Me and a policeman. Fergus sticks to the regulations. He will want a kosher cop at the interview. He'll also demand a guarantee from Slocombe that he won't publicize the cast in any way. It has to remain a secret until the killer's arrested.'

Claudia pulled a face. 'Well, we can but try.'

Thorneycroft watched her cross to the telephone and punch in numbers. He couldn't believe that she'd get Slocombe on board.

Everyone knew about Max Slocombe but very few people could claim to know him.

Born at the end of World War II, he was one of the world's great palaeoanthropologists. As a schoolboy he'd spent his holidays hunting for fossils. At twenty-seven he left Cambridge with a doctorate and joined a team of professionals on an important fossil site.

From then on, he made news, not only because what he retrieved from the earth was newsworthy, but because he was deeply involved in the dialogues and controversies of his chosen field.

That second half of the twentieth century was a period of vast scientific advances. A mass of knowledge was building about the earth, its structures, climate, vegetation, and the creatures that had emerged, evolved and become extinct over the millennia.

In the laboratories, new methods of dealing with this mass of material were being devised. There were new techniques for dating the rocks in which fossils were found. The ancient bones could be probed by tomographic X-rays and DNA tests. Climatologists, archaeologists, geologists and biologists provided the backup information that helped to define how, when, where and why long-gone species had lived and died.

Slocombe absorbed and used this kind of knowledge. To his flair for locating significant fossils, he added a hunger for empiric certainty. He tested his theories as far as was humanly possible.

Some people described Slocombe as a genius, others said he had the luck of the devil. Whatever the case, by the time he was forty-five, his place among the glitterati was assured.

Then in 1988 his luck deserted him.

He took his wife and only daughter on a long-promised holiday to France. The train carrying them to the Pyrenees was wrecked, his wife and daughter were killed, and he himself was so badly crushed that his left leg had to be amputated. He never regained full physical strength. His days of active fossil-hunting came to an end.

He embarked on a second career. With the help of sponsors, he set up the Slocombe Research Centre. He wrote for prestigious journals in various parts of the world. He was the *éminence grise* who could swing a decision this way or that. But he avoided the public scene.

He lived in a large house near St Albans, looked after by an elderly housekeeper and a gardener/chauffeur. He was offered lecture tours, honorary degrees and a title, none of which he wanted.

Some said he had Alzheimer's. Thorneycroft thought he was alive and well and living the life of Riley. No way would he agree to entertain a recycled SAS dropout who wouldn't know a fossil if he trod on one.

But Claudia returned smiling. 'He'll see you and your policeman next Tuesday morning at eleven o'clock. I give you fair warning – he's an oddball. When I told him you'd engaged me to rebuild the skull of a murdered man, all he said was "There's no accounting for tastes." But when I mentioned the cast, he was really fired up. He said you're to take along all the pictures and information you can muster.'

'Will he sign a secrecy guarantee?'

'Yes, provided it's lawful and doesn't offend his conscience.'

'If he does sign, will he keep his word?'

'Yes. No question.'

Claudia wrote Slocombe's address and phone numbers on a slip of paper and handed it over.

'And now,' she said, 'we'd better discuss my programme for the next two or three weeks.'

VI

Fergus was delighted to hear that Claudia would take on the reconstruction job.

'When can she start?' he asked.

'She'll arrive on Monday afternoon. She says if you can provide her with a computer, she'll bring all her other equipment. I'm to book her in at a bed and breakfast.'

'Nonsense, she'll stay with us. I've had the kit-bag and its contents shifted from the mortuary to the nick. Bunce has got it locked up in the security storage on the top floor. Claudia can work up there. Does she need an assistant?'

'No. She did ask if there was a tomograph in Abbotsfell.'

'A what?'

'A machine that takes X-rays of specific layers within a bony structure. You can make a sort of layer-cake of the results and build up a picture of what lies under the surface . . . like the inside of an ear, or the honeycomb structure of a frontal sinus.' Thorneycroft tapped his own forehead. 'Everyone's different. It's almost as good as a fingerprint. Clo says, with a tomograph, she can put a face on the skull in half the time.'

'Then I'll locate one. Taft can help.' Fergus made a note. 'We need results as fast as possible. The press is already heckling me, wanting the names of missing persons. I've a good mind to give them those.' He waved a hand at the lists piled on his desk. 'That, let me tell you, is the shortlist. We've taken Taft's word for it that the victim died about two years ago, and we've excluded any person who was known to be alive eighteen months ago. We've also ruled out women and juveniles. The computer helps us sort the names on the lists, but there are still hundreds of people who've never been declared missing. Vagrants, migrant workers, errant husbands, crooks whose pals prefer not to talk to the police.'

'Taft also told us the skull was buried in loam soil. Does that help?'

'Not really. The victim didn't necessarily live in the area where he was buried. He may have come from anywhere in the world. Checking lists, trying to match fuzzy photos with the skull, could take months. Claudia's our best hope.'

'Have you told Taft she's to do the job?'

'Yes. He just grunted. He's in a foul mood. Yesterday Barry caught him trying to climb up to the landfill, and when he was stopped, he lost his temper. Threatened to get a court order. What for, I can't imagine. There's nothing left up there. The diggers have reached the bottom of the fill. It's only old compacted soil. No bones.'

'Was Taft raised in Abbotsfell?'

'No, in Bath. He's never fitted in here. Always a tricky bugger.'

'Can he handle the inquest?'

'Oh yes. He's told me exactly how he intends to present his evidence. He may be bolshie, but he's perfectly clear in the head.'

The next few days passed quietly. Fergus was buried in his office, setting up the routine investigations of a murder case: questioning people who might legitimately have had access to the tip before or after it was closed to the public; monitoring the search of the refuse from the landslip, and from the river area; dealing with the queries and complaints of the townsfolk, and the gadfly attacks of Momple and his fellows.

Thorneycroft spent time with the team combing the river bank, a task becoming easier as the floodwaters subsided. No more human bones were found. It was clear that the kit-bag was a one-off, a strange incident that seemed to bear no relation to Abbotsfell's normal life.

Late on Saturday evening, he decided to walk up the Mount so that he could look down into the hole that had once been Abbotsfell tip.

The light was nearly gone, and the lanterns of the workers below were small glow-worms on the velvet river meadows. The air was cool and fresh. It would be a starry night yet he felt uneasy. Reaching the chain-link fence, he turned towards the tip and moved forward. As he approached the edge of the chasm, the fence curved away so that he found himself facing uphill, towards the summit of the Mount.

It was only then that he saw the figure on the opposite side of the tip. It was moving back and forth on the slope, in a curious, loping gait, its body bent double like an animal sniffing a trail. A pinpoint of light spun and danced round it. A dark garment draped its shoulders and at times swept the ground.

Thorneycroft could not tell if it was man or woman, but watching it, he felt the hairs rise on his neck. It had no right to be there. It boded no good.

Thinking to attract the attention of the men on the road, he shouted. At once, the figure jerked upright and stared across at him. The torch it carried illumined a devil mask, huge greedy mouth, blood-red cheeks, thrusting horns. It swirled its draperies like wings and its feet described a few prancing steps. Then the torch went out, and the figure turned and ran up the hill, crossed the skyline and disappeared.

There was no way Thorneycroft could follow. He ran down the

hill to the road, alerted the workmen, and called Fergus on his mobile.

'An interloper on the Mount,' he said, and gave details. 'He'll be gone before you can get anyone round to the Limford side, but you might find traces of him; a devil mask or a cloak, car tracks maybe.'

He didn't think they'd find anything.

He went back to the house and checked the locks on doors and windows.

The creature on the hill had meant to be seen, had deliberately flaunted its presence on the forbidden ground of the tip. The devil mask announced evil intent, lack of human compassion, human reason.

Thorneycroft was neither a superstitious man nor a coward, but he poured himself a whisky and drank it fast.

The Sunday papers gave headlines to the Abbotsfell Skull, with the result that on Monday the courthouse was besieged by a capacity audience of townsfolk.

The coroner, Dr Bedver Smythe, was a large man with raisin eyes in a pale dough face. His temper was acerbic, and as Fergus had foreseen, he was far from satisfied with the facts presented to him.

Any fool, he told Taft, could see that the owner of the skull had suffered a potentially fatal blow to the head and was therefore to be counted a victim. But a victim of what? Murder? Culpable homicide? An accidental slip in the bath tub?

These questions required answers. Further dredging of the river was necessary, to see if other skeletal remains could be found. The police believed, rightly or wrongly, that given time they could establish the identity of the victim. They must be given that time. It was to be hoped that while this investigation was in process, the media would curb their propensity for publishing salacious and inaccurate stories.

What was needed, across the board, was more fact and less idle gossip. When the facts were properly assembled and presented, it might be possible for reasonable people to come to a reasonable verdict.

Fleas having been duly planted in the ears of the police, the chief pathologist, the media and the public at large, an adjournment was agreed upon, and Dr Smythe shook the dust of Abbotsfell from his feet.

Claudia arrived in Abbotsfell at 3.30 that afternoon. Thorneycroft and Fergus escorted her and a large number of boxes to the top floor of the building, where they were met by a policewoman and a uniformed man.

'Molly Field will help you with anything you need,' Fergus said. 'Charlie Bunce is in charge of this floor, including all the material in the security lock-ups. You'll have a pass to allow you into this sector, and the big room at the end will be your workroom.'

'Fine,' Claudia said. 'And the material I'm to work on? The skull and the cast?'

'Charlie will bring them to you as soon as you're ready.'

'Good, then perhaps Molly can help me to set up my equipment and I can start work right away.'

Fergus dropped a hand on her shoulder. 'Thanks, Clo. I can't tell you how grateful I am for your help.' He hesitated a moment, then said, 'We've had a prowler around so don't wander about the town alone. Molly will act as your guide. And when you're ready to go up to the house, let John know and he'll follow you. Your room's ready for you, so make yourself comfortable.'

He moved off, taking Thorneycroft with him. Quite like old times, Claudia thought, when the soldiers went to war and the wives and sweethearts shut up and did as they were told. And how comfortable could one be reconstructing the face of a murdered man under the watchful eyes of the police?

She smiled at Molly Field and began unpacking her equipment.

VII

At 11 a.m. on Tuesday morning, Thorneycroft and DS Kelly arrived at Max Slocombe's house, a rambling villa couched between twin spurs of land, like a bone between a mastiff's paws.

Slocombe met them on the driveway. He was of medium height, thin-framed, and he leaned heavily on a walking stick, yet approaching him Thorneycroft received an impression of power.

His face was long, its angular planes resembling the strokes of a palette knife. His hair, thick and silver-grey, stood up like an aura; his large and crooked nose was both commanding and inquisitive. His mouth, full and curling, might widen in laughter or explosive rage. And the eyes, very dark, very brilliant, might be the eyes of a prophet, or an iconoclast ready to trash the cherished illusions of the world. Slocombe, thought Thorneycroft, could be a lot more devious and ruthless than Claudia believed him to be.

He received Thorneycroft's introductions with an unnervingly fixed stare, then led the way into the living-room of the house. This seemed, like Topsy, to have just growed. The furniture looked comfortable but nothing matched. A brilliant Rorke's Drift tapestry hung cheek by jowl with a pegboard loaded with press cuttings. Coir matting covered the floor. The centre of the room was taken up by a massive yellow-wood table. Over by the French windows stood a map rack and a set of African drums. To the right of the drums hung a painting of a cheetah, racing belly to the ground, mouth wide for the kill.

Thorneycroft studied the painting, compelled by its vigour, the force of the brushwork, the light that informed every inch of the canvas.

'That's magnificent,' he said, and Slocombe smiled.

'Yes. The artist did that when he was seventeen. I have a couple more of his pictures in my bedroom.'

'Do you know the man?'

'Never set eyes on him.' A lie, Thorneycroft thought, and wondered why.

Slocombe guided them to a circle of chairs set close to a book-lined wall. Thorneycroft scanned titles. Palaeontology, archaeology, the related sciences, and also a sizeable collection of religious works. Was that the common ground between Claudia and their host?

Slocombe came straight to the point. 'I understand you're involved in a murder investigation. Give me the details.'

Thorneycroft described the finding of the skull and its companion cast, the need to identify the victim, and the attendant need for secrecy.

Slocombe nodded impatiently. 'Yes, yes. You've seen this cast, I understand. What did you make of it?'

Thorneycroft hesitated. 'I know very little about fossils. It looked to me like a hominid . . . a recent species . . . something close to modern man.'

'Do you think it's genuine?'

'I'm no judge of that. Dr Taft thinks it's a fake.'

'May I see the photographs?'

'I must first have your promise of secrecy, sir. To publicize the cast at this stage could seriously prejudice the success of our investigation.'

Slocombe frowned. 'I understand that the police have a duty to

bring a criminal to justice but as a scientist I have my own imperatives. If it turns out that this cast represents an important fossil
find, then I can't give you a blanket promise to hold my tongue
indefinitely.'

Thorneycroft held the older man's gaze. 'Do I have your word
that you will not divulge what you see and hear today to anyone,
unless you first consult the police authorities in charge of this
case?'

'You have my word.' Slocombe stretched out a hand. 'Now, the
photographs.'

Thorneycroft handed over Levine's folder. Slocombe took it
eagerly, lifted out the photos and examined them one by one.
Presently he selected a few and spread them on the low table in
front of him, studying them through a magnifying glass. Finally he
returned them to the folder. His hands were shaking and he
pressed them together on his knee, fixing Thorneycroft with his
bright gaze.

'How much do you know about evolution, Doctor?'

'Only what I've read or seen on TV.'

'And you, Sergeant?'

Kelly merely shook his head.

Slocombe drew a long breath. 'Then listen carefully. This plaster cast is important to your case. To solve your case, you need to
have a glimmering of what you're dealing with. You need to think
like fossil-hunters. You have to adapt to a different time-scale.
Forget months, years, and centuries. Think in millions of years.'

He leaned back in his chair. 'I'll spare you the dawning of planet
earth. Let's start with the dinosaurs the kids are so keen on. They
flourished over 200 million years ago, lasted for 160 million years,
and became extinct 65 million years ago. We've recovered some
fossil remains and put them in museums for you to goggle at, but
the point is that those heavyweights died out because they could-
n't adapt to a changing world.

'Planet earth, since its beginning, has been in constant change. Continents have cracked apart, mountains risen, ice-sheets formed and melted; and as earth's physical form changed, climates changed, vegetation changed, environments changed.

'Any species, be it flesh, fowl or good red herring, if it is to survive must thrive in its environment. Elude predators, propagate successfully. Faced with a changing environment, a species has three choices: move to a more suitable place, adapt to the present place, or become extinct.

'Some twenty million years ago there existed an ape – scientific name Dryopithecus, commonly known as Proconsul – which diverged from the main group of apes in Kenya. The textbooks describe Proconsul as a reasonable model for the ancestor of modern apes and modern humans.'

Kelly made a choking sound, and Slocombe laughed. 'Take comfort, Sergeant, we've made great strides since Proconsul. Between seven and five million years ago, earth went through a cooling period, and in parts of Africa tropical forest gave way to savannah; fewer trees, less food and shelter for the apes. A species of hominid made a crucial adaptation. It learned to move on two legs instead of four. It was bipedal, but it wasn't yet Homo sapiens.'

Slocombe paused, half-smiling. 'Our descent isn't a nice straight line from Proconsul to Homo sapiens. In fact, we spring from a sort of bush, made up of many species. We are the sole survivors of all the branches on the bush. The others are extinct. But along the way, we not only learned to walk on two legs, we developed big brains, hands that can wrap around a hammer or hold a paint-brush in two delicate fingers.

'Somewhere along the way, our spinal cords became larger, allowing us to breathe better, and the larynx moved lower in our throats, so that we became capable of speech. We made and used tools. We mastered technical, artistic and scientific skills. We embraced religion, philosophy, all the characteristics that we consider to be the marks of our humanness.'

Kelly moved restlessly in his chair, and Slocombe turned towards him.

'You think this is irrelevant, Sergeant? You think it doesn't concern your murder investigation? It does, indeed it does.' He picked up the folio and rose to his feet. 'Come with me. I'll show you what I mean.'

They followed him through a door into a room lined with electronic equipment and filing cabinets. At its far end, chairs faced a television screen. Slocombe signed to them to sit down. He selected a cassette from a rack, slotted it into the video machine, and pressed the play button. A picture appeared; three skulls ranged side by side. Slocombe froze the tape.

'The gorilla's on the left,' he said. 'Note the heavy bone structure. The face protrudes in a snout, the jaw is square, with huge teeth suited to chewing tough vegetation. The nose is merely two large holes level with the face. The brow-ridge is massive and the cranium is narrow . . . containing a brain that's small for an animal of that great size.

'The chimp, in the middle, is smaller, lighter, probably smarter, but it's unmistakably ape.

'The modern man, on the right, has a slightly bowed face, no snout, a protruding nose. The jaw is curved in a parabola and the teeth are much smaller than the gorilla's. The longer cranium contains a large brain.

'The skulls you're looking at are not fossils, they're modern. It's worth noting that tests show that after seven million years of evolution, modern man's DNA – the material that shapes his body and his life – differs from modern chimp's DNA by only about two per cent. That two per cent, however, is a world of difference.

'I won't show you all the species that have appeared and disappeared over the millennia, but I'll touch on just a few, to help you grasp the importance of that lump of plaster you've found on your rubbish dump.'

Slocombe touched fast forward, stopping the tape at a picture of footprints frozen in rock, like tracks in the cement of a city pavement.

'The Laetoli footprints,' he said, 'found by Mary Leakey in 1974 in Tanzania, Africa. Dated at 3.6 million years old, yet they display a foot very like that of modern man. Proof that the species that made them was bipedal, and had been for centuries. Fossil bones found near the Laetoli site are believed to be those of a primitive form of man.

'Again, this picture.' The tape moved on. 'Australopithecus afarensis, Southern Ape from Ethiopia, otherwise known as Lucy. Small, long-armed, short-legged, pot-bellied like an ape. Lucy was a bipedal apewoman, but with human traits.'

Slocombe shifted to a picture of a small skull. 'The Taung Child, named by Raymond Dart Australopithecus africanus, Southern Ape of Africa – 2.5 million years old, a small, ape-sized brain, but very human teeth and jaws. Dart believed it proved Africa is the birthplace of modern man.'

The tape scrolled through several pictures. 'Homo habilis,' Slocombe said. 'Handy Man, Smart Man, our ancestor who said, give us the tools and we'll finish the job.' He stopped the tape at a picture of an almost complete skeleton.

'The Nariokotome Boy,' he announced. 'Found in Kenya by Kamoya, working with Richard and Maeve Leakey and Alan Walker. An example of Homo erectus, Upright Man. Recognizable as early man, but not yet very large of brain, and probably incapable of proper language. It was Homo erectus who over a million years ago migrated from Africa and colonized the Middle East, much of Asia, and Europe.'

'Our ancestors?' asked Thorneycroft, and Slocombe gave a rueful shake of the head.

'That's where the big debate starts. There are two main theories about the origin of Homo sapiens.

'The first group believes that all modern populations are descended from that million-year-old influx of Homo erectus into Asia and Europe. Supporters of that theory hold that over many centuries, these immigrants developed regional variations of appearance and language. They hold, for instance, that the difference in face, form and language between the modern Chinese and the modern French developed in separate regions, over a very long period of time. That is known as the Multi-Regional theory.

'The second group believes that that early erectus population was entirely replaced by a new species, which evolved in Africa much more recently . . . perhaps as little as 200,000 years ago. This new species migrated into Asia, Europe and the rest of the world, 150,000 years ago or less. And it entirely replaced the existing population of Homo erectus. That argument is known as the Out of Africa theory. The Noah's Ark theory.'

'Which do you support?' Thorneycroft said.

Slocombe gave a faint smile. 'It's not as simple as picking sides,' he said, 'but I think DNA research, and the fossil evidence, favours the Out of Africa argument. That said, there are experts who have doubts, and we are all of us hoping that one day someone will find the Holy Grail – the fossil that will tell us which is the right theory. That's what makes your photographs so vitally important.'

He shifted his chair so that he faced his guests. Choosing one of the photographs from the folio, he held it up against his chest.

'Tell me, Sergeant Kelly, how do you think this compares with the last couple of pictures on the video?'

Kelly stared, brows knit. 'Looks more human than the others,' he said. He moved a hand in front of his own face. 'I mean, it doesn't stick out so much round the mouth. It's got a better nose, and the head's not so pinched up, on top. If I bumped into this joker on a dark night, I wouldn't yell for the zoo keeper.' He grinned. 'I wouldn't stop to chat, either. He's a bit of a plain child, isn't he?'

Slocombe nodded. He selected another photograph that showed the underside of the cast.

'And you, Dr Thorneycroft. When you first saw this object, it struck you as "nearly man". This picture supports that opinion. This hole here – the foramen magnum, through which the spinal chord joins the brain – it's larger than the foramen of other early species I've examined, and it's placed well under the skull, not towards the back, as an ape's would be. It suggests a creature who walked upright, and possessed a thicker spinal cord than that of earlier hominids.'

Slocombe tapped his chest. 'He had a thicker spinal cord, more nerve cell bodies serving this thoracic region than did, say, Nariokotome Boy. That meant he had better control of the muscles that worked his ribcage and abdomen. He breathed better.

'Without that firm breathing control, speech isn't possible. The creature in this picture very likely possessed speech . . . language . . . the gift that enabled him to outclass earlier species like Homo erectus, in Europe and Asia.'

Slocombe leaned forward, his dark eyes glittering. 'If you had the real fossil in your possession, I would demand to be allowed to examine it at once. I would want to estimate its brain size, the position of the larynx in its throat. I would study the vestibule and inner labyrinth of the ear, because that would tell me if its owner was adapted to swinging through the trees, or running upright with a weapon in his hand.

'If this cast proved to have derived from a genuine fossil, I would spend my last strength finding out where it came from and whether other parts of the skeleton existed. If this fossil exists, then it is definitive. Important beyond my wildest dreams.'

He laid the photograph down. 'Of course, it could be a fake.' He looked at Thorneycroft. 'How did your friend Taft describe it?'

'As something a tourist might buy in a kitsch shop.'

Slocombe waved an impatient hand. 'Not that, no. It's much too accurate. If it's a fake, it was made by someone who knew exactly what to make. Knew fossils. Had exact knowledge of the early species. These photographs are believable, do you understand? Just thinking how believable brings me out in a cold sweat.'

Kelly looked unconvinced. 'Why would anyone fake a fossil?'

'To express a dream, perhaps,' Slocombe answered, 'or as a joke, or to defraud a rich collector, or bamboozle the world. That's been done before. The Piltdown Man.' The bright gaze switched back to Thorneycroft. 'Did the cast belong to the murdered man?'

'Perhaps,' Thorneycroft answered. 'It's not established.'

'When will Claudia finish her reconstruction?'

'She hopes, within a few days.'

Slocombe regarded him broodingly. 'I gave you my word I wouldn't advertise what I've learned from you today. I've tried to make you understand that I can't be silent for too long. I have a request I would like to put to your boss. When Claudia'a reconstruction is complete, will you let me see it at once? I may be able to put a name to it, which will spare you the need to blazon it abroad.'

'I'll talk to Fergus Lowry. It's his decision.'

Kelly spoke suddenly. 'Sir . . . Dr Slocombe . . . if this is a copy, what would the real fossil be worth?'

Slocombe shook his head. 'One can't put a price on it.'

'But there's people will want to. How would the palaeo folk value it?'

'Priceless. You can't put a price on the Holy Grail.'

Kelly pursed his lips. 'Reckon there's folks would give a lot to grab a hold of that bit of bone. They'd sell it, or flog the story to a newspaper, make a nice bit of cash.'

'I suppose that's possible.'

'To my mind,' said Kelly flatly, 'there's some that'd even kill to get their hands on it.'

61

The housekeeper gave them an excellent lunch – lobster bisque, a whole fillet done medium rare and served with salads from the garden, and apple pie with double cream. The red wine came from France, the white from South Africa.

They ate in a room overlooking the hills. Thinking of what Slocombe had told them, Thorneycroft found himself wondering what those rounded humps might contain. He found he had caught the trick of thinking in aeons rather than years. What strange bones might lie buried in the rock beneath their feet?

Slocombe did not revert to the topic of the cast. Instead, he talked about his early days in Africa, and the fossil-hunters he'd sought to emulate – Dart and the Leakeys, Tobias, Broom and Robinson, Walker.

Yet Thorneycroft felt that Slocombe was in some way guarding his tongue. He was not talking about the new generation of palaeoanthropologists, and he was offering no thoughts about the man whose skull was lying in Abbotsfell's police station.

Slocombe, he decided, might express a decent concern about the fact of murder, but his real interest lay in the discovery, excavation and proper classification of an important fossil . . . if it existed. There was no doubt that Slocombe could and would gather a team to find it. The Holy Grail would not lack for knights eager for the search, and Fergus might find himself faced with publicity fiercer and more greedy than any he'd envisaged.

During a pause while Slocombe circled the table to pour wine, Thorneycroft broached a question. 'Tell me, how would you set about looking for this fossil? If we got a lead to its whereabouts, how would you follow it up?'

Slocombe halted in his tracks, frowning. 'I'm an old man with a tin leg. I couldn't work alone, but I would set up an expedition to make the search.'

'So you haven't abandoned palaeoanthropology?'

'In one sense, I have. It's no longer my job, but I'll always have an interest in old bones buried under, and this one, as I've said could be definitive. A sort of Rosetta Stone among fossils. I couldn't resist the pull of that.'

He returned to his place, and glanced from Thorneycroft to Kelly as if coming to a decision.

'I've promised to keep my mouth shut about the cast, and your enquiry,' he said. 'Now I want the police to give me *their* pledge of secrecy. I want an assurance that details concerning the cast will not be publicized except after consultation with myself or some other authority in my field. This is not a selfish demand. Loose talk about a fossil like this one could prove to be would cause a stampede of people mad to lay hands on it. The hunt would not be confined to professionals who know what they are doing. It would include the ignorant, the greedy, possibly the criminally inclined. Do you understand?'

The two men nodded, and Thorneycroft said, 'I'll ask Fergus to discuss it with you.'

Slocombe appeared to be satisfied with this, and at Thorneycroft's request, he switched to describing the sort of sites where the dream fossil might be found. At last he said:

'So you see, the thing might be buried in many places across the world, but I believe . . . I hope . . . it will be found in Africa. I'll admit that that's because I want my theory of modern man's descent – the Noah's Ark theory – to be proved right. However, hoping isn't enough. To start any sort of search we need very definite information, and if the man who owned this cast is dead, who the hell are we to get it from?'

VIII

They parted from Slocombe on cordial terms. He limped out to the car with them, and then asked Kelly to go back to the kitchen door to collect a bag of fruit and vegetables from the housekeeper.

'I wanted a word with you alone,' he said as Kelly departed. 'It's about Claudia. She tells me you want to marry her.'

'Yes,' Thorneycroft answered. 'It's becoming a sort of household joke. I ask, she refuses, everyone falls about laughing.'

Slocombe made an irritated sound. 'She should marry again. Have children. I know she's very fond of you.'

'That may be, but she won't marry me.'

'Why?'

'I don't know. The other day she said it's because I don't have any faith.'

'Is that true?'

'No. I believe in God. An abiding order, a presiding spirit. I'm a Christian. I mean, I haven't given enough thought to religion, but I'm not against learning. I'm not a basket case.'

'You're sure of that?'

'Yes.' Thorneycroft spoke with firmness, and Slocombe smiled grimly.

'Then start learning, my friend. Work at it. Faith is hard work. Hope's easier. You can use hope as an aid to faith but not as a substitute. Don't give up, hear? I'm telling you this because I know what's bugging Claudia. It's not a flaw in you, it's the flaw that existed in Vincent. He was devoid of faith. He wasn't even a pagan with an idol to worship. He did not believe in any god, great or small, past present or to come. Zilch.'

'As a soldier—' began Thorneycroft, and Slocombe silenced him with a sharp movement of the hand.

'No. Nothing to do with soldiering. Vin believed that when he died, he would rot in the ground, and that would be that. He never wanted a divine presence, in life or in death. He felt no curiosity about the creation, the universe, life itself. He deliberately stamped out every vestige of religious feeling in himself, and having cold hell in his own heart, he tried to create it in Claudia's. He tried to cut Claudia off from God.'

Thorneycroft spread his hands wordlessly, and Slocombe sighed. 'No fault of yours, of course, but Claudia sees you as Vin's right-hand man, part of that ruthless career of his. You shared his battles and his battle honours.'

'We had a job to do and we did it. Vin saved a lot of lives in his time. You can thank God for his ruthlessness.'

'The trouble was, he made Claudia part of his battleground. He tried to crush her spirit. She's afraid you might repeat the attempt.'

'Why? I'm not Vin's clone. I'm nothing like him.'

'Then you'd better convince her of that. I'll put in a word for you when I can, but you have to do the convincing.'

Before Thorneycroft could reply, Kelly returned, carrying two brown paper bags stuffed with fruit and vegetables. As he reached them, Slocombe said cheerfully, 'Remember to let me know, the moment she puts a face on that skull.'

He stood on the driveway to watch them drive away, lean and wind blown, a prophet in the wilderness.

'We did OK,' Kelly said, stacking the paper bags next to his feet. 'The old girl gave us all this stuff, and the recipe for that soup, and the old boy gave us the motive for the murder. Joe Soap was slugged because he'd found the fossil everyone wants.'

'If the killer was after the fossil,' Thorneycroft answered, 'why did he put the cast in the kit-bag and throw it on a rubbish dump? Why didn't he keep it, and clear out and set up a search for the fossil, right away?'

'Well, for one thing, like the old boy said, he didn't know where to look. Funny old geezer, wasn't he? I couldn't understand the half of what he said, except he thinks we're a lot of monkeys.'

And Slocombe, thought Thorneycroft, is the cleverest monkey of us all, and as ruthless, in his way, as Vin ever was.

Aloud, he said, 'We'll make a full report to the chief as soon as we reach Abbotsfell.'

This plan came to nothing, for as they reached the outskirts of the town, the mobile phone on the dashboard yodelled, and Fergus's voice spoke urgently.

'John? Where abouts are you?'

'Just passing the soap factory.'

'Come straight to the mortuary garage. Levine's been mugged, and his pass keys stolen. Looks as if someone may be planning to get into the morgue.'

Minutes later, Thorneycroft swung the Rover into the cavernous mortuary garage, and parked next to a blood-wagon. With Kelly, he joined Fergus and the uniformed policeman guarding the double doors through which cadavers were admitted to the morgue.

'What happened?' Thorneycroft asked. 'Is Levine OK?'

'He's alive,' said Fergus grimly. 'In hospital. They're operating. The mugger hit him several times with something heavy. Broke his nose and front teeth and knocked him cold.'

'Where did it happen? Here?'

'No. He went home for lunch. At 2.30 a friend, Gustav Kriel, was walking his dog and decided to drop in and borrow a book.

He started up the path and the dog began whining and dragging on its leash. Kriel ran up to the house, found the back door open and Levine lying on the kitchen floor, bleeding heavily. He called us, and an ambulance.'

'Did he look for the mugger?'

'Not at once. He's a retired paramedic and attended to Levine first. The back gate was unbolted. It gives on to a quiet lane. By the time we arrived, there wasn't a vehicle or a pedestrian in sight. We're questioning the occupants, but most of them are working people.'

'And the mugger took Levine's keys. Nothing else?'

'Yes, the photographs in Levine's filing cabinet.'

'Including the photos of the skull and the cast?'

'Yup. We're running the usual checks for prints and traces. A back window had been forced. The man was probably hiding in the house, waiting for Levine to come home. I've posted a guard on the house, and there's a locksmith in this building, changing the locks Levine had keys to.'

'So, someone assaulted Levine in order to get hold of his keys to the morgue premises, not knowing that the skull and the cast have been moved to the police station. Someone crazy enough to think he could walk in here without being challenged.'

'That's it.'

'Were you able to speak to Levine?'

'No. The hospital registrar will phone me as soon as he's able to talk. Later tonight, he thinks.'

'Does Taft know about this?'

'I called him. He's at a two-day conference in Bath. He barely gave me the time of day. According to him, Levine was attacked because he interrupted a break-in. Says it was "some nutcase looking for easy pickings". I told him the nutcase was aiming to break into the morgue. Taft didn't want to know. He slammed the receiver down.'

'He's a damn fool,' Thorneycroft said. 'There's a maniac loose.

Levine's lucky to be alive, and Taft could be the next target. Tell him to get back here, Fergus. Tell the silly sod not to take chances.'

'I did. That's when he slammed down the phone.'

Fergus directed Kelly to join the detachment at Levine's home, and asked Thorneycroft to give him a lift back to the police station.

'The news of the mugging's leaked,' he said, 'and the press are baying for blood.'

They drove the short distance in the Rover. Some fifty persons were milling round the doors of the station; two local reporters, one from out of town, and a gaggle of goofers. The latter were giving off that high buzzing noise that warns of electric tension. Fergus stood for some time on the steps, answering questions, trying to soothe nerves. Presently a car rolled up, and delivered the mayor and the town clerk.

Thorneycroft left Fergus to cope, and went upstairs to talk to Claudia.

He found her in her appointed work room, sorting through a pile of computer print-outs. She wore a white slack suit, and her hair was hidden under a theatre cap. Hearing him arrive, she turned quickly.

'How's Levine?'

'Battered, but alive.' He told her as much as he knew of the attack. When he finished, she looked at the skull on the workbench across the room.

'Is it connected to that?'

'It must be. The only things stolen were Levine's keys to the morgue, and his photographs of the skull and the cast.' He put his hands on her shoulders. 'I wish I hadn't got you into this.'

She didn't pretend not to understand him. 'We're all targets, I know. I'll be careful. The important thing is to catch this madman.'

'How's the work coming?'

She walked with him to the workbench. The skull had been

mounted on a revolving plate for easy access. Thorneycroft leaned to examine it. Slender pins had been attached to numerous points on the face and cranium, and fine wires stretched between the pins to form a delicate network.

Claudia gestured at the papers she'd been sorting. 'Those are the statistics that tell me the likely thickness of the flesh at each point on the skull. I'll feed the figures, together with measurements I've taken of the wires, into the computer. I've already entered the proportions of the skull, and working on the data I add, the computer will build up "flesh" on the surface of the skull. It will reconstruct the head of the victim, and produce pictures of it from all angles ... recognizable portraits. A material model can be constructed with great accuracy.

'Fergus can show the pictures around, and perhaps get a positive identification. If necessary, the computer can make changes – add signs of age, scars, define the colour of the eyes, skin and hair. It's faster and more exact than working with clay.'

'Sounds great.'

Claudia nodded. 'It was invented by an American woman.' She rubbed a hand over her head, drawing off the cap. 'How was Max?'

'Fine. He sent you his love.' Thorneycroft was about to enlarge on the meeting when his mobile rang. It was Fergus.

'The hospital called,' he said. 'We can go and see Levine in an hour's time. Come on down – I want to hear how things went with Slocombe.'

They left Charlie Bunce to stow the skull in the security lockup, and took the elevator down to the real world.

Fergus shut his office door and ate leftover Tandoori while Thorneycroft described the interview with Slocombe.

'He gave us a crash course on the ascent of man,' he said. 'Ape to astronaut. He's very interested in Levine's pics of the cast; thinks it was made from a genuine fossil. He said if it's a fake, the faker knows fossils and the hominid species.'

'Valuable, is it? The fossil, I mean.'

'Priceless, he said. Also a passport to fame for whoever claims the find.'

Fergus groaned. 'Fame and fortune. If that idea gets about, we'll see the vultures gather. Taft could be right, you know. Some chancer's got wind of the cast and sees a chance to get rich quick. Murder for gain.'

Thorneycroft was silent, thinking. Financial gain was the motive for many murders, but he felt that this case wasn't so simple. The killing was more complicated, the killer more devious and dangerous than the surface facts suggested.

'If the killer was after the fossil,' he said, 'why didn't he dispose of the skull in a safe place, and keep the cast? Why dump them in Abbotsfell?'

'Could be a local killer,' Fergus said. 'Could be the victim was killed elsewhere, and his body safely disposed of, but the killer believed that if the skull and cast were found, they would be linked to him. He chucked the bag on the dump, knowing it was to be closed to the public soon. He felt safe, but then the storm brought the stuff to light, and now he's desperate to recover it. Levine was mugged to gain possession of the keys to the morgue. The killer searched his house in case the skull and cast were there. When he opened the filing cabinet, he found the photos and took them.'

'The killer needn't be a local man,' Thorneycroft said slowly. 'He could have an accomplice who does know Abbotsfell, knows the layout of the town and the mortuary. Someone who could stage the devil dance on the Mount.'

Fergus gave him a sharp look. 'You have someone in mind?'

Thorneycroft hesitated. 'I have this question about Taft. What's he hiding? Who's he shielding?'

Fergus scowled. 'If he's withholding material evidence, I'll break his bloody neck.'

'Better get him back here before someone does it for you.'

'Barry's phoning him every half hour, telling him to come back here at once. He's not listening.' Fergus pushed aside his greasy plate. 'We're digressing. Go on about Slocombe.'

'Well, he thinks the fossil – if it exists – may be the skull of a hominid more highly evolved than Homo erectus. He says it could be the immediate predecessor of Homo sapiens, a species that migrated from Africa to Asia Minor and Europe round about 150,000 years ago, and replaced the various species that were there at that time. The big takeover bid.'

Fergus leaned on his elbows. 'So this fossil – if it exists – is really important, scientifically speaking?'

'Crucially important, Slocombe says. It could prove that Homo sapiens evolved in Africa, and that the takeover of the rest of the world happened fairly recently, palaeologically speaking. Not a million years ago, but plus-minus 150,000 years ago.'

'There'll be other experts to say he's wrong. There always are.'

'Slocombe's one of the best there is, Fergus. He wants to see Claudia's reconstruction of the skull as soon as it's ready. If the victim is connected with the fossil – if he's a palaeoanthropologist – Slocombe might be able to identify him right away, before you pass the job to the general public.'

'It looks to me as if Slocombe wants a head start in looking for the fossil.'

Claudia spoke indignantly. 'That's not fair. Max is thinking of protecting the fossil site. If you advertise that there's an important fossil find, it'll become the target for fortune-hunters, crooks, even folk who want to destroy the thing.'

'Who'd want to destroy a piece of old bone?'

'Plenty of people: flat-earth bigots who hate the whole theory of evolution, ordinary folk who resent being told they're descended from apes, crooks paid by any of the above, vandals who get a kick out of destroying anything precious.'

Thorneycroft said placatingly, 'Slocombe has shown he wants that head start, Clo. Fergus has to consider all the angles.'

She rounded on him. 'Surely you can't suspect a man like Max of murder?'

'We have to look carefully at everyone who may have a reason to commit murder. Fame and fortune are powerful motives.' He turned to Fergus. 'Slocombe's eager to help us, and we can use his help. He has terms of his own.'

'What terms?'

'He undertakes to hold his tongue about the cast, he won't tell anyone about the fossil find, he'll give us reasonable time to complete our investigations. He hopes that won't take long. In return for his co-operation, he wants your assurance that you won't publicize the cast without prior reference to an approved authority in the field of palaeoanthropology.'

As Fergus started to protest, Thorneycroft said, 'It's a reasonable request, for the reasons Clo's just stated. Slocombe is a leader in his field; he has to protect its interests. I told him it was your decision, not mine.'

'It's not my job to protect fossils,' Fergus said angrily. 'I'm here to protect human beings.' He raised both hands. 'All right, all right, I'll think about it.'

There was a tap on the door, and a policewoman appeared.

'The hospital rang, sir. Dr Levine's conscious and he wants to talk to you.'

Fergus stood up. 'Good. Ask Sergeant Kelly to bring a car round. You'll come with us, John?'

Thorneycroft looked at Claudia. 'You'll be all right here? We won't be long.'

'I'll be upstairs,' she said, 'working on my model.'

Kelly drove Fergus and Thorneycroft up to the hospital on the northern side of the town.

Levine had been given a private room, and a uniformed police-man was on guard outside his door. As Fergus made to enter, his way was barred by a cerberian nurse.

'Don't you tire my patient,' she warned. 'He's suffered severe trauma and shock. He needs rest, as you would understand if you'd ever been bludgeoned with a heavy instrument.'

'I have, several times,' said Fergus unwisely, and she gave him an icy look.

'Not hard enough, it seems.' She studied the watch pinned to her expansive chest. 'Five minutes you have. Starting now.'

They went into the sickroom. Levine was lying with eyes closed. His nose was covered by sterile dressings. There were stitches in one cheek, which was already stained by bruises. His mouth looked like a squashed plum. As they approached his bed, he opened his eyes and raised a sheltering arm.

Fergus stood still. 'Take it easy, Doc. We heard you wanted to see us.'

Levine's arm dropped. 'Glad,' he said thickly.

'You're safe here.' Fergus approached the bedside. 'There's a man on your door. Can you answer a couple of questions?'

'Yesh.' Levine's lips barely moved.

'Did you see your attacker?'

'He wore a balaclava.'

'How did he make the attack?'

'I was having lunch. At the kisshun table. Heard him. Turned round an' he hit me. I don' remember after. Woke up here.' A bandaged hand fluttered. 'Why? What'd he want?'

'The intruder ransacked your house. He stole your keys, and your photos of the fossil cast that were in your filing cabinet. The rest seemed undisturbed, but we'll check with you later.'

Levine's gaze, blurry and reddened, switched to Thorneycroft. 'You have the copies?'

'Yes, they're safely locked up at the police station.' Levine heaved a sigh of relief. Then anxiety returned. 'The morgue keys. You must . . .'

The locks have already been changed,' Thorneycroft said. 'Don't worry.'

'Thank God.' Levine was silent for a moment, touching fingers to his cheek. 'When I woke up. So thankful to be alive, you know? Didn't think. Just cried.'

'I know the feeling.'

'Taft? Is Taft all right?'

'He's been recalled from Bath,' Fergus said. 'Until he arrives, Clancy will look after things. It's all under control.'

'Yesh.' Levine's eyes were closing again. He drew a long breath and seemed to slide into sleep.

There was a tap on the door and the nurse entered.

'Time's up,' she said. 'Out!'

Molly Field spoke to Claudia on the intercom.

'Feel like going out for a bite?' she said, and Claudia readily accepted.

'I've a couple of things to fix,' Molly said. 'Meet you at the front, ten minutes' time.'

Claudia locked her work away, and made her way to the front entrance of the station. She stood on the steps, breathing in cold air, scanning the almost deserted main street. A sound behind her made her swing round and she found herself facing a heavily built man with a tangle of black hair. Before she could move he had reached out and laid hold of her wrists. He was grinning, but it made his expression no pleasanter.

'Mrs Hibberd. Did I scare you? No need – I'm an admirer of yours. Momple's the name, and I want to congratulate you on the job you're doing to catch this dreadful murderer. Making a model of the poor victim, that's a tough job, but they tell me you're a real whizz at it, eh?'

'Let go of me at once,' Claudia said, and he complied, raising both hands in apology.

'I'm sorry, I'm sorry. It's my work makes me impatient. I'm a reporter. You may have seen my stuff in *The Herald*. I see it as my duty to help the investigation along but it's not easy. People don't like to talk to the press. Any hope you can put a name to the victim?'

'None whatsoever.' Claudia tried to sidestep him, but he blocked her path.

'I'm in a position to put the word out to millions of people, speed the case along. If you'd let me do an interview . . .'

'I most certainly will not,' said Claudia furiously. 'You've been told by the police that there will be no such publicity, and if you really want to help the investigation, you'll do as you're told and exercise constraint in what you write.'

Momple fell back, still wearing the unpleasant smile, and Molly Field arrived to sweep Claudia off to the steakhouse.

Driving back from the hospital, Fergus said, 'If Levine's friend and his dog hadn't arrived, Levine would have been a goner. The first blow laid him out cold, but the perp hit him five or six more times.'

'Didn't kill him, though,' Thorneycroft pointed out. 'Didn't smash his windpipe or crush his temple. Which looks more like blind fury than calculated murder.'

'How does this fit your theory of two assailants?'

'I'd say this attack was made by the killer, not by the accessory who dumped the bag. Levine's attacker is physically strong, cold-bloodedly determined, and reckless. This attack was made in broad daylight, in a suburb where people chat across fences, a place where strangers and strange vehicles are noticed.'

'We're working on that. You say the killer is reckless. Do you think he's sane?'

'Legally, perhaps, but in my view he or she's psychotic, and will kill again if threatened in any way.' Thorneycroft's eyes went to the road that forked away up the back of the mount. 'For some reason, he didn't himself dispose of the exhumed skull and cast. He persuaded . . . bribed . . . coerced some other person to do that for him. And that person, again for reasons we don't know, reneged on the job. Instead of obeying instructions, and destroying the kit-bag and its contents, he tossed the lot on to Abbotsfell tip.'

'Perhaps he thought he could reclaim the cast later, and make money from it.'

'Very difficult to do,' Thorneycroft demurred. 'The tip wasn't stable. The access road was officially closed. Retrieval of the bag was well nigh impossible. No. I think he had other reasons. The way the bag was packed was . . . almost ritualistic. Everything cleaned and carefully wrapped. The person who did that wasn't reckless, wasn't motivated by rage, or fear, like the killer. So what did drive him? We need to know the answer to those questions. What motivated the killer, and what the accomplice? What was the connection between two very different people?'

'What I'd like to know,' said Fergus, 'is did one of them attack Levine, and if so, which one?'

'There's no guarantee either of them did,' Thorneycroft said. 'As Taft says, it could be Levine surprised an interloper.'

'Who stole the keys of the morgue and photographs of the cast? No, the attacker knew about the cast. Too many people know about it. Some of our own people; outsiders like Slocombe; Taft, and the morgue staff. There's been a leak.'

As the car swung into the station yard, Fergus said savagely, 'The only way to keep a secret is to tell no one. Taft knows that. He's been playing his own game, and when he gets back here I'm going to have a talk with him. I'm going to show him there's a price to pay for withholding information from the police.'

*

Within the building, the night shifts had taken over, but there was still work for Fergus to do, reports to be heard, and plans to be laid for the following day. It was after nine o'clock when Thorneycroft drove him and Claudia back to the house. She insisted on cooking supper, a massive fry-up which they all consumed in silence.

Over coffee, Claudia said, 'Do you think it was the man in the devil mask who attacked Dr Levine?'

Fergus set his cup down. 'It's possible. The mask wasn't bought in Abbotsfell. There's only one shop that deals in masks. It's run by old Fred Campbell. He's a staunch Presbyterian, and set in his ways. He'll sell you a mask of Nixon or Beckham or any number of wild animals, but devils are out. But there are plenty of towns near here that aren't so fussy. And wherever the mask came from, it doesn't mean the owner is anything more than a stupid sensation-seeker.'

Claudia shivered. 'Pulling a stunt like that is wicked,' she said. 'Mask or no mask, there's a real devil out there.'

IX

Thorneycroft was awakened by a bright light in his eyes. The bedroom light had been switched on, and Fergus was standing by the open door. His face was very pale.

'Taft's dead,' he said. 'Shot dead, in Helford Woods. It's in my manor. I must get a squad over there at once. Will you come?'

He waited only for Thorneycroft to roll out of bed, and headed back to his bedroom. Thorneycroft went to rap on Claudia's door. She answered quickly, flinging a dressing-gown round her shoulders, saying, 'What? What's happened?'

'It's Taft,' he said. 'He's been murdered. Fergus and I are going with the team. You can't stay here – we'll drop you at a hotel.'

'No. At the station. I must get on with my work. We can't lose any more time on it now.'

He dropped a kiss on her forehead, and went to get dressed.

Fergus, Kelly and Thorneycroft raced to the murder scene in a police car with driver. Sergeant Barry and the murder squad followed, and an ambulance brought up the rear.

Fergus's shock had turned to rage.

'Why didn't Taft do as he was bloody well told?' he said. 'I spoke to him – I warned him Levine had been savagely attacked. I told him the attacker was probably still in the area. I ordered him – *ordered* him – to leave Bath at once and come straight back to

Abbotsfell, using the major roads. The road patrols were to pick him up and escort him all the way, he knew that, and instead of doing the intelligent thing, he ducked the arrangements and went off on the Helford road. What the hell possessed him?'

'He went to meet someone,' Thorneycroft said.

'His killer? After all I said, he made a rendezvous with his killer?'

They swung off the main road and entered the road to Helford Woods. It struck Thorneycroft as a good place for a murder. Willed to an ungrateful nation by a fast-food magnate, its hills and dales were frequented only by wildlife and conservationists. The access to it was winding and dark, trees and undergrowth crowded close, and the air was dank.

'Who found him, sir?' Kelly asked, and Fergus scowled.

'A gamekeeper by the name of Greenstone. Should be Greenhorn. He trampled all round the car, moved the body, and phoned the Bramwell division instead of us. Why move the body? Taft was shot through the head at point-blank range. He was stone-cold dead.'

They reached the crest of a rise, and saw Taft's Ford drawn up on the grass verge. A uniformed constable was stationed next to it. As they climbed out of their own car, a plain-clothes man came across to them and introduced himself as DI Fox from Bramwell.

They went with him to the Ford. Taft's body was still in the driver's seat, but it was obvious from the distribution of blood and matter on the passenger seat and the left-hand door that he'd been thrown sideways by the impact of the bullet.

'Not wearing a seat-belt, and the window was open,' Fergus said. 'Expecting someone he knew?'

Fox nodded. 'Greenstone, who found him, swore he didn't touch the window. He says he came along that path, over there, saw the car, came to have a look, saw the body lying on its side, then walked round and round "to see if there were other victims".

He's thick as two planks. Next he opened the driver's door, leaned in and hauled the body back to where it is now. Thought it might be lying on the gun. Finally, having pawed over everything in sight, he called us, and I called you.'

'Yes, and thanks for all you've done. How did you identify the victim?'

'ID in his pocket and, as he hasn't much face left, we checked the car registration. Prints and DNA will confirm.'

Fergus was looking about him. 'No obvious signs of any other vehicle parking hereabouts. There was a lot of rain last night. Maybe the shooter stopped on the tar and left no tracks. Or he could have walked, or used a cycle or a horse. Taft opened the window to talk to him, and got a blast full in the face.'

As they spoke, Barry and the team were sealing off the area with blue police tape, and setting powerful lamps to illuminate the whole stretch of road.

Fergus, accompanied by Kelly and Fox, converged on Greenstone who was perched morosely on his mountain bike. He proved to be not only stupid but belligerent. When Fergus questioned him about moving the body, his lip jutted.

'Yus, I moved un. I could see he'd been shot and I wondered where was the gun. Can't have guns lyin' around. Some'um might go after my birds, or a badger or such.'

Fergus breathed deeply. 'Mr Greenstone,' he said, 'it is illegal to move a body before the police have had a chance to examine it, and the scene of the crime.'

'Well, I dunno about that, but I'll not have trespassers shootin' my animals.'

'When you arrived and looked into the car, how was the body positioned?'

'Eh?'

'How was the dead man lying?'

'On 'is side, with 'is 'ead on the other seat. I took a hold of 'is jacket and brought 'im back this side. I thought the gun might be under 'im, but it weren't.'

'Was the window down and the door locked when you arrived?'

'Winder was open. I never tried the door. I just leaned through and grabbed 'im.'

This fact was noted at once by the medical officer from Bramwell when he arrived a few minutes later. He had pungent things to say about persons who messed with murder victims. He nodded to Fox, shook hands with Fergus and set about pulling on surgical gloves.

'Bellamy,' he said. 'I'm qualified, I can do the prelims for you, but you'll handle the autopsy, I take it. In Taft's own morgue – there's irony for you.'

He set about examining the body with speed and efficiency.

'A single bullet through the brain,' he said. 'Heavy calibre. The exit wound's very large.'

'A double-action revolver?' suggested Fergus. 'We haven't found a cartridge case. The weapon must have been compact enough to be concealed in a large pocket or a bag. Taft wouldn't have sat and waited for someone openly carrying a gun.'

'The post mortem will tell you more,' Bellamy said. 'He's been dead several hours, I'd say. Stiffening's advanced. It's cold up here, though, and the car window was open. Say eight to ten hours? Why did that oaf move the body?'

'He was looking for the weapon. He thought it might be a suicide.'

'Not from this angle.' The doctor mimed a figure standing on the tarmac, arm outstretched, hand pointing slightly downward. 'The entry wound's in the middle of the forehead, the exit wound's at the base of the skull. What's left of the projectile could be lodged in the back of the passenger seat.'

'It is,' Fox said, indicating the torn and bloodied fabric of the seat.

Thorneycroft ventured a question. 'Dr Bellamy, were you by any chance at the pathologists' conference in Bath, these past two days?'

'No. I can't stand those talkathons.' Bellamy signed to everyone to move back. 'I must take samples for forensic testing.'

He set about scraping blood, tissue and fragments of bone into sterile packets, which he stowed in a box and handed to Kelly. Finally he stripped off his gloves and tossed them into a disposal bag.

'If you want my guess,' he said, 'this man knew his murderer. There was no struggle, no argument, it was over very quickly. He lowered the window to greet someone, who shot him dead.'

He stayed to see Taft's body zipped into a body-bag and loaded into the ambulance. After spending a few minutes with Fergus to discuss formalities, he climbed into his car and drove away. Fox and the constable from Bramwell followed soon after.

Fergus and Kelly stood by while Barry and his squad went through their routine. The flattened bullet was dug out of the passenger seat and bagged. A truck arrived to tow Taft's car back to Abbotsfell, where it could be examined for fingerprints and trace elements. Plaster casts were made of the tracks of a number of vehicles left on the soft verge, but Barry shook his head over these.

'Too old,' he said. 'Been here for two or three days.'

Fergus questioned Greenstone again and warned him to present himself at the Abbotsfell station next day to make a formal statement. The gamekeeper, grumbling fiercely, then departed on his mountain bike.

Thorneycroft took no part in these activities. He watched, and brooded, trying to piece together the events of the past two days. Levine's mugging. Taft's murder.

Taft had kept an appointment with death. Arrived at this place and parked his car. A short time later his killer arrived from the same direction and stopped alongside Taft's Ford. Climbed out. Came close. Taft wound down the window of his car and leaned to face it. He knew the murderer and didn't expect trouble.

As Dr Bellamy had said, there was no discussion. The killer fired a bullet into Taft's brain, and left. Judging by the angle of the shot, he wasn't a tall man. About the same height and build as Levine's mugger, but the two attacks were different. Levine's attacker was taken unawares, lashed out, used far more violence than was necessary. Taft's killer knew what he meant to do, and did it swiftly and efficiently. The killing was totally cold-blooded. It was premeditated, done by someone Taft knew and trusted.

His fatal mistake.

It was near dawn before Fergus consented to leave the Helford Woods scene to Barry and his squad. Kelly drove the police car back to Abbotsfell, with Fergus and Thorneycroft slumped in the back seat, mute with fatigue.

On the outskirts of the town, Fergus's mobile rang. He listened, responding to a discourse with grunts. The call concluded, he said:

'That was Voysey. He's heard about Taft. He says sod the doctors, he's coming back to work, to take over the investigation. I'll argue the toss with him tomorrow.'

'You can't afford to,' said Thorneycroft. 'You need every experienced man on the strength.'

Fergus didn't answer, and Thorneycroft read his mind. 'You think he won't relish my presence?'

Fergus sighed. 'Voysey's competent, but he's the sort who regards reinforcements as a challenge to his authority.'

'Umh.' Thorneycroft yawned. 'I've been thinking about something Max Slocombe said. He talked about "old bones buried under". He meant fossils, but in another sense, that's what we're dealing with. Old bones, old stories, the past. Taft's past. It's linked in some way to the skull and the cast. He refused to talk about it and that cost him his life. We have to find out what it was that he didn't care to discuss. I could do some work there. Dig around in the archives. Talk to people he knew.'

'Yeah. Good idea. Sleep on it.' Fergus rubbed his eyes. 'I could sleep for a week.'

But when they reached the station precincts, all thoughts of sleep were dispelled by Claudia. She met them in the charge office, eyes shining, and presented them with computer pictures of a head.

'Roughs,' she said, 'but it'll give you a good idea.'

The face they saw was square, strong-jawed, high of forehead. The mouth was full and sensual, the eyes somewhat prominent, their expression belligerent. Claudia had made them brown. The cranium and jaw were still hairless.

Not a forgettable face, Thorneycroft decided. Aloud, he said, 'I think we should invite Slocombe over, at once.'

X

Slocombe arrived within the hour, and accompanied Fergus, Thorneycroft and Kelly to Claudia's workroom. Claudia had set chairs facing her workbench, but Slocombe ignored them and stood at her side, staring at the pictures that rolled down the computer screen. Thorneycroft, watching his face intently, saw recognition there, and something else. Slocombe looked like a man tasting victory, a man who sees the enemy dead at his feet. He sucked in a breath and exhaled slowly. 'It's brilliant. A brilliant likeness.'

'You know who it is?' Fergus said.

Slocombe turned to face him. 'It's Martin Parady. Not a doubt of it. The eyes are the wrong colour, though. He had eyes like a lion, pale, cold gold.' He gestured towards his own scalp. 'A lot of light brown hair, tangled. A small beard. The Lion King.'

'Was he a palaeontologist?'

'Palaeoanthropologist.' Slocombe returned to staring at the screen as Claudia tapped keys. Pictures appeared. The head was adorned with a tawny mane and a small tuft of beard. Golden eyes watched them, unblinking.

'That's him,' Slocombe said. 'It's terrific, Claudia. You'll be making a 3-D model, I take it?'

'Yes. Starting today.'

Fergus touched the old man's arm. 'Sit down, please, sir. I need to ask you some questions.'

Slocombe complied, sitting upright, his hands folded on the head of his walking stick. Fergus sat facing him.

'How do you spell Parady?'

'P-A-R-A-D-Y.'

'How well did you know him?'

'As well as anyone could know Parady.'

'A loner, was he?'

Slocombe's mouth twisted. 'Hardly. He didn't form close friendships, and he preferred to work alone. On his digs, he'd employ only a few local workers. He trained a couple of them to spot fossils, and clean and pack them. But in between times, he sought company, female company. There was always some woman dancing attendance, seeing to his every need. It's the lionesses who do the hunting, you know.' He closed his eyes suddenly, as if shock had suddenly hit him. 'God, what a thing. What a bloody waste.'

'Good at his job, was he?' Fergus said.

'Superb,' Slocombe answered. 'He was the best of the younger men. He was a brilliant student, and he never overlooked the academic side of the work. He kept in touch with the research – there's been a mass of it in the last three decades. Parady made use of the advances, radiometric dating, tomography, DNA. But his great gift was in the field. He found new fossil sites, he knew how to handle the fossils he found, how to identify them and place them in the right species. He was never blinded by science. He used his instinct. He wasn't afraid to offer theories, and they were nearly always proved right. He's a great loss to the world.'

Fergus cut him short. 'Have you any idea who would want to kill him?'

'Just about everyone who ever crossed his path, I imagine.'

'Why do you say that, sir?'

'Because Parady was a brilliant bastard. He was arrogant, totally self-centred, quarrelsome. He did his best to destroy anyone who challenged his views, he destroyed reputation, self-respect. He exploited women and deserted them, leaving them without a shred of belief in themselves or the world.'

'Can you name any potential killer?' Thorneycroft asked, and Slocombe turned to look at him.

'I wanted to kill him myself, once. He seduced my daughter. She was fifteen years old. I wanted to kill him, I wanted him taken to court, but my wife persuaded me that that kind of action would only cause Emma further distress. I sent Parady packing. After that, he badmouthed me for years. But time passes. One learns that hate's a bad master and a worse servant.'

'When last did you see Mr Parady?' Fergus said.

Slocombe frowned. 'Let's see. At a conference in Bournemouth, three years ago. Since then I've not seen or heard of him.'

'Unusual, isn't it, for a man so prominent in the field to drop out of sight?'

'Ach, Parady was prone to these vanishing tricks. He'd go off on an expedition, leave no address, be away for months on end. Then he'd reappear without warning, the jack-in-a-box tactic. The press loved it. He wouldn't let the media use him, but my God how he used them.'

Thorneycroft said, 'Did he have a favourite stamping ground?'

'Africa. He was an Out of Africa man. I believe he'd wangled dual citizenship in the UK and South Africa. He did one stint in the Middle East, but his main focus was Africa, particularly the southern states.'

Slocombe was silent for a moment, then he said, 'If Martin found the fossil that matches those pictures of the cast, it's possible he was working on a new site. The established sites – Sterkfontein, Swartkrans, the Kenya digs – are under the eye of people who guard their territory well. My guess is, Parady discovered a new site and it turned up trumps. There's a good chance that other parts of the skeleton are there. Waiting.' Slocombe's eyes shone. He seemed to be sliding into an inward dream, and Fergus brought him back to earth.

'If, as you say, the rest of the skeleton is there, waiting to be dug up—'

'You don't just "dig up" fossils, Chief Inspector. It's a delicate, skilled business, and it takes a long time.'

'My question is, why didn't Parady stay at the site to complete the job? Why did he make a cast of the fossil and bring it to England? Why not bring the fossil itself?'

Slocombe spread his hands. 'Who knows. Perhaps he needed to raise money fast. Perhaps he wanted to stake a claim to his find. Perhaps he ran into difficulties with the authorities governing the site, and they wouldn't let him take his find to another country. Perhaps he wanted legal or political backing, or more money. Whatever the case, he came, he was murdered, and that is going to raise a huge dust in a lot of places. Thank the Lord you kept the news of the cast from the media. Now at least the find can be followed up by suitable people who know what they're doing.'

Thorneycroft said quietly, 'At least two highly unsuitable people already know about the cast. The killer, and an accomplice.'

Slocombe's eyes clouded for a moment, then he shrugged. 'They're hardly likely to go public about it, are they? It would be an admission of guilt.'

'They may not go public, but they may well take action. In fact, they already have. The attack on Dr Levine – you've heard about that – was probably an attempt to regain possession of the skull and the cast. And I have other questions. Martin Parady returned to this country at least fifteen months ago. There must be other people who worked on this new site you talk of. Yet we've heard nothing from them about any fossil. There's been no enquiry about Parady. Isn't that silence extraordinary?'

'Not if others are exploiting the find,' Slocombe retorted.

'That's true. But didn't Parady speak to anyone, here in England, before he was murdered? Does he have no family?'

Slocombe moved restlessly in his chair. 'He was married, but his wife died years ago. She bequeathed all her money to her daughter, because Parady had run off with an air hostess.'

Fergus intervened. 'Do you know where to find this daughter? She must be informed of the death, and we need her for DNA comparisons.'

'I never met her,' Slocombe said. 'She's a scientist of some sort, I believe. Her name's Inez Parady. She's a doctor.'

Claudia said, 'She's a botanist, a great conservationist. I've read her books. I have one of them here with me. I expect her publishers can tell you where to find her. It's the Calydon Press, in south London.'

Fergus glanced at Kelly. 'Try them, and the botanical bodies,' he said, and Kelly left the room. Fergus returned to Slocombe.

'I need to know everything you can tell me about Parady.'

'Well.' Slocombe cleared his throat. 'That's a tall order. I've lists of his achievements at my home. Records of his important finds over thirty years. Copies of articles he wrote for *Nature* and other journals. Papers and lectures he gave. There's a mass of stuff. You're welcome to come and look through it, and borrow what you want.'

Thorneycroft remembered the peg-board in Slocombe's living-room. 'How about press cuttings? From what you've told us, Parady must have made the gossip columns from time to time.'

Slocombe looked weary. 'Less often than you'd think. Folk paid to keep the family name out of the gutter press. But yes, there were some big scandals. Famous names among his conquests. Lady Sabrina Truscott. That singer, Linda Hulley. A newscaster on TV – I don't recall her name.'

'Helena Buckingham,' Thorneycroft said.

'Right.'

'How about at Cambridge?'

Slocombe pursed his mouth. 'There was a tale about a don's wife but it was hushed up. Parady wasn't sent down. He graduated with distinction, and joined a team on a dig in Kenya. He clashed with the team leader, who believed he'd found a Homo habilis. Parady, newly hatched chicken, announced it was Australopithecus, and he was proved right. After that, he set up his own expeditions and blazed a successful trail.'

'Who paid?' asked Thorneycroft.

'In the early days, his wife. After her death, he finagled backing from American and European sources. I imagine he also conned his besotted mistresses into giving him money.'

'If he did indeed find our most recent ancestor,' Thorneycroft said, 'it could be money well spent.'

'And that,' said Slocombe, 'is the nub of the matter.' He suddenly got to his feet, and his eyes had a hard glitter. 'I would like to know, Inspector Lowry, if you intend to keep the news of Parady's death quiet?'

Fergus stood to face him. 'We're bound to inform his daughter and his lawyers of his death. If we can locate Inez Parady without delay, we can tell her quietly. If we can't find her quickly, we may have to work through the networks – police and media – which means trouble for everyone but the sensation-mongers.'

'If Parady's name becomes known,' Slocombe said, 'and the fossil cast also hits the press, the floodgates of hell will be opened. On its own, the cast is just a lump of plaster, possibly a cheap fake. Associated with Parady's name – his murder – the cast is given authenticity. Your plans and mine will be crushed in the ensuing stampede.'

Fergus held his gaze. 'I'll keep it in mind,' he said. 'I'd like to take you up on your offer of material about Parady. Sergeant Kelly will collect it, any time that's convenient.'

'Send him tomorrow,' Slocombe said. He smiled at

Thorneycroft. 'Come too, and bring Claudia. I may have some scuttlebutt for you.'

Thorneycroft and Fergus went with Slocombe to the parking lot. As they reached his car, Fergus spoke.

'Dr Slocombe, there's something you must know. Dr William Taft was murdered last night. Shot dead in his car, in Helford Woods.'

Slocombe stared in blank amazement. 'Why? What reason could there be to kill him?'

Fergus said, 'It's our belief that Taft withheld information about Parady's death. He may even have guessed at the murderer's identity. I have to warn you, sir, that anyone who follows that example exposes himself to the same risk. If you know anything about Parady's actions over the past two years . . . His liaisons, his associates, anything that could touch on his death, please tell me at once.'

'I will. I assure you, I've no desire to become a victim. You will have my full co-operation.'

He climbed stiffly into his car, started the engine, and with a lift of the hand drove away through the gate to the high street. Fergus watched the tail-lights disappear.

'I don't trust him,' he said. 'He admits he hated Parady, and it's plain he'd sell his soul to find that fossil. That's two motives for murder.'

'Parady bedded his daughter,' Thorneycroft said. 'Slocombe may have wanted to kill him, but he didn't. And it was years ago.'

'He still wants to go after that fossil.'

'Sure. He's probably already planning his expedition, but he doesn't know where the site is.'

They turned back to the building. Fergus said, 'The two murders are linked. Parady and Taft were killed by the same person. What links them?'

'The cast,' Thorneycroft said, 'and also the past. Taft's past, Parady's past. There's a connection there we need to find. When does Voysey come back to the coalface?'

'As soon as he can discharge himself from hospital. Maybe tomorrow. But that doesn't mean you're off the case, John. You answer to me, not to Voysey.'

Kelly was waiting for them in the charge office. He handed Fergus two message slips.

'Dr Inez Parady is in Rio de Janeiro,' he said, 'campaigning for the preservation of rainforests. Her publisher says she won't be back for another six weeks.'

'I'll see about that,' said Fergus, and strode away to make phone calls.

Thorneycroft went back to the house, showered, ate, and slept for five hours. By two that afternoon he was with the police team engaged in searching Taft's house.

It was the property of a misanthrope. Patchy lawns and sallow shrubs surrounded a yellowish bungalow that had no grace notes. Inside the house, the furnishings were functional but colourless. Only in the kitchen were there indications of the owner's tastes – the culinary equipment was state of the art, and an expensive Relaxa chair faced a flat-screen TV with satellite receiver, DVD and music centre. Here, Thorneycroft decided, was where Taft lived.

Fergus was in the living-room, going through the contents of Taft's desk. He had set aside the routine material of receipted bills, accounts and stationery, and was sorting the contents of the lower drawers – Taft's professional documents, his birth and marriage certificates, his insurance brochures, and his bank and investment statements.

He waved the statements at Thorneycroft. 'The man was bloody rich,' he said. 'Money from his father, no doubt. He seems to have invested cannily and spent carefully. There's a copy of his will, made three years ago. He left most of what he had to charity. Nothing to his ex-wife, nothing to anyone in Abbotsfell.'

A policewoman handed Fergus a list of Taft's outgoing phone calls for the past month, and he scanned it, frowning.

'All Abbotsfell numbers,' he said. 'Tradespeople, his own mortuary office, the newspaper office. If he made the appointment with his killer by telephone, then it was from an outside number, or perhaps from the conference in Bath.'

'Or the call was to one of the numbers on that list,' Thorneycroft said. 'The killer could be in Abbotsfell.'

Fergus nodded wearily. 'Yes. We'll have to check all the people he called.' He laid the papers aside. 'I spoke to Inez Parady. She was pissed off because I hauled her out of a meeting. She didn't seem too upset about her father's death, but she did agree to come back here at once. She'll arrive late on Sunday. She gave me the phone number of her flat in Belgravia.'

'Cosy.'

'Yuh. From what Slocombe said, she inherited plenty from her mum, who I find was a Burne-Wilkins. That's merchant bankers. Martin Parady got nowt from the estate, so if Inez killed him, it wasn't for the money.'

'How about Taft's ex?' Thorneycroft asked. 'Has she been told about his death?'

'Yes, the Birmingham division handled it for us. Apparently Maisie Taft received them politely, was shocked to hear he was murdered, but not much grieved. I spoke on the phone to her brother. He said Maisie hadn't spoken to Taft for years, and doesn't care a fig for him, alive or dead. It seems that's one thing Taft and Parady had in common – their relations didn't much like them.'

Fergus rubbed reddened eyes. 'I'm bushed. I'm going home to catch some sleep. Kelly's up in the attic; there's a couple of cartons of Taft's stuff you might like to look at.'

Thorneycroft made his way up to the attic. It was surprisingly bare of the usual household junk. Kelly was squatting on the floor, pawing over the contents of a large carton. As Thorneycroft joined him, he waved a dusty hand over the piles of paper.

'The story of Taft's life,' he said. 'A levels from the best school in Bath, studied medicine at Edinburgh University. No mention of bursaries or such, so his folks must have been loaded. He got a good degree, but there's no mention of other skills. No sports clubs, no hobbies, just work, work, work.'

Kelly tapped a second pile of documents. 'After he graduated, he served as a surgical registrar, first in Liverpool, then in Paddington, London. Studied some more to increase his skills, especially in forensic medicine. Became a state pathologist in Bath, then took the job in Abbotsfell. Married, no kids, wife left him.'

'Were they divorced?'

'Yes. The final decree's here. She didn't ask for alimony.'

'The marriage certificate's downstairs in his desk. The divorce decree's up here. Odd.'

'Taft was odd. Another thing, there's all this stuff about his professional life, but no records of his cases. Also odd, for a man who was keen on his job. Maybe there's more in the second box.'

Kelly reached a hand into the second carton and lifted out a plastic bag. It proved to be stuffed with news cuttings of post mortems and inquests, not those that Taft had handled himself, but notorious cases from the past two decades. Thorneycroft set them aside for further study.

Kelly dredged up a number of small boxes.

'Photos,' he said. 'In date order. The top ones are the most recent.' He brushed dust off his hands. 'Man, I hate other people's photographs.'

They examined pictures of Taft's Abbotsfell years, in and out of the mortuary building, attending meetings, being interviewed by the press. There were wedding groups. His wife was a doe-eyed blonde with a nervous expression. One enlargement showed her gazing not at her husband but at a stocky man with a belligerent mouth. Thorneycroft checked the names on the back of the photo.

'Edwin Fayre,' he said. 'Maisie's brother. He gave her away, and then he came and took her back again.'

Succeeding boxes contained photos taken in Bath, Bristol, Edinburgh and London. All of them showed Taft formally dressed, unsmiling, somehow not part of the group. Thorneycroft studied the body language, arms folded, head tilted back. He pitied the dead man, unloving and unloved.

The last box dealt with Taft's childhood. They studied prints of a prosperous house in Bath, a Chrysler sedan parked at its front door; interiors crowded with overstuffed furniture and too many ornaments; frequent shots of a florid man, small of eye and large of tooth, and a handsome blonde who struck a faint chord in Thorneycroft's memory. He couldn't think why.

The last picture in the box showed a young boy, seated on a sofa between the man and the woman. On the back of the print, in an adult hand, were the words, 'Me with Mum and Dad. Fifth birthday'.

Thorneycroft stared. Taft at five years old. There was nothing earlier. Why?

Had no one cared to take pictures of him, his parents, his home during the first five years of his life? Had a box of pictures been lost during a move? Had Taft or some other person destroyed the pictorial record of that time?

He considered the two cartons. They told him nothing that would help him understand why Taft had been murdered. They threw no real light on his life. Just the facts, the bare bones. His parents had been well off, had lived in Bath, had given their boy a good education.

Mrs Taft appeared in her son's wedding group, but Mr Taft did not. Dead by then, perhaps?

It must have been Taft money that laid the foundation for Taft's very healthy bank balance. Money he'd never learned to enjoy, it seemed.

Taft died because he withheld information relating to the death of Martin Parady.

Why did a man withhold lethal information?

Out of guilt, a fear that he might incriminate himself.

Out of fear, induced by the threats of guilty associates.

Out of greed, a hope of private gain, against the law.

Out of a desire to protect someone else, someone loved, someone for whom responsibility was felt.

Kelly was dumping the boxes back in the carton. 'Waste of time, this was, if you ask me. Nothing to tie Taft to the victim, or to the fossil cast, is there?'

'Something did,' Thorneycroft answered. 'Something or someone. That's the link we have to find.'

XI

Early on Thursday morning, Thorneycroft, Kelly and Claudia set out for Max Slocombe's home.

This second visit differed from the first. Slocombe had discarded the role of amiable host and mentor. His manner was brusque. He greeted Claudia with a perfunctory kiss, nodded to her companions, and marched ahead of them to the living-room.

The long table in the centre of the floor was loaded with files, journals, official reports and computer print-outs. There was a small stack of photographs and newspaper cuttings.

Slocombe waved a hand at the collection. 'That's everything I can find on Parady. Sometimes it's a two-line mention in a conference report, sometimes it's fifty pages of Parady's own creation. I haven't had time to sort the stuff. Perhaps Claudia and Kelly can start on that? Divide the items by subject, then by date, get them into some sort of order? I can't give you my file copies, but I'll photocopy anything you want to take away.'

He turned to Thorneycroft. 'Can we talk, Doctor? Over here, if you will.'

They settled in the chairs by the bookshelves. Slocombe said abruptly, 'I want to clarify my position. I appreciate that you and Lowry are trying to solve a double murder. I am trying to decide what must be done about the fossil cast. These two concerns may become irreconcilable.'

Thorneycroft met the brilliant gaze. He said quietly, 'You gave your word that you'd do nothing about the cast without Inspector Lowry's permission.'

'And I'll keep my word, within reason. It's my responsibility to locate that fossil, if it exists. It's of world importance. It must be retrieved, protected, examined and classified by people who know what they're doing, not by incompetent amateurs.'

Thorneycroft smiled. 'And you, of course, are ideally suited to launch and conduct such a project. I understand your eagerness to get it under way.'

Slocombe's sallow face reddened. 'Don't imagine that I intend to claim the fossil as my own discovery. I will certainly go in search of it – I'm already making plans to do so – but it will not be to cover myself with glory. This fossil is Martin Parady's find, and in due course that will be acknowledged. I shall see to that.'

'A generous undertaking, in view of the fact that you disliked Parady.'

'I hated his selfish, immoral guts, but I can't deny the excellence of his work. That can't be taken from him, ever.' Slocombe sat back in his chair. 'That's my standpoint, Thorneycroft. What's yours?'

Thorneycroft was puzzled. 'As you've said, I'm working to catch a double murderer.'

'Why? To help your policeman friend? To bask in public approval? To be near Claudia?'

'All three, perhaps.'

Slocombe laughed softly. 'Surface reasons. Dig deeper.'

'It's my job,' Thorneycroft said. 'I'm programmed to do what I can to combat crime, to discover why people steal, rape, murder. To reach the truth.'

'The truth. The reason why.' Slocombe seemed to be talking to himself. 'That's the motivation that drives scientists, policemen, religious devotees.' Louder, he said, 'You believe Parady was killed because of the fossil?'

'I think the fossil was part of the reason, not the whole reason. Someone who was intent on searching for the fossil wouldn't have thrown the cast on the Abbotsfell tip. He'd have kept it, organized a search for it – and there'd have been rumours spread as a result. You would have heard about that, wouldn't you?'

'Yes, very likely.' Slocombe closed his eyes. 'If Parady wasn't killed because the killer meant to find and claim the fossil, then why was he killed?'

Thorneycroft took his time answering. 'Because of what he was,' he said at last. 'Because of what he did in his past, in his last days maybe. From the little I know of him, he was a man who invited attack, all his life.'

'That's true. But what about Taft? Taft had high moral standards. He wasn't liked, but he earned respect.'

'And he trusted others,' Thorneycroft said. 'He trusted his killer, even though he suspected that person was involved in Parady's murder. This case is full of contradictions: they arise from the character of the people involved in it. I've told Fergus Lowry I'd like to probe that aspect of things, which means going back to the past. Taft and Parady are linked in some way, perhaps not directly, but by the people they knew. At some point in their lives, their paths crossed. I want to know the truth about Taft and Parady; not just the facts, but the scuttlebutt, as you called it. Do you have the scuttlebutt on Martin Parady?'

'Ah.' Slocombe gave a satisfied sigh. 'I thought we would succeed in striking a deal.' He reached into his pocket and withdrew a sheet of paper, holding it up between thumb and forefinger. 'This is a list of the women Parady seduced. It includes the name of my daughter. That should convince you of my honesty. I'll continue to feed you any information about Parady that comes my way. I'll hold my tongue about the skull's identity, and about the fossil. In return, if you discover where the fossil was found, you will advise me before making it public knowledge.'

'You want a head start,' Thorneycroft said.

Slocombe held his gaze. 'Yes. For the reasons I've given.'

'The police don't make deals,' Thorneycroft said.

'Try him. See what he says.' Slocombe released the list he held into Thorneycroft's grasp. It included seven names:

Lady Sabrina Truscott	*(socialite/racehorse owner)*	*1986*
Ms Linda Hulley	*(blues singer)*	*1990*
Helena Buckingham	*(newscaster)*	*1992*
Dodo Mboweni	*(model)*	*1995*
Crystal Dark	*(journalist)*	*1999*
Sybilla Klug	*(air hostess)*	*2002*
Emma Slocombe	*(scholar)*	—

Slocombe had scrawled a note under these names. 'There were dozens of others, but they were passing affairs, they never made headlines. My daughter was never in the news because she was under the age of consent. She cannot be questioned, because she and my wife were killed in a train accident in France.'

Thorneycroft looked up from the page. 'What about the wife of the Cambridge don?' he said.

Slocombe shook his head impatiently. 'I told you, there was no truth in the story. Parady was a tomcat, he tried to lay anything that moved, but he was never accused of that particular exploit. He was never penalized in any way. You'll find, if you investigate the names on that list, that he was seldom censured for his randy lifestyle. The tomcat had ninety-nine lives.'

Thorneycroft folded the paper into his pocket. 'I'll tell Fergus of your request. I doubt he'll make you any promises.'

Anger flared in Slocombe's eyes. 'Tell him that if the fossil is damaged or lost through the actions of greedy and unskilled scroungers, the blame will be on the shoulders of the police.'

'That's nonsense,' Thorneycroft said, 'and you know it.'

For a moment Slocombe looked ready to argue the point, then he relaxed. 'You're right,' he muttered. 'You must forgive my over-eagerness. Suggest to Inspector Lowry that his best hope of finding the fossil site is through Parady's daughter Inez.'

'I thought there was no love lost between them.'

'That may be so, but Inez was the main sponsor for Parady's expeditions.'

'How do you know?'

'He boasted of it. He told me once that getting money out of Inez was like getting blood out of a stone, but he knew how to do it.'

'By fair means, or foul?'

'That he didn't say.' Slocombe got to his feet. 'We must go and help sort out those papers,' he said. 'It's going to be a long job.'

Claudia and Kelly had made inroads into the task, and Thorneycroft and Slocombe joined them. By one o'clock they had brought some order into the material on the table, and they paused to eat ham rolls and salad.

Last to be examined were the photographs, pictures of Parady alone and in diverse groups. The earliest showed him as a toddler, flanked by his parents.

'They had him late,' Slocombe said. 'He was an only child, probably spoiled rotten. His mother died at sixty, while Martin was at Cambridge. His father's still alive, but he's in a home in Brighton, quite gaga.'

'You know a lot about him,' Thorneycroft said.

'Oh yes. After he wrecked my daughter's life, I made quite a study of him.'

Thorneycroft studied the later photographs. Parady had possessed the physical magnetism coveted by actors and politicians. The women on Slocombe's list probably never stood a chance.

By four o'clock they had the material sorted and packed into three cartons. Carrying one of them out to his car, Thorneycroft paused by the painting of the hunting cheetah. The painter's signature was in the bottom right-hand corner – the initials 'E.B.', interwoven.

Claudia stopped beside him. 'Beautiful, isn't it?'

'Very. Who is "E.B.", do you know?'

'No. Max doesn't, either. He just bought it because he liked it. He says it'll be worth a lot of money one day. He's a very shrewd judge of art.'

Shrewd, thought Thorneycroft, was the right word for Max Slocombe.

It was on reaching Abbotsfell High Street that they saw the newspaper board with the headline 'EXPERT EMPLOYED TO IDENTIFY ABBOTSFELL SKULL'. Thorneycroft bought a copy of the paper, and saw Claudia's face on the front page, with a caption describing her as 'the veteran of several murder investigations' and a text proclaiming her skill as a reconstruction artist.

He carried the paper to Fergus's office, fuming. 'It's Momple,' he said. 'He cornered Clo a couple of nights ago, wanting her to tell him who the victim was. It shines a spotlight on her, Fergus. It increases the danger to her.'

Fergus shook his head. 'It isn't Momple. That's the *Oxford Courier*, and they could have picked up the news that Clo was doing the reconstruction from a dozen sources. Calm down, John. We're looking after Clo. I give you my word.'

It was Claudia herself who dissuaded Thorneycroft from calling Momple to account. 'We'll be announcing the victim's name soon enough,' she said, 'so what's the difference? I'm being careful, really I am. Show Fergus the list Max gave us of Parady's conquests.'

Fergus was unimpressed by the list. 'Old hat,' he said. 'The last public scandal was back in 2002.'

'The year Parady went abroad,' Thorneycroft said. 'He was out of Britain for a year, probably in Africa. During that year there'll have been women in his life, probably several.'

'That's guesswork.'

'It's probability. Two things drove the man: one was his love of palaeoanthropology, the other was an insatiable sex drive. We have to look for the women in his life. When will you release the news that Parady's the victim?'

'I want Inez Parady to confirm it before I go public. Once the media get the story, all hell with break loose. Voysey's coming in tomorrow; we can make plans then. What's your programme?'

'I'd like to go to Bath,' Thorneycroft said. 'I want to check on Taft's early background.'

'I'll have to clear it with Freddy Plomer,' Fergus said. 'He's in charge there. They're questioning the people who were at Taft's conference – officials and delegates. I'll have a word with Freddy, tell him you'll be over tomorrow.'

Thorneycroft and Claudia lugged Slocombe's cartons to the Rover. Although it was just past seven o'clock, the sky was dark, heavy clouds pressing on the surrounding hills. There were few people in the main street, and the shop windows were dimmed.

Claudia shivered. 'Everyone's scared the man who killed Taft is still around, watching. Do you think he is?'

Thorneycroft toyed with comfortable lies, and discarded them. 'Here, or within striking distance,' he said. A description that applied to half of England.

'The skull and the cast are safe,' she said, 'locked in the strongroom.'

Thorneycroft opened the car door for her. 'The way to get into a strongroom is to take hostages, and make their survival dependent on the delivery of the goods.' He closed the door and went round to take his own place.

'That would take a gang,' Claudia said. 'You believe there are two people involved in these murders, not a whole gang.'

'If the story gets about that Parady found a fossil of immense value, the whole picture could change. I don't believe we're facing gang action, but it's a possibility, so don't take chances, Clo. Don't dispense with your police protection, don't risk becoming a hostage, because if you became one, I'd hand over the goods myself.'

The Rover moved out of the car park and headed up the road that led through the outskirts of the town, to the Mount. Claudia said, 'I don't know why you love me. I'm not what you've always liked. I'm not clever, or fashionable. I'm not like Louise. Vin told me once she could light up a room.'

'So can Lucifer,' Thorneycroft said. 'Marriage to Louise was great for six months. I was often away, and when we were together, it was everything to excess – sex, parties, drink. As time went on, I realized Louise was . . . all on the surface. Her talents didn't make her contented. She needed constant change, constant excitement to fill the emptiness inside her.'

They were approaching the house, turning into the double garage. He stopped the car and turned to face her.

'I love you, I desire you, I want to marry you and have kids with you. I need you because of what you are. You have strength and calmness. Something flows from you that I want to share. When I'm near you I feel at home. Safe.' He sighed. 'I can't explain.'

She smiled at him. 'You have explained,' she said. 'Let's go and make supper. I'm starving.'

They spent the evening studying Martin Parady's own writings, and the few brief references made to his childhood.

'According to Slocombe,' said Thorneycroft when they called a halt, 'Martin was spoiled rotten by elderly parents.'

Claudia looked mutinous. 'They packed him off to boarding school when he was eleven. I'd say they gave him material things because that was easier than giving him time and love. His mother was busy being social, and his father did what he was told. Martin didn't get love, so he never learned how to give it.'

'He loved his work,' Thorneycroft said. 'Even his critics admit that – in that area, at least – he had complete integrity.'

'And he loved Africa.' Claudia was gazing at a photograph of water cascading over red rocks. 'He loved Africa and he was welcomed there, enough to earn him dual citizenship in at least one country. He believed that we evolved in Africa, that it was the launch pad of Homo sapiens.' She stretched her arms, sighing. 'I dream about travel, but I never get around to it.'

'Come to Bath with me, tomorrow.'

She smiled, but shook her head. 'I have to start on my reconstruction of the cast. Max says it's important to have the features in 3D.'

Thorneycroft nodded sagely. 'We need to know how we looked 150,000 years ago.'

XII

Thorneycroft's duty call at Bath's main police station produced results.

Detective Inspector Fred Plomer, grey haired and corpulent, presented him with a typed report that set out the dates of William Taft's birth, admission to schools and university, job appointments, marriage and death. His research had obviously gone beyond mere statistics, for when Thorneycroft produced the photograph that Taft had labelled 'Me with Mum and Dad', he chuckled.

'That'll have been taken right after the wedding,' he said. 'William wasn't born in wedlock, but Mortimer always treated him as his own, so the lad gets the benefit of the doubt, eh?'

'Did you know Mortimer Taft?'

'Not to say know. My dad was foreman in one of Mortimer's factories, so I saw the great man on high days and holidays. He made his pile out of synthetic fibres. He was free with his money, I'll say that for him. Gave a mint to charity.'

'What about his wife?'

Plomer's grin became leery. 'Her I never met. My mum used to say she was no better than she should be. She called herself Eleanor Venables, but that was just her stage name. Her real surname was Nicholls. Ellie Nicholls, she was.'

'And a stage performer?'

'Yes. A dancer, a good one. Trained for the ballet, but she got too tall for that, so she took up modern dance. Went to America and was in some big shows. Then she came back to London. Didn't work for a year, then bobbed up as a dancer in revues and musicals.'

'Why the year's break? Was she pregnant?'

'That I can't say. Anyways, Mortimer spotted her in some revue, and set her up in a fancy apartment. He used to go up to town weekends for a bit on the side. That went on for five years, then Mortimer decided to make an honest woman of her. Brought her back here for a fancy wedding. William was page boy – that was a titbit for the cats.'

'How did Mortimer and Eleanor react to William's marriage?'

'Mortimer never lived to see it. Died in his sixtieth year, of liver cancer. Ellie was happy about the match, so far as I know, but she didn't live long to enjoy it. Went under a bus, DOA at the hospital. She left all the family cash to William. Not the house, though. That went to the city, for a public library.'

Plomer licked a finger and turned a page of his report. 'Fergus asked me to check on the conference William was at – a pathologists' pow-wow. You should see the agenda. Seventeen ways to cut up a corpse. I interviewed everyone I could – officials, delegates, catering people. I didn't pick up anything to do with Taft's murder. Nobody knows if he made an appointment to meet someone in Helford Woods. There was a phone bank provided for the delegates, but he didn't use it. Either he made the date before he came to Bath, or he left the conference hall and used an outside phone.'

Thorneycroft nodded. 'And got a bullet through his head as a result.'

'There's a lot more delegates to be seen,' Plomer said. 'I'll keep plugging away, let you know what comes up.'

Thorneycroft accepted a copy of the report, with thanks, and left the station.

The air was humid; he fancied he could smell sulphur. Healing baths, or the devil? He felt depressed. This had been a wasted journey, in a sense. Routine enquiry was best left to the police. Voysey and Plomer had the training, the contacts, and the authority to seek out and establish facts. To compete with them would be a waste of valuable time.

Thorneycroft climbed into the Rover and drove slowly away from the business centre, heading for the classical squares and terraces of Georgian Bath. After some wandering, he found the Mortimer Taft Public Library, a graceful mansion flanked by emerald lawns and a discreet parking lot.

William Taft, born out of wedlock, had nevertheless had what most people would consider a good start in life – loving parents, a fine home, education, the opportunity to develop and practise his skills. Yet happiness had eluded him.

Did the answer lie in the first five years of his life? The years spent with Ellie Nicholls in London before she became Eleanor Taft of Bath? What happened to turn him into the misanthrope who was unable to make friends, who failed in marriage, who ended up a murder victim?

If routine couldn't discover the truth about him, what could?

Instinct? Gut feeling? Hunches?

This case wasn't routine. The killer wasn't normal. Abnormal circumstances had led to the killing of Martin Parady and William Taft.

There was no point in staying in Bath.

He turned the car from the Georgian colonnades, the Roman ruins, and climbed the steeps to the road that led westwards.

The entrance to Abbotsfell Police Headquarters was clogged with people clamouring for admission. A television van was blocking the road, and as Thorneycroft climbed out of the car, he was surrounded by reporters baying for news about William Taft's death.

He thrust past them, saying that he had no comment to make, and reaching the main door was bundled through it by a uniformed policeman. Inside, Kelly met him.

'The chief wants to see you,' he said. 'He's in his office with Voysey. They're both of them spitting tacks. There's a piece in the first edition of the *Gazette* suggesting there's a serial killer loose in town.'

Thorneycroft grimaced and edged through the crowded charge office to Fergus's office. Voysey was seated in the visitor's chair. His right arm was in a sling, and above the brace on his neck, his face was pale. The look he gave Thorneycroft was less than welcoming.

'You're back early,' Fergus said. 'What went wrong?'

'Nothing.' Thorneycroft pulled a chair to the desk and dropped Plomer's report between the two men. 'DI Plomer's done the donkey work for us.'

Voysey sniffed. 'Plomer knows his job; he doesn't need help.'

'I agree,' Thorneycroft said. 'We don't have time for duplication.' He looked at Fergus. 'Did you speak to Slocombe about his request?'

'Yes, I did. I let him know that if he goes public about the cast, I'll have his guts for garters.'

'He won't renege.'

'You hope,' Voysey said. He was staring at Thorneycroft with dislike. 'I don't hold with making deals with people outside of the force. It brings nothing but trouble.'

Thorneycroft thought of the informers, the friendly press-men, the specialists like himself, but now wasn't the time to argue. He looked at Fergus. 'For the moment, you don't need me cluttering up the scene, but I can work round the fringes.'

'Doing what?' Fergus said.

'For a start, I'd like to talk to Maisie Taft.'

'You won't get past her brother.'

'I might, with your help. You told me that when Maisie was caught shop-lifting, you and Tessa got her off the hook. Now's the time to call in the debt. Phone her during the day, when the watch-dragon is at work. Ask her to meet Claudia and me, somewhere he can't call the shots.'

'And if she agrees?'

'I'll talk to her about Taft, his likes and dislikes, his hang-ups.'

Fergus chewed his lip. 'I suppose it's worth a try, but I doubt Maisie Taft can tell you much. Taft treated her like a retarded child. He didn't confide in her.'

'He didn't confide in anyone – he wasn't the type. He was aggressive, abusive, but above all, secretive. Maisie lived with him for several years. She may be able to shed light on his secretiveness – the things he refused to discuss, the things that aroused his hostility. It's what people won't tell that betrays them, Fergus . . . the deafening silence they maintain to conceal their guilt, rage, pain, failure.'

Voysey muttered, 'All these bits of gossip, they're not what'll make a case stand up in court.'

'We piece 'em together,' Thorneycroft said, 'and see what shapes.'

Voysey got to his feet. 'If we're done here, sir, I ought to go and sort out that lot outside.'

He moved off, and Fergus smiled apologetically. 'He'll come round in time. When do you plan to meet Maisie Taft?'

'Tomorrow, if possible.'

'I'd better get busy, then.' Fergus reached for the telephone. Keeping his finger on the receiver cradle, he said, 'Birmingham tomorrow. Then where?'

'Cambridge. I want to chat to Theo Brink, about Parady.'

'Umh. Have you made an appointment?'

'I will do.'

'And Claudia? Will she go with you to Cambridge?'

'I hope so.'

Fergus grinned. 'Always the patient fisherman, John.'

'What other kind is there?' Thorneycroft said.

Patience was rewarded. Thorneycroft and Claudia arrived in Birmingham on Saturday morning, and found their way to the coffee shop Maisie Taft had designated – a place, she said, where no one would recognize her. Over coffee and cake, she questioned them about Fergus, Tessa and the boys.

'It's a good thing she's in New Zealand with them,' she said. 'All that horribleness going on, they're well out of it, and Fergus must be glad to have them safe.'

Watching her, Thorneycroft decided that she was no bird brain. Her round blue eyes were shrewd, and her button of a mouth suggested both caution and determination.

She received their condolences on the death of her ex-husband with a shrug of her plump shoulders. 'Of course I'm shocked that he was taken in such a dreadful way,' she said, 'but I'd be lying if I pretended I was grieving. We weren't suited and he made me very unhappy. But that's all in the past. He's gone; I don't need him or his money. I've made a new life for myself.'

She stretched out her left hand to display a handsome cabochon ruby ring. 'I'm getting married again in July.'

Thorneycroft held her gaze. 'Does your brother approve?'

Maisie chuckled. 'That'd be a first, wouldn't it? I'll tell you right out, I've had enough of people deciding what's best for me. Ifor's what I want. He doesn't boss me about, and what's more he's an actuary with his own business, so if my brother threatens to cut me off, I can tell him where to go.' She drained her cup and settled back in her chair.

'You didn't come here for a chit-chat,' she said. 'What's on your mind?'

Thorneycroft leaned his elbows on the table. 'I'm helping Chief

Inspector Lowry in the investigation into your ex-husband's death. We need to establish the motive for his murder. You were married to him for some time . . .'

'Seven years.' Maisie grimaced.

'During that time, did he appear to have enemies? Was there anyone who held a grudge against him?'

Maisie picked cake crumbs off her plate, thinking. 'Will didn't have enemies or friends,' she said. 'He never let anyone close enough for that. It was like he lived behind a wall. I used to wonder why he married me. It wasn't for sex; he was never much for bed. Maybe he thought having a wife would help him in his career, and I was never much for that! It got to the point where he couldn't stand the sight of me. Criticized me all the time; I couldn't do anything right. I was young and soft, and I went sort of crazy. I expect Fergus told you, I was caught shop-lifting. Fergus and Tess were wonderful; they saved me from going to jail.

'My brother came and fetched me away. I got a divorce and Erwin built me a cottage in his garden. I came right, but it seems poor Will didn't. He just never got the hang of what life's about.'

'Did he know a man called Martin Parady?'

'Parady?' Maisie looked mystified. 'Not that I recall. Mind, it's years since I left Abbotsfell. I don't remember everything that went on there. Don't wish to, either. Why d'you ask?'

'It's part of our general enquiries,' said Thorneycroft vaguely. 'Mrs Taft, we believe that William may have withheld information from the police . . . and that it's possible he was killed to prevent his changing his mind.'

'Wouldn't surprise me. Withholding information, I mean. Will could never share anything. He kept everything bottled up inside him.'

'What sort of things?'

Maisie launched into a saga of Taft's reticences. Thorneycroft let her deliver a list of trivialities, and at length said, 'Was there any particular subject he refused to discuss? Anything that made him angry, or upset, if you mentioned it?'

'Like Bluebeard's chamber?'

'Yes, exactly.'

'Kids,' said Maisie promptly. 'Having kids.' Her round face was resentful. 'If I talked about starting a family, he'd blow his top.'

'From what I'm told, his own childhood was happy.'

Maisie pursed her lips. 'Well, maybe, but sometimes things look good on the surface but underneath there's weevils. I remember once, we argued about having a family. I told him any normal couple wants kids. He started to yell, and I lost my rag, I yelled back. I said I'd been brought up in a happy home, and I wanted my own family. I said, "You don't know what it means; that's why you're such a misery to yourself and everyone else." Will freaked. He gave me a great shove, and I fell down and cut my face on the kitchen fender. I thought he was going to kill me. It was after that, I had a sort of breakdown. Tried to steal a teddy from the shop.'

Maisie gave her shoulders a shake, as if to throw off past misery. 'And that was the end of that marriage,' she said. Her voice was brisk, dismissing past failure, looking forward to future happiness.

'Did William get on well with his parents?' Thorneycroft asked.

'Well enough, I think. He never spoke about his dad . . . I never met him; he died before I married Will. Will was fond of his mum and she doted on him. Came to see us often.'

'What was she like?'

'I liked her. She was down to earth, you know. A bit of a loud voice. She laughed a lot. Some folk said Mortimer Taft married beneath him, but what I say is, outsiders will never know the truth about a marriage.'

'She died in an accident, I believe?'

'Yes. She was shopping, and a bus mounted the pavement and hit her. She was killed outright. Will lost the one person that really loved him.'

Though Thorneycroft continued to question her, Maisie had little more to say about William Taft and his parents. She promised to let him know if she remembered any other facts, but it was plain that her thoughts were focused on happiness to come, not on the bleakness of the past.

She drove away in her Mercedes roadster, a present, she said, from Ifor the actuary. Claudia looked at Thorneycroft.

'What did you make of her?'

'She's a survivor, unlike her husband. She's a good witness, very honest, and observant. I think she put her finger on William's problem.'

'Which was?'

'My guess is, the first five years of his life – the time he lived in London – were happy. When Maisie told him he'd never known a happy family life, he was so enraged he knocked her down. I think that when William was taken away from London, he was driven out of his personal Eden.'

Thorneycroft dropped an arm round Claudia's shoulders. 'Let's get going. We'll find a pub on the road to Cambridge, and talk.'

XIII

Once clear of Birmingham, they bypassed Coventry and followed A roads eastward. Approaching Rugby they found a wayside steak-house, ate fillet and green salad, and talked about Maisie Taft.

'Don't be fooled by that fluffy look,' Claudia said. 'She's a toughie. It doesn't bother her that her ex was murdered. She never asked you for details. It's terrible that a man can die and there's no one to mourn him.' She sipped her black coffee and watched Thorneycroft slice figs on to camembert cheese. 'What makes you think Taft was driven out of Eden?'

'Lots of things.' Thorneycroft pushed the jar of figs towards her. 'The photographs in his house. There's nothing that shows the first five years of his life. His mother was a stage dancer, but there's not a single picture of her in that guise. Not one that shows her, or William, or Mortimer in London.'

'Photos get lost.'

'Or deliberately destroyed. Ellie Nicholls the dancer wanted to become Eleanor Taft, respectable Bath matron. She destroyed the evidence of her stage career.'

'How could that have upset William? He was five years old. It wouldn't have worried him that his mother was a dancer.'

'If he was happy in London . . . if leaving London destroyed his happiness, his sense of security . . .'

'How could it? If something terrible had happened to him, if he'd been abused, or raped, that might wreck his life, but just leaving a city . . .'

Thorneycroft was staring past her, unhearing. 'His father,' he said. 'If he was separated from his natural father, the man he'd known from birth . . .'

'You told me everyone accepted that Mortimer Taft was his natural father.'

'That's what DI Plomer, the Bath copper, led me to believe. He said Mortimer treated William as his son, gave him everything he could need or desire. That doesn't mean to say he sired William. What if, in those first five years of his life, William knew another man as his father? Loved him, was loved by him?'

'Mortimer would have found out if Ellie was two-timing him.'

'Not necessarily. Mortimer was the weekend lover; the other man had the other five days. Ellie let Mortimer think William was his son. And when he started talking of marriage, maybe she weighed up her prospects and decided she'd do better with Mortimer than the London man. She left her old life, took her child with her, took him from his true father. That could be an injury from which he never recovered. All the photographs of him at school, at university, as an adult, show him withdrawn, unsmiling. Taft had no sense of belonging, no sense of his own worth.'

Claudia sighed. 'That may be so but I don't see how it ties him in with Parady's murder.'

'I'm convinced the murders are linked. Taft made an appointment with his killer, it was someone he knew. He was killed to prevent his revealing how he was linked to Martin Parady. God, if we only knew how.'

'Couldn't they have met through university activities?'

'They could, yes. Voysey will be checking on that, but so far we haven't found anything to show they ever met. Of course, Parady was famous, he appeared on television and his name was often in the papers. Taft could have known of him, but that's not enough. There has to be something more.' Thorneycroft fell silent, fingers drumming on the table top.

'Maurice,' he said. 'Maurice might do it.'

'Maurice who?' Claudia demanded.

'Maurice Topman. He was a theatre critic in London through the period of the big musicals and knew all the performers – he's written biographies of several stars. He was kind of an investigative journalist to the acting profession.' Suddenly invigorated, Thorneycroft signalled for his bill.

'I'll call Maurice as soon as we reach the hotel,' he said. 'He's just the man to dig up the facts of Ellie Nicholls' life.'

The Unicorn Hotel at which Thorneycroft had made reservations was of the family type, in the newer part of the city. As soon as she had signed in, Claudia departed in search of a bath and change of clothes. Thorneycroft, after a critical look at the dinner menu, used the desk phone to book a table at an Italian restaurant down the road.

Up in his bedroom he made two more calls. The first was to Theodore Brink, recently retired from the faculty of Chemistry at the university, where he'd distinguished himself both as a lecturer and a pioneer of research. He possessed a phenomenal memory and impeccable discretion, gifts which had made him sought after by a wide range of organizations. One of these was the SAS, which was how he'd become friendly with Fergus and Thorneycroft.

He greeted Thorneycroft's call with enthusiasm. 'John, this is nice. It's been too long. But you're a full-time sleuth now, I understand. And assisting Fergus on this Abbotsfell case. How is he these days?'

Meaning, does he approve of this interview you're planning?

'He's fine. He sends you his regards.'

Meaning, he approves. It's kosher.

117

'Good, good. Come at ten. You have the address? The Daintry Haven. Should be the Disney Haven, to look at some of my neighbours, but live and let live.'

He gave directions for reaching the place. 'Buzz number twenty-five at the main gate and I'll let you in. Then take two lefts and a right to my cottage. I look forward to seeing you.'

Thorneycroft's second call was to Maurice Topman. It reached a message machine. Thorneycroft left his name and number, and filled in the waiting time with a shower and a shave. Topman returned his call at six o'clock, sounding impatient.

'I'm playing a billiards match,' he said. 'If it's anything less than life or death, John, forget it.'

'It's death,' Thorneycroft said. 'I'm on a case, and I need your help.'

Grumbling noises gave way to a sulky, 'Well, what?'

'Ellie Nicholls,' said Thorneycroft. 'You heard of her?'

'Yup. Dancer, yards of leg and red hair, everything from ballet to bosom tassels. Venables was her stage name, but she was born Nicholls. What's your interest?'

'I need all the information I can get about her, especially the years she spent in London. Her work, her associates, her love affairs. One of the lovers was Mortimer Taft, a manufacturer from the West Country. She married him. She had a son, William Taft, who was murdered a couple of nights ago. I'm helping the police with their enquiries.'

'I thought that meant they suspected the helper.'

'Not in this case.'

Topman snorted. 'The things I do for a laugh. OK, I'll nose around. The people who knew Ellie are probably six foot under by now, but I'll try.'

'Thanks, Morrie.'

'It'll take time, going back to the sixties.'

'Make it as fast as you can. There's a killer loose. I'll pay any reasonable expenses.'

'You can buy me some beers, next time you're this way.'

'Deal.'

Thorneycroft dropped the receiver back on its cradle.

It was true, what Maurice said. It would take time to track down and question the people who could give information about Ellie Nicholls' past. But time was a commodity in very short supply.

Fergus needed facts, fast. Slocombe was straining at the leash, panting to go in search of Parady's fossil. And out there, a murderer could be moving in on victim number three.

The Italian restaurant was all it should be, providing simple decor, a host who spoke to every guest, soft music, and a menu that took carbo-loading to new heights.

Thorneycroft and Claudia ate, drank, and avoided talking about murder. They returned to the hotel in mellow mood. Crossing the foyer, Claudia clung to Thorneycroft's arm.

'Bumpty carpet,' she said, and he smiled.

'Smooth vino.'

'I'm sober,' she declared, and after a moment added, 'Ish.'

Outside her bedroom door, Thorneycroft bent to kiss her. She kissed him back, her mouth open, her body soft and yielding, but when he reached to unlock her door, she thrust him away from her.

He faced her, out of patience at last. 'Make up your mind, Clo. Do you want me or not?'

'Yes. No.' She rubbed her hand across her mouth. 'I don't know.'

He reached for her hand, put the door key into it and folded her fingers together.

'If you want to be a nun,' he said, 'say so. It'd be a terrible waste, but if that's how you see your life, I'll stop bothering you. I've said all I bloody care to on this subject. Good night, Clo.'

He turned and crossed the corridor to his own room; heard her door closing behind him and didn't look back.

He didn't sleep well. His mind swerved from panic at the thought of losing Claudia, to certainty that it was time to make a beginning or an end. In the early hours, he dozed off, and dreamed vivid and frightening dreams. Waking at seven, he saw that an envelope had been pushed under his door. He rolled out of bed and collected it. It contained a note from Claudia.

Dear John

About last night, I'm so sorry. You see, the flesh is willing but the spirit is weak, and the mind is hopelessly confused. Please don't be angry, just give me a little more time. I shouldn't ask it, when you've been so patient, but let me finish my work on the skull and the cast, and I promise I'll give you an answer. I know I'm not being reasonable, but you mean so much to me that I can't bear it if you just walk away. You don't need me this morning, so I've gone to the early service in King's College Chapel. I'll see you at lunch.
    Yours unreasonably,
    Claudia

Thorneycroft read the note several times. 'She took the bait', he told himself. 'Now reel her in carefully.'

XIV

'Arthritis,' said Professor Brink, limping ahead of Thorneycroft to his living-room. 'That's why I'm here. Old folk need facilities, and this place provides them.'

'It seems very pleasant,' said Thorneycroft, contemplating a vista of lawns, flower-beds and discreetly placed cottages. The room they were in was comfortable and colourful, though not everyone would choose to have a fossilized lizard on the chimney-piece.

'Tea? Coffee?' As Thorneycroft shook his head, Brink lowered himself into an armchair. He was a small man, corpulent, with a bald head fringed by a tonsure of curly hair. His bland expression was deceptive. Thorneycroft knew him to be sharply inquisitive, with a puckish sense of humour.

Now he steepled his fingers and smiled at his guest. 'The Abbotsfell Skull,' he said. 'How did you become embroiled in that murky scene?'

'I was staying with Fergus. A storm exposed the skull, and I found it. It aroused my interest.'

'And so far, the victim has not been named?'

'No. But we're close.'

'Ah?' Brink tilted his head. 'You know, but you're not telling. I understand.'

And he did, the old conniver, thought Thorneycroft. He was promising co-operation and silence. It was safe to speak the truth.

'I'm interested in a man named Martin Parady,' he said. 'He was a student here. Did you know him?'

Brink did not answer at once. His face showed shock and dismay. He shook his head and said slowly, 'Indeed, yes. A star in his field. And a pain in the arse, to some. He couldn't take discipline of any kind, and annoyingly he achieved top results without it. He was a fine athlete, cricketer, tennis player. Also a compulsive womanizer, as no doubt you've heard.'

'Yes. There was some story about an affair with a don's wife. Max Slocombe said it wasn't true.'

Brink's eyelashes flickered at the mention of Slocombe's name. 'Max knew Parady better than I, being in the field of palaeoanthropology. But I agree. Most of the dons' wives were middle-aged and dowdy. Parady liked 'em young and gorgeous, and he got what he wanted. He was very good-looking. Amazing eyes. But he was a predator, he collected scalps, he never cared for the girls he bedded. He used to boast about his sexual prowess. He was despicable, really, except in his work. Is Slocombe a friend of yours?'

'An acquaintance. He's helping on the case. He gave me a potted introduction to evolution.' Thorneycroft met Brink's mild gaze. 'He told me that Parady seduced his daughter.'

Brink made no comment, and Thorneycroft said, 'Slocombe didn't press charges against Parady. So he got his first class degree and left for pastures new, is that right?'

'It is. He wasn't an academic. He went straight into fossil-hunting, became a thorn in the flesh of the people he hunted with, and pretty soon started to head his own expeditions.'

'How did he manage to get a place in that first one?'

'He was recommended by his professor, Adrian Baldwin. Adrian was a recognized expert. He got Parady his chance, and

was always ready to put in a good word for him. We all were.'
Brink caught Thorneycroft's questioning look, and sighed.
'Parady was poison to deal with but he was a top talent in his
field. Time and again his finds, his opinions, even his quarrels,
took the science of palaeoanthropology to new levels. One had to
give the devil his due.'

'Tell me about Baldwin.'

'He was a fine scholar, generous in his views, a great teacher.'
Brink's gaze rested briefly on the fossil lizard on the chimney-
piece. 'Parady was at least grateful for what Adrian taught him. He
showed respect for him, I must say.'

'Can I meet Professor Baldwin?'

'Sadly, no. Adrian took early retirement. He was a diabetic,
and his heart was weak. He died quite suddenly, a couple of years
ago. He was due to speak at a forum here in Cambridge, but a
few days before, he went into a diabetic coma, and never came
out of it.'

'What was he due to speak on?'

'Mitochondrial DNA, its application in dating fossils. Adrian
held to the multi-national theory of evolution, and he had doubts
about the reliance some people placed on DNA dating.'

'Was the paper published after his death?'

'Not to my knowledge.'

'Was he married? Did he have family? I need to talk to the
people who remember Parady.'

'He was married. His widow Marian lives in Simnell. It's a
village not far from here. Adrian bought a house there, and
Marian's never moved away. There's one son, an artist, who lives
in Spain or some such place. After Adrian died, I rather lost touch
with Marian. She was never interested in the academic scene,
though I admit she made Adrian happy. We exchange cards at
Christmas time, and that's about it.'

Brink wrote down the Simnell address for Thorneycroft, with

a telephone number that he warned might have changed. Stowing the paper in his pocket, Thorneycroft said, 'Would you by any chance remember the names of any of Parady's conquests?'

Brink's face puckered up. 'No, I would not. I found his goings-on most distasteful. I never could understand why a young man with such splendid talents should wallow in such sordid little affairs. I concentrated on what was good in him and turned a blind eye to the rest.' Brink met Thorneycroft's eyes. 'Martin Parady will be remembered for his work. His private life is best forgotten.'

Thorneycroft spent some time trying to elicit more information about Parady's spell in Cambridge, but learned little that wasn't contained in Slocombe's collection of papers.

As he prepared to leave, Brink stood up and crossed to a desk in the corner of the room. His distorted hands raised the lid and fumbled through pigeon-holes, alighting at last on a battered newspaper cutting. He handed it to Thorneycroft. It was a report of the eulogy read at Adrian Baldwin's funeral. The reader was Brink himself.

'You can keep it,' he said. 'I have other copies.'

He accompanied Thorneycroft to his car, and offered his hand in a careful handshake.

'Good luck with your investigation,' he said. 'I hope you find the killer. Murder is the ultimate cruelty.'

Once clear of Daintry Haven, Thorneycroft pulled to the side of the road and read Brink's eulogy. It was clear he'd loved Adrian Baldwin as much as he'd disliked Parady. The praises delivered, he'd made a brief reference to Marian Baldwin, who he described as 'a much-loved wife, a devoted mother, a woman of this county who has the sympathy of all of us here today'.

Thorneycroft sat for a few minutes, thinking. Then he fished the road map from the side pocket of the Rover, and after some searching found the very small dot that represented Simnell village.

He called Fergus on his mobile phone. 'Brink gave me the home address of the widow of the man who taught Martin Parady at Cambridge,' he said. 'I'll call on her, on the way back to Abbotsfell. She must have known Parady.'

'Good,' Fergus said. 'See you later.'

Claudia was waiting in the foyer of the Unicorn Hotel. She said anxiously, 'Did you get my letter?'

Thorneycroft smiled at her. 'Yes. Thank you for it. Did you enjoy the service?'

She relaxed. 'It was great; the singing was angelic. Was Professor Brink helpful?'

'Yes. He confirmed that Parady was a brilliant shit, which we already knew, but he also gave me the address of Adrian Baldwin's widow. Baldwin was Parady's professor. I thought we could visit the widow on our way home. Would you mind a detour?'

'Of course not.'

'Right, then. You pack your bag while I phone for an appointment, then we'll have an early lunch and be on our way.'

Simnell had outgrown Brink's memory of a small village. The nucleus of antique cottages clustered round a seventeenth-century church was now ringed by a supermarket, two banks, three pubs, a street of small shops, and a petrol station. Beyond these were several Victorian villas, a housing estate and a motel. The outer limits were set by scattered houses in large grounds.

Marian Baldwin's property was at the end of an untarred lane: a bungalow encircled by fine old trees. The gate stood open and they drove through into a garden foaming with spring blossom. A woman in a green trouser suit was spading round the rose bushes in a circular bed. She straightened at their approach, and waved Thorneycroft to a brick apron fronting a double garage.

The garage doors stood open; a red Polo and a Yamaha motorbike were parked in the left-hand space, and the right side was taken up by a motor mower, garden tools, and sacks of manure and compost.

Mrs Baldwin came up to them as they climbed out of the Rover.

'Dr Thorneycroft, welcome. I won't offer to shake hands.' She waggled earth-stained fingers. Thorneycroft introduced Claudia to her and she smiled. 'Are you a gardener, Mrs Hibberd?'

'Yes, but I'm not in your class. You're obviously an expert.'

'When we moved here,' Mrs Baldwin said, 'it was just a rough field. The advantage was we could plant what we liked.'

Gardening had kept her fit, Thorneycroft thought. She was of medium height and firmly built, and her skin was clear with colour on the cheeks. Her eyes, slightly prominent and set wide apart, were of the bright blue that one sees in young children.

She led them past the front door and along a path that bordered a wide flower-bed. The air was heavy with the scent of roses, lilies, jasmine and an exotic plant that smelled of cinnamon. At a break in the path they turned on to a flagged walkway and saw ahead of them french windows, standing open. To each side of these, wire trellises had been erected against the wall of the house. Honeysuckle trailed on the left-hand frame, and on the right young plants reached curling green tendrils to the wire.

'Sweet peas,' Claudia said, and Marian Baldwin beamed at her.

'Yes, indeed. My husband loved all scented plants. I used to put in what he'd enjoy, and I keep up the custom.'

The room they entered was an extension of the garden. The walls were painted pale yellow, and against this sunny background stood ferns and pot plants, and a vase filled with pink and white tiger lilies.

Mrs Baldwin held up her muddy hands. 'Sit down and relax,' she said. 'I must wash and then I'll make tea. I won't be long.' She bustled away through an inner door.

Claudia obeyed the instruction to sit, but Thorneycroft wandered round the room. A low bookcase stretched along one wall, and on it were ranged a number of framed photographs.

Most of them featured Marian: standing arms linked with a tall, thin man, presumably her husband; holding aloft a beribboned trophy; embracing a young man wearing calf-length jeans, sandals and dark glasses. Thorneycroft examined that picture more closely. The houses in the background were painted red, blue, yellow. Spain, perhaps, and the young man Marian's son?

Right at the back of the collection was a snapshot of a man sitting astride a motorbike, with a young blonde girl standing beside him. The son and girlfriend?

Above the fireplace hung an oil painting of an elderly man with gentle eyes and a lop-sided smile. The portrait was unsigned.

Nowhere in the room was there evidence of Adrian Baldwin's profession. No certificates, no Cambridge group photos, no fossils. The books in the bookcase were mostly well out of date, and there was no non-fiction to be seen.

Hearing footsteps beyond the door, Thorneycroft went to relieve his hostess of a large tray that bore a fat china teapot, crockery, hot scones, strawberry jam and a bowl of whipped cream. Settled at a low table, she dispensed her wares, talking all the while.

'You say Theo Brink gave you my address? How is the old boy? He never visits us. He always kept himself to himself, though Adrian was one of his few friends. Try the jam, Doctor, I made it myself, but the cream's from the supermarket. I don't run to cows, I'm afraid.'

Her guests served, she helped herself, lavishing jam and cream on a scone. Smiling at Claudia, she said, 'And what's your line of work, my dear?'

'Computers,' said Claudia rather thickly, and Marian laughed.

'Machines are a mystery to me, except for my Mastermix. And you, Dr Thorneycroft? Are you a specialist?'

'I'm a forensic psychiatrist,' Thorneycroft answered.

She stared at him blankly, but he had the feeling her mind was busy. 'Like on the TV,' she said. 'but how did you meet Theo, then?'

'At a party,' Thorneycroft said. 'Tell me, that portrait over the fireplace, is it of your husband?'

'Yes.' Her gaze softened. 'It's a good likeness; it's caught his expression exactly. He was such a kind man.'

'It's not signed, which is a pity.'

'Evan, my son, wouldn't sign it. He didn't like doing portraits; he says it's his job to paint the truth, not what people want him to paint. He's making a name for himself with landscapes and wildlife. Nice bright pictures with lots of sun in them.'

'Is he here in England?'

She turned from the portrait. Her eyelids flickered. 'No. He's in Spain. He'll come back in June, I expect, to stage his summer exhibition. It'll be a sell-out, like his last one.'

'You must miss him,' Claudia said, and Marian nodded.

'Well, I do, but I'll never stand in his way, or try to keep him by me. He has his career to make, his reputation.'

'Where did he train?' Thorneycroft asked. The question seemed to irritate her. Her mouth compressed and she said flatly, 'In London, Paris, America. That's where he learned the techniques, but I say it's his natural inspiration that will make his name. You can't teach inspiration and you can't buy it, either.'

She brushed crumbs from her bosom and said briskly, 'What brings you to see me, Dr Thorneycroft? If it's Evan's work you're interested in, I can't help you – you'll have to speak to him your-self.'

'I hope to, some day.' Thorneycroft saw that she was watching him closely, and he spoke with care. 'Theo Brink told me when I saw him this morning that Martin Parady was one of your husband's brightest students. Did you know him?'

She sighed, leaning back in her chair and gazing at the flowers beyond the French windows. 'Yes, I knew him, though not very well. I met all Adrian's students while we were in Cambridge. They used to come to our house for tea and talk.' She smiled faintly. 'I remember Martin because he caused Adrian so much trouble.'

'What sort of trouble?'

'Well, Martin was wild, you know. He went to parties where they did drugs, he drank too much and chased the girls. I know that's part of student life, but mostly they grow out of it, don't they? They settle down. Martin didn't. He seemed to need to live on the edge, know what I mean? He made dangerous decisions, and Adrian would try to sort him out.'

'Were you a student before you married?'

'No. I was never in college. I was a masseuse in the new town.' She smiled suddenly, showing strong white teeth. 'That's how I met Adrian. He had a frozen shoulder, and the doctor sent him to me. I'll always be grateful to that doctor. Adrian was a wonderful husband, and a wonderful father.'

'I understand he died two years ago.'

Her wide-set eyes clouded. 'Yes. He had a fall. That's bad for a diabetic patient. He went into a coma. We rushed him to hospital but they couldn't save him. He died two days later.'

'Were you living in Simnell at the time?'

'Yes, in this very house. I've never wanted to leave. Adrian's here, for me, and I have my garden.'

'You don't find it lonely?'

'No. I'm not one for the social life. I have all I want.'

'Did Martin Parady keep in touch with your husband after he left Cambridge?'

'He wrote to Adrian, and when he was in England, he'd come and visit. That wasn't often. He was always off somewhere, digging up fossils. Adrian followed his career. He felt he'd launched Martin, and he was proud of his success.'

'When was the last time you saw him?'

She was silent for a space, frowning. 'Oh . . . I suppose it must have been four or five years ago. Adrian took me to a lecture Martin gave after one of his expeditions. It was way over my head, I'm afraid. I don't expect I shall see him again. I'm out of that world now, since Adrian went.'

Her eyes brimmed with tears, and she groped for a handkerchief and wiped them away. Very soon, Thorneycroft saw, they would have to leave. He leaned towards her.

'Mrs Baldwin, you've been very patient, answering all my questions. There's one more I have to ask you. Did you ever know a man called William Taft?'

'Taft?' Her gaze wandered; she seemed hardly to be listening. 'I don't think so. I've met so many people over the years. I'm bad at remembering names. Why do you ask?'

'Taft was the pathologist at the Abbotsfell mortuary, in the Chilterns. He was murdered two nights ago.'

Marian's head jerked round. 'Murdered? How? What happened?'

'He was shot.'

She stared at him, shaking her head. 'How terrible. What a terrible thing. But I'm sorry, I can't recall that name.'

'It's I who should apologize, for bringing such news into your home. Tell me, are you alone here? Is there no one to keep you company?'

She straightened, and her face coloured. 'I don't mind being alone. I prefer it.'

'And when your son comes home from Spain—'

She cut him short. 'We'll have time together but I don't know when that will be. I don't impose on him.'

The bonhomie she'd shown when they arrived seemed to have gone. She glanced at her watch and rose to her feet.

'I'm afraid I have a meeting to attend. The Rose Club.'

Thorneycroft and Claudia moved with her, out into the garden where the shadows were beginning to lengthen round the fringes of the lawn.

They thanked her for her hospitality, and she accepted their thanks with a smile and a nod, but she remained close to the house as they drove away. As they passed through the gate, they saw that she had returned to the house, and closed the French windows behind her.

'Poor woman,' Claudia said. 'We certainly wrecked her Sunday afternoon. And you upset her, asking about her son. Obviously he doesn't take much care of her, and she doesn't like to talk about it.'

Thorneycroft grunted. 'I'd very much like to talk to Evan Baldwin.'

'You can't. He's in Spain.'

'Is he? Then who owns the motorbike I saw in the garage?'

'Even if it's Evan's, that doesn't mean he's in England. Perhaps he leaves it here when he goes abroad.'

'Perhaps.' Thorneycroft swung the Rover from the unmade lane to the road that would take them westward to Abbotsfell.

He had memorized the Yamaha's registration number. Kelly could find out easily enough if it was owned by Evan Baldwin.

Other thoughts jangled in his mind.

Evan Baldwin had painted the portrait of his father.

Max Slocombe had a painting of a cheetah, signed 'E.B.'

Theo Brink kept on his mantelpiece a fossilized lizard probably given to him by Adrian Baldwin.

Links existed, but he didn't know what they meant.

Slocombe hadn't wanted to talk about Evan Baldwin. Brink had claimed to know little about him. His mother became defensive when his name was mentioned.

All of which made Thorneycroft very anxious to meet him.

XV

They reached Abbotsfell soon after six, and drove straight to the Lowry homestead. Fergus was there, slumped in an armchair. He eyed them over the rim of a whisky glass.

'So what did you learn from Maisie Taft?'

'Not much.' Thorneycroft fixed a gin and tonic for Claudia and a beer for himself. Coming to sit down, he said, 'She has no feelings left for William, doesn't mind that she was left out of his will, she's about to marry an actuary who will supply the comforts of life.' He took a long pull at his tankard. 'She did give us one useful piece of information. She's convinced that Taft's gloomy character stems from his lack of happy family upbringing.'

'He had good parents, didn't he?'

'He never appeared to love them. I think Maisie's right. Taft's troubles go back to his childhood, in particular the first five years, in London.'

Fergus looked unconvinced.

Thorneycroft continued: 'His mother, Miss Venables, real name Ellie Nicholls, was a dancer who did well on the stage. Mortimer Taft set her up in a flat in London, and visited her as often as he could. The affair dragged on for five years. William lived in the flat with Ellie.

'Now, let's suppose that Mortimer was the sugar daddy, but that

133

she had another lover, who spent a lot of time with her and her son. Let's suppose that William loved this other man and viewed him as his father. But the man couldn't marry Ellie, or keep her in the style she enjoyed. He couldn't give her respectability. So in the end, she married Mortimer Taft, and moved to Bath. She took William with her. He was taken away from the person he loved most, who represented security and love to him. He lost his little Eden.

'It shaped his life; it determined what choices he'd make. It caused him to withhold information about the skull. I believe Taft knew who dumped the bag on the rubbish tip. It was someone from his past. I have a gut feeling that Taft's past and Parady's past are linked in some way.'

'Gut feelings don't count in a court of law,' Fergus said. His voice held the sharpness of exhaustion. 'I need facts, John, not wild guesses.'

'I'm trying to find the facts,' Thorneycroft answered. 'I've asked a journalist named Maurice Topman to find out what he can about Ellie Nicholls' London life. Perhaps you can get the Metro police to do some digging along those lines.'

'I can try.' Fergus set down his empty glass. 'We've had some developments here. That fool Momple came in to see me. He's scared shitless we'll tie him to Taft's murder. He admits he staged the devil mask episode.'

'He can't have,' Thorneycroft said. 'He's too big. The man I saw was medium height.'

'Momple didn't do the job himself. He paid a layabout twenty quid to do it for him, so he'd have a story for his miserable newspaper. I described the laws he'd broken and the penalties he could face. I don't think we'll have any more trouble from him.'

'Stupid prat. How's Voysey doing?'

'Fine. He's been working on Taft's financial situation. The man never spent money on himself – you saw what his house is like –

but his financial adviser in Bath says that he gave away large sums, mostly to charities caring for children. He always said where the money was to go. But seven years ago he sold investments worth £100,000, and refused to say what he planned to do with it. Could be it went to someone who fits into your scenario . . . someone from his past, his natural father, maybe. We'll follow it up.' Fergus straightened in his chair. 'That's all speculation. Tell me about your meeting with Professor Brink.'

Thorneycroft made his report, and ended by saying, 'The same story, really – Parady was a star and nobody could stand him. Brink said the man who gave Parady his start was Professor Adrian Baldwin, now deceased. Brink gave me the widow's address, and we called to see her at her home in Simnell.'

'What's she like?'

'Good housewife, great gardener, defensive of her son who's a talented artist. She knew Parady, though not well. Didn't like him because he bucked authority and gave her husband trouble. But she was upset by the news of Taft's death, despite the fact that she claimed not even to remember his name. I think she was worried on her son's account.'

'Why do you say that?'

As Thorneycroft hesitated, Claudia intervened. 'Marian Baldwin is the sort of woman who devotes her life to her family and her home. When John told her Taft had been murdered, she went as white as a sheet, and I saw her glance at the photograph of Evan on the bookcase. Perhaps Evan knew Taft.'

Fergus nodded thoughtfully. Turning back to Thorneycroft he said, 'Did you meet this Evan?'

'No. Marian told us he's in Spain, but there's a Yamaha motorbike in the garage that could be his.' Thorneycroft handed Fergus the registration number. 'Have the plate checked. If it belongs to Evan Baldwin, Voysey should try to establish if Evan was in the UK on Wednesday night, and where he is now.'

'Are you suggesting he killed Taft? And Parady? That he slugged Levine?'

Thorneycroft shrugged. 'I'm shadow-boxing, Fergus. We need to check on anyone and everyone who knew Parady and Taft, see if they shared a common factor. Evan Baldwin could have met Parady on one of his visits to Simnell; they could be acquainted, even friends.' He glanced at Claudia, conscious of the delicate truce they'd achieved. 'There's one more thing.'

'What?'

'Evan Baldwin's a painter, a very good one. His mother has one of his portraits in her lounge. Max Slocombe owns a painting of a cheetah, signed "E.B.", and Max said he had other examples of Baldwin's work.

'However, when I asked who E.B. was, Slocombe didn't answer. He seemed reluctant to admit he knew Baldwin. I'd like to know why.'

Before Fergus could comment, Claudia said furiously, 'What are you getting at, John? Max collects good art – that doesn't mean he knows all the artists personally. If he says he never set eyes on "E.B.", that's the truth.'

Fergus held up a hand. 'As John said, we're shadow-boxing, but I must tell you that to my mind, Slocombe's a possible suspect. He had a double motive for killing Parady. Parady seduced his daughter, and Slocombe would give his eye teeth to lay hands on the fossil Parady seems to have found.'

'That's ridiculous!' Claudia was trembling with rage. 'Max is the most honourable man I know. He detests violence. He could never commit murder.' She rounded on Thorneycroft. 'You can't believe such horrible rubbish.'

Again Fergus cut her short. 'Wait, Claudia. Slocombe has been in my mind's eye all along. No, listen, please. In 2003, Martin Parady came to England. It was an unexpected visit, none of the usual press brouhaha. He apparently brought with him the cast of a fossil head that Slocombe defines as the most recent predecessor of Homo sapiens. Such a fossil would be of immense scientific and monetary value. Parady would have been looking for many things – authentification, protection for the fossil site, money to advance his search. So what would be the first thing he'd do? He'd seek out an authority in his field, someone who could confirm the fossil's value, enlist expert support, raise funds. Am I right, John?'

Thorneycroft nodded. 'Probably.'

Fergus turned back to Claudia. 'He couldn't go to his teacher, Adrian Baldwin. Baldwin was seriously ill, too frail to be of any help to Parady. But there was Max Slocombe, a man of knowledge and power, who could cut through legal and political red tape.'

Claudia glared at him. 'Parady wouldn't go to Max. Max despised him.'

'As a man, yes. Not as a palaeoanthropologist. Slocombe knew that if Parady made a claim, he must be listened to. Parady visited Slocombe, and Slocombe, with the double motives of personal revenge and burning ambition, killed him.'

Thorneycroft saw that Claudia was ready to start a shouting match, and caught hold of her hand, saying quietly, 'I don't think that theory holds water, Fergus. Slocombe doesn't fit what we already know about this killer.

'Slocombe is clever, organized in all he does. He wouldn't have buried Parody's body and later exhumed the skull, he wouldn't have knocked out its teeth. He'd have got rid of the whole skeleton, and he'd have hidden the cast somewhere safe. He certainly wouldn't have thrown it on a rubbish dump. The person who killed Parady made mistakes that Slocombe would never have made. Slocombe doesn't fit my profile of Parady's killer.'

Fergus said deliberately, 'You know as well as I do that a clever killer may fake evidence to mislead the forensic experts.' He put a hand on Claudia's shoulder. 'I hope sincerely that John's right, my dear, but I have to examine every possibility. And if Max Slocombe is innocent, we need to prove it.'

His expression forbade any further argument. The policeman was in charge, not the friend.

Claudia was silent, and Thorneycroft said, 'What about Inez Parady? Is she back in the UK?'

'Yes,' Fergus answered. 'I spoke to her on the phone. She'll come here tomorrow, to look at Clo's reconstruction of the skull. She promised to bring photographs of her father, and some letters he wrote to her. I'd like you both to sit in on the interview.' He got to his feet. 'I'm due back at the nick,' he said. 'I'll bring Voysey up to speed. Don't keep supper for me.'

They heard his car drive away. Claudia said angrily, 'He's mad to suspect Max.'

'It's his job, love.'

Her mouth tightened. 'You'd better find out who did kill Parady, and Taft. You'd better find out, pretty damn quick.'

XVI

Fergus ruled that the interview with Inez Parady should take place in Claudia's workshop.

'She'll want to see the skull as well as the reconstruction, he said, 'and I don't doubt she'll have questions aplenty. Voysey will conduct the interview, with Kelly in support. You and Claudia will be there as observers, but you'll be given the chance to speak. I shall meet Dr Parady at the front desk, downstairs, and bring her up to the workshop. She should be here in fifteen minutes.'

Voysey, Kelly, Claudia and Thorneycroft settled in chairs round a central table. The skull and Claudia's reconstruction head were placed on the enamel workbench, with a screen drawn round them so that Inez Parady shouldn't be confronted by them as she stepped out of the lift.

Thorneycroft spent the fifteen minutes studying the CV of Inez Parady that Kelly had compiled. Father, Martin, born 1947, married in 1974 to Charlotte Burne-Wilkins, a wealthy socialite. Daughter Inez born 1975. Martin quit the family nest in 1988. Charlotte died of cancer, 1989, leaving her considerable fortune to her only child, and nothing to her defaulting husband.

Inez grew up devoted to her mother, clever, and very rich. Became a botanist of note, travelled widely, wrote several books that sold well. Was a dedicated conservationist.

A list of her career achievements followed.

Thorneycroft sighed. The girl had been parted from her father when she was fourteen years old. It was unlikely they'd get much information, from her.

He laid the CV aside.

The atmosphere round the table was not convivial. Claudia seemed nervous, wondering perhaps how the bereaved woman would react to the sight of her dead father's skull. Voysey thumbed through papers, tight-lipped. Plainly he saw Fergus's arrangements as irregular, and a reflection on his own skills. Kelly moved to switch on the in-house video that gave a continuous picture of what went on in other parts of the station. In due course they saw Inez Parady arrive at the front desk, where Fergus was waiting. The two stood talking for some minutes, Fergus obviously offering his sympathies, and explaining the current situation to her.

Thorneycroft studied her.

She was above average height, strongly built, her skin darkly tanned. She wore slacks and a designer shirt, and carried a small briefcase. As Fergus turned to conduct her across the charge office to the elevator, her face came into clear focus, and Thorneycroft saw that she didn't resemble her father. Her hair was dark and straight, short but elegantly cut. She had a high forehead, a Roman nose, a pointed jawline. An air of self-sufficiency. The word patrician crossed his mind.

The elevator ascended, the doors opened, and Inez stepped out and advanced towards them. She pulled off her dark glasses, revealing eyes that were dark brown, large and bright.

She was not beautiful, not even pretty, but she compelled attention. The Parady power was hers, if not the appearance. Voysey would be no match for the brain behind that piercing gaze.

Fergus made the necessary introductions and departed. Inez Parady turned at once to Claudia.

'Dr Hibberd, you did the reconstruction?'

'Yes.'

'Show me, please.'

They walked together to the workbench. Claudia drew aside the screen and stood back. Inez folded her arms and stared first at the skull, and then at the model head. At last she nodded.

'It's my father,' she said. 'You're very good at your job.'

Claudia lifted the skull back into its metal box and locked that. Voysey came to conduct Inez to the chair opposite his own.

'This is a very sad time for you, Dr Parady,' he said. 'We appreciate your coming to our help. You feel that Mrs Hibberd's reconstruction is a good likeness of your father?'

'It's my father. Martin Parady.' Inez sat down and placed her briefcase on the table.

Voysey cleared his throat. 'Your father left home when you were only fourteen years old—' he began, but Inez interrupted him.

'I've seen him at intervals since then. I'm sure that that model is taken from his skull. I'm sure that the skull is my father's skull, and so are you, Inspector, or you wouldn't have hauled me back from South America to make the identification.'

She snapped the clasps of the briefcase and lifted out an envelope. 'I've brought some photographs of my father. You can make comparisons with the skull. I'm ready to give blood for DNA testing. That will clinch the matter.'

Voysey took the envelope and drew out four portrait-sized photos. Inez watched him calmly. She gave no sign of grief, no tears, no tremor of the voice, but Thorneycroft sensed the electric tension in her.

Voysey laid the photos aside, and Inez spoke. 'Chief Inspector Lowry told me that you're treating this as unnatural death; accident, culpable homicide or murder. I asked him what was the basis of that decision. He said that there are circumstances which you are not at liberty to divulge.'

She pronounced the last words in a sardonic tone, and Voysey stiffened. 'The coroner's court met last week, ma'am, and post-poned the inquest, pending the completion of our search of the area where the . . . ah . . . remains were found.'

'It was murder,' said Inez flatly. Her hands clenched on the table top. 'Someone crushed his head. There are chisel marks on his jawbone.'

As Voysey opened his mouth to reply, she said impatiently, 'Don't let's waste time fencing, Inspector. My father was murdered, and his skull was thrown on a rubbish heap. I read in this morning's paper that there's been a second murder, of the man who did the post mortem on the skull. A Dr Taft?'

'That's correct,' Voysey said. 'Dr Taft was shot dead on Wednesday night.'

'Are the two deaths connected?'

Voysey folded his hands. 'I'll ask the questions, Dr Parady, if you please. Tell me, did your father have enemies?'

'Dozens,' she said wearily. 'He made enemies the way other people make friends . . . in his work environment, his love affairs, his business dealings. He was a genius, you understand, and genius is seldom popular.'

'When last did you see him?'

'About . . . four years ago. In 2001. We didn't often meet. We both moved about the world a lot.' She rubbed a hand across her eyes. 'Let me explain. He was a lousy husband, and he didn't care a damn about me. My mother died of cancer in 1989. It was very rapid in its course. I sent for my father, but he never even answered my letter. My mother cut him out of her will and left everything to me.

'As soon as the estate was settled, my father wrote to me, asking for money. He made no apology, just said he needed it for excava-tions he was doing. He felt he had the right to ask. He felt no guilt for his desertion, his callous disregard of Mum and me.' Inez ran a finger along the edge of her briefcase. 'He was contemptible, I despised him, but I sent him the money. I knew his work was important, and he did it better than anyone else on earth. I felt he was entitled to support.' She surveyed her listeners with a half-smile. 'I don't expect you to understand.'

Surprisingly, Voysey nodded. 'Honour where honour's due. When was the last time you sent your father money?'

'Christmas, 2002,' she said at once.

'Were was the money sent to?'

'To a bank in Johannesburg, South Africa.' For the second time she reached into her briefcase, this time pulling out several sheets of paper. 'These are the statements of money paid by me to Martin Parady over the past five years. I thought you might need them.'

Voysey scanned the papers. His eyebrows rose, but he made no comment.

'Have you seen him or heard from him since this last . . . gift?' he enquired.

'No. I've heard nothing since Christmas 2002. He never troubled to acknowledge the money. I last saw him in September 2001. He was in England to deliver lectures. We had an hour together. He didn't mention that he planned to go to Africa. He said he didn't know where he'd be heading next – he thought perhaps Kenya, but he must have changed his mind.'

'Four years ago,' Voysey mused. 'That's a long gap, seeing as you were such a generous sponsor.'

Inez regarded him with growing irritation. 'I've tried to make it clear to you. I didn't miss Martin, I didn't feel the need for his presence. As a person he meant nothing to me. It didn't surprise me when he did one of his disappearing acts. That was typical of him.'

Thorneycroft reflected that Slocombe had said much the same thing.

Voysey rubbed his cheek. 'The pathologist was of the opinion that the condition of the skull indicated that death probably occurred some two years ago. In 2003, that would be. Were you in England at that time?'

'No.' Inez spoke calmly. 'I was in India for the whole of 2003. India and Nepal.'

Thorneycroft, watching her closely, saw her neck muscles grow taut, her breathing rate increase. Her rigid self-control couldn't quite mask her mounting anger, her mistrust of Voysey's questioning. So far, she'd told them little they couldn't have learnt for themselves. Somehow she must be persuaded to trust them.

He got to his feet, crossed to the far side of the room and approached the counter where the security guard was seated. He reached for the intercom and pressed the number for Fergus's office. Fergus answered at once and Thorneycroft said softly, 'We have a stalemate. She has more to tell, but she's clamming up. I'd like to show her the fossil cast.'

'No way. Absolutely not.' Fergus sounded annoyed.

Thorneycroft persisted. 'We need to get her to talk about Parady's last African safari. I want to assure her that we won't put his work at risk.'

There was a pause, then Fergus said, 'I'll come up. You can talk, but you are not to mention the cast. Not a hint, understand? Step out of line and you're off this case.'

'Right.' Thorneycroft returned to the table. 'Fergus is coming up,' he said. No one answered. Voysey was studyinq the bank statements Inez had brought, and muttering to Kelly. Claudia sat quietly, eyes lowered. Inez Parady gazed into space.

Fergus arrived and took the chair at the head of the table, between Voysey and Inez. He nodded to Thorneycroft.

'Go ahead, John.'

Thorneycroft leaned an elbow on the table so that he faced Inez. 'Doctor,' he said, 'as Inspector Voysey has said, we know this is very hard on you, and I'm afraid it will get harder. Very soon we'll have to reveal that the skull found on Abbotsfell tip is that of

Martin Parady. He was a public figure. There'll be great public concern and interest.'

Inez made a grimace of distaste, and Thorneycroft said quietly, 'You're right, some of the interest will be morbid and cruel. The sensation-mongers will dig up old scandals and quarrels. But there will also be an enormous response from the world of palaeoanthropology. Experts will be quick to acknowledge your father's brilliance, his total commitment to discovering the truth about our human history. Do you agree?'

'I suppose so.' She did not look at him. Her gaze was fixed on her clasped hands.

'Inspector Voysey asked you if your father had enemies, and you said he had plenty. Isn't it probable that some of them hated him not for his bad qualities, but for his virtues? His ability to find and identify important fossils, for instance?'

'It's possible.'

'So.' Thorneycroft leaned closer to her, speaking as if they were alone in the room. 'Reliable sources have told us that he dropped out of sight in 2001. They suggest he went to South Africa and remained there from early 2002 until April 2003. That period is, we believe, critically important to our investigation. We need to gather every scrap of information we can that relates to that period. We suspect that while in Africa, he discovered a fossil site, and recovered from it a fossil of great scientific significance.'

Inez's head jerked up. 'Why do you think that?'

Thorneycroft ignored the question. 'We think that it was that discovery that led to his murder in April of 2003. We need your help, Dr Parady, not only because his murderer must be brought to book, but because if we're right . . . if he indeed found a new site, a valuable fossil, then those finds must be protected against exploitation by greedy and incompetent scavengers.'

Inez was staring, her face set.

'We don't have much time,' Thorneycroft said. 'In a short while the murder of your father will become public knowledge. Rumours will fly. Some person may get wind of your father's discovery – if indeed there was one – and the hunt will be up. His right to claim the find will be beyond protection.'

Inez shook her head violently, both hands raised. 'Why should I help you?' she demanded. 'Why should I believe that you care about anything except your precious investigation? And how do I know that what I tell you will remain private? I'm damned if I'll have my life pawed over in smutty newspapers.'

'I can't promise you privacy,' Thorneycroft said. 'No one can. But surely you agree that what you need, and what we need, is the truth about that last year of your father's life. The truth, not the scandals and innuendoes that the media will invent if the truth isn't available.'

Inez glared at him, eyes narrowed. Then surprisingly, she turned to Claudia.

'Can I trust these people?' she said.

'Yes,' Claudia answered.

'What must I do? I don't know what to do.'

'Do what your father would have wanted you to do.'

Inez bent forward, elbows on her knees. At length she straightened and reached into her briefcase.

'My father wrote me other letters,' she said. 'I'll tell you what's in them.'

XVII

'In June, 2002,' Inez began, 'I received a letter from my father. He gave no address, but the envelope was postmarked Johannesburg, South Africa.

'As usual he wanted money, but this time it was a lot more than before.' She pointed to the bank statements she'd given to Voysey. 'The amounts are all listed there.'

She gazed round the ring of watching faces. 'He wrote that he'd found a new fossil site,' she said. 'He described it as the probable cradle of mankind, the Eden of mitochondrial Eve.'

'Wait,' Voysey interrupted. 'What's that mean?'

'DNA,' Inez said impatiently. 'Geneticists study human cells. Most of the genetic information is in the nuclei of cells, but a few genes are to be found in structures called mitochondria. They're inherited from the mother only. My father believed that the hominid from whom our species – Homo sapiens – derived, lived in Africa. She was African Eve, mitochondrial Eve.'

Voysey started to speak, but Fergus waved him to silence. 'Your father was saying that he'd found a fossil that would prove that the Out of Africa theory of evolution was the correct one?'

'Yes.'

'Did he say where this site was?'

'No. He described it a little. He said it was on the edge of a plateau that drops down to the river valley of the Limpopo River. That means the northernmost part of South Africa. He said that in prehistoric times, the area would have been covered by tropical forest, but now it was grassland and scrub bush. He mentioned wild stinkwood and wild olive trees. He said there were fruit farms in the lower valleys.'

'Why was he so vague? He must have known the importance of exact knowledge.'

'He was always secretive about his work,' Inez said drily. 'He suspected everyone of wanting to steal his finds. I was no exception. He told me what he knew would interest me as a botanist, because he wanted me to give him a great deal of money. He made special mention of a rare plant with pink flowers and a root that tastes of liquorice.'

Thorneycroft said quickly, 'Rare? Then it could be protected. Did you try to identify the plant?'

'Yes. I wrote to a colleague in Africa. She couldn't pinpoint the site, but she told me there are four areas where the plant is found. Its papilionaceous.' Inez saw Voysey scowl, and sighed. 'Its upper leaves have a butterfly shape and are pink in colour. It's beautiful to look at, and its roots can be used medicinally. It prefers a lime soil.'

'Lime?' Thorneycroft struggled to recall schoolboy geology. 'Calcium carbonate plus magnesium,' he said. 'Magnesian limestone. Dolomite rock, which is a good place to look for fossils.'

'So I understand. It won't help you to pinpoint that site. Do you know how big Africa is, how long the northern edge of that plateau is, how many valleys and rivers you'd have to explore to find one small fossil site?'

'Yes, Dr Parady, I do know, but it has to be done. As a scientist, you have to admit it has to be done.'

'All right. I admit that now my father is dead, we have to find the site, but that's not my job. Maybe it's yours. If so, you'd better get on with it.'

Claudia said quietly, 'There's more, isn't there? Another letter?'

Inez shot her a sullen glance, and it seemed she would refuse to answer, but at last she nodded.

'Two more. He wrote in September 2002, wanting more money, this time because he'd run into heavy opposition.'

'From whom? The South African authorities?'

'No, he never mentioned them. I think he must have had that clearance at least to begin his search. I don't know if he was cleared to launch an expedition or set up a dig.'

'Then who opposed him?'

'Just about everyone.' Inez linked her hands on the table top. 'He said the rural people of the area are black and very poor. The valley gives them water, pasture for their goats, space to plant subsistance crops. Their religion is ancestor worship and the ancestral graves are in the valley. They don't want those disturbed.

'The conservationists made waves for Martin. They're hyped up because of the liquorice plant, scared that a rush of fossil-hunters will damage the environment.

'There's also a white-run church nearby, flat-earthers who think evolution is heresy and a denial of the book of Genesis. And finally, there are the mineral prospectors. Along that border there are deposits of platinum, copper, tin, and there are people anxious to exploit them.'

'So your father's site could be close to a mineral area,' Fergus said. 'Did he mention who was doing the prospecting? Was it the South African government? A foreign company?'

'I don't know.' Inez looked at the metal box on the work bench, then at Thorneycroft.

'Doctor, you believe he came to England in April of 2003. That he was . . . killed around that time. He never told me that he meant to come home. I think perhaps he didn't have time.'

She paused, and Thorneycroft prompted: 'What do you mean,

he never had time?'

'He felt a threat to his work,' Inez said. 'He felt his site was threatened, and he wasn't easily scared. He wouldn't have been fazed by religious humbugs, or a gaggle of greens, but I think he recognized that mining operators had the money and the influence to put pressure on higher authorities. He didn't appeal to his colleagues for help – you say none of them knew where he was. He didn't tell me he was going to England. I think it was a snap decision.'

'Do you know of any person or group that could have posed such a threat?'

'No, I don't.'

Voysey said impatiently, 'We need facts, Dr Parady, not guesses.'

She glanced at him with dislike. 'The friend I wrote to about the liquorice plant sent me an email with the information I wanted. She also gave me news of my father. She said she'd seen a picture of him in a Johannesburg paper. He was with a woman – a beautiful woman, she said – and they seemed very matey. The caption gave the woman's name as Mrs Runa Vaughn. Perhaps she can provide you with facts . . . if you can trace her.'

She addressed Fergus. 'I'll leave the letters with you, Chief Inspector. They've been handled only by my father and me. You may like to check them for prints. And you'll need a sample of my blood for DNA testing. Can you arrange for me to give that now? I'd like to get back to London as soon as possible.'

Fergus rose and took the letters from her. 'Thank you. You've been extremely helpful.' He hesitated. 'I have to tell you that we'll be releasing the news of your father's death, very soon. There will be a lot of publicity. I'm afraid you'll be a target for the media.'

'They won't find me,' said Inez grimly. 'I'm leaving for France tonight. I have a cottage in Brittany. I'll give you the address and contact numbers.'

She nodded to the listeners round the table, and moved off with

Fergus. As the lift doors closed after them, Voysey said explosively, 'Well, that was a bloody waste of time. All that crap about religious nutters and grizzling greens and mining buffs, that's not going to help us solve this case. Parady wasn't topped in bleeding Africa, he was topped here, so we'd better get on with finding the perp here, in England.'

He slid the papers Inez had given him into a sample bag and handed it to Kelly. 'Have those checked,' he directed, and to Thorneycroft he said, 'I'll see you get copies. That lady's touched in the attic. She didn't even like her dad, but she gave him close on a quarter of a million over the past few years. That's a lot of moola to spend on digging up old bones.'

He hurried off, with Kelly in his wake.

Claudia saw the skull and her model of it locked in the security safe, and she and Thorneycroft went down to Fergus's office. He gave Claudia a quizzical look.

'Why did that tough woman appeal to you for advice instead of to us pillars of the law?'

Claudia touched the silver brooch on her lapel, the silhouette of a fish.

'She's a Christian,' she said. 'What are you going to do now?'

Fergus grimaced. 'Try to trace this Runa Vaughn. If Parady was bedding her, she may have learned something about where he was working. We'll also have to try to establish which mineral prospectors are at work in South Africa. Needles in a haystack, I'd say.'

Claudia fiddled with her brooch, frowning. 'Why don't you ask Rollo for help?' she said.

Both men blinked. Rollo had been their commanding officer in the SAS. He was now involved in activities that provided him with a great deal of privileged information, and not a little power. Claudia had always disliked and mistrusted him, saying there was a whiff of sulphur about him. For her to suggest that they ask for his help was an astonishing about-face.

Fergus said flatly, 'We can't go to Rollo. We have to work through the proper channels, police channels.'

'Which grind more slowly than the mills of God,' Thorneycroft pointed out.

Fergus raised both hands, and Thorneycroft sighed. 'All right. You're the boss.'

'Kelly's been checking on your visit to the Baldwins',' Fergus said. 'That motorbike you saw in their garage is registered to Evan Baldwin. Seems his mum lied when she told you he was out of the country.'

'Maybe he parks his bike with her when he's abroad.'

'She lied,' Fergus insisted. 'Evan Baldwin's in London, staying with an art dealer named Dustin Bloom, who owns the Alessandri Gallery in Kensington. Baldwin's work is to be exhibited over the next two weeks. It covers three years, most of which time he's spent out of England. I'll ask the Metro mob to have a word with him.'

Thorneycroft demurred. 'If Ma Baldwin is trying to protect him, she'll have warned him that we've been asking questions about Parady and Taft. And if he has something to hide, he'll have his answers ready. He won't bare his soul to a copper. He must be interrogated by someone who knows the full details of the Parady and Taft cases – it can't be a hit-or-miss affair.'

'Tomorrow,' Fergus said, 'the media will carry the news that the victim in the Abbotsfell Skull murder is famous palaeoanthropologist Martin Parady. If Baldwin's implicated in the murder, he may skip the country.'

'If he's implicated, he already knows Parady was the victim. He hasn't bolted. If he's not implicated, he has no need to bolt. Handle him with care and you'll get the information you want. Rush him, and you could end with nothing.'

Fergus puffed out breath. 'I'll work something out with Voysey.' He touched the plastic bag that held Inez Parady's letters. 'We'll

get in touch with the South African police, to see if they can identify Parady's site. He's given us a few clues. The geological and
botanical experts may help. And we'll work on identifying the
mineral prospectors. But it all takes so much time.'

The two men fell to discussing the way forward.

Claudia returned to her workroom upstairs. She had started
work on building a model of the fossil cast, but her attention
wandered.

Everyone railed against the lack of time. The police, the media,
Max Slocombe, all wanted quick solutions to their problems. A
matter of life and death, literally.

She sat for some time, staring into space. Coming to a decision,
she put through a call to Mrs Maggie Hogan, Rollo McLeod's
personal secretary.

Reaching Rollo, even with the aid of an old friend, involved being
passed through several sieves, human and electronic; but at ten the
next morning, Maggie ushered Claudia into his presence.

He rose from behind his desk and saw her settled in the visitor's
chair. He hadn't changed, Claudia thought. Still the sleek grey
haircut, the cold grey eyes, the exquisitely tailored grey suit. His
smile acknowledged past acquaintance, but made no promises. He
waved aside her attempt at thanks.

'Good to see you, Claudia. How can I help?'

She began hesitantly. 'I need information, not for myself, but for
John and Fergus. They're working on this investigation.'

'The Abbotsfell Skull murder. Very Grand Guignol. Do John
and Fergus know you're here?'

Claudia swallowed. 'No. They won't break protocol.'

Rollo looked amused. 'A first for them. I know the basics of the
case. Give me the details.'

Claudia described the conversations Thorneycroft had had with
Maisie Taft, Professor Brink and Marian Baldwin. 'They all said

153

the same thing,' she told him. 'Parady was a wizard at his job, and no one could stand the sight of him.'

Rollo sighed. 'So there are suspects, no proven motive, and no grounds for arrests.'

'John doesn't believe Parady was killed because he was a pain in the neck. He says he was killed because he found the fossil. We showed pictures of the fossil cast to Max Slocombe, who's an expert, and Max said if such a fossil exists, it could be a hitherto unknown species, the immediate predecessor of Homo sapiens. You can see the importance . . .'

'Yes. Immense.' Rollo's voice had lifted a shade and Claudia was encouraged.

'Yesterday we met with Inez Parady. She saw my reconstruction of the skull and identified it at once as her father. She said he went to South Africa in early 2002 and discovered a fossil site. It contained the fossilized bones of a hominid which he claimed is the most recent ancestor of modern man.'

'And you're assuming that the fossil cast dumped on the Abbotsfell rubbish tip was made from the fossil bones Parady described to his daughter?'

'It's obvious, isn't it?'

Rollo pursed his mouth, but didn't argue. 'Where is this fossil site?'

'Parady never told Inez where it was. He was murdered, probably in early April of 2003, before he could report his find to the palaeoanthropological boffins.'

'And was this incredibly valuable site taken over by the South African authorities? Has it been developed?'

'Apparently not. There's been no report of its existence from them, or the palaeos, or the media. It seems no other individual or group has tried to locate or work the site.'

'That,' said Rollo bluntly, 'boggles belief.' He sat silent for a moment. 'Do you imagine Parady was hoping to handle the dig on his own?'

'According to Inez, he hadn't yet set up an investigatory team. He encountered a lot of opposition, from local farmers, black and white, from a hellfire church, from conservationists, and from mining prospectors.'

'So many fingers in the pie.'

'And Martin Parady pulled out the plum, and was killed for it. Inez said he wrote to her in December 2002, asking for money to work the site; but then, in April 2003, he made an unannounced trip to England. Her theory is, his dig was under threat from the mining hopefuls, and he brought the cast here to persuade the leaders of his profession to head off the prospectors. He was killed before he could put his case to anyone.'

'Did Ms Parady name the prospectors?'

'No. But she told us that Parady was having an affair with a woman in Johannesburg, name of Runa Vaughn. If we can trace her, she may be able to tell us where Parady was working, and who else was interested in that piece of ground.'

'Runa,' mused Rollo. 'An unusual name. Maori, I believe.' He reached into a drawer of his desk and lifted out a file. 'When Maggie gave me your message yesterday, that you were looking for a woman named Runa Vaughn, it rang a bell. We put some facts together.'

He leaned back in his chair. 'Runa Vaughn is the wife of Lance Vaughn, who calls himself a mining engineer but is in fact a crook. Not a top ranker, but nasty enough. His front in London is Vaughn Prospectors. His real job is pimping for the major villains.

'Under cover of sniffing out gold, or copper, or some other mineral deposit, he enlists criminal customers, and brokers their deals. If you want illegal arms, or drugs, or child porn, Vaughn's your boy. He'll help you set up an illicit-documents trade or plan a military coup. He's smooth, streetwise and never lacks for capital. He uses catspaws to take the really big risks. He knows who to bribe and who to kill. He's never been nailed in a court of law, but he's persona non grata in a good many countries around the world. In South America he's known as Fer-de-Lance: the poisonous viper.

'Of recent years he's been operating in Africa, but they're fast getting wise to him. In late 2002, South Africa gave him the heave-ho, because he was suspected of running consignments of mandrax from India via Mozambique.'

'Did Vaughn clash with Parady in Africa?' Claudia asked. 'Was that what made Parady hightail it back here?'

Rollo tilted his head. 'The question you should rather ask is, 'Did Parady put a spoke in Vaughn's wheel? Did Parady become a threat to Vaughn? That would have put him on Vaughn's hit list.'

'Vaughn has hit men?'

'And women.'

'What about Runa Vaughn?'

Rollo leafed through the file under his hand and extracted a photograph, which he handed to Claudia.

It showed a woman with curling dark hair, and the sort of face beloved of chocolate merchants. Her skin was lustrous as a pearl, her mouth made promises which her green eyes denied. Her splendid body was entirely nude.

'Lance uses her as bait,' Rollo said. 'Customers who can't be bought may be bedded and blackmailed, you know how it goes. She probably tried to entrap Parady, but she's none too bright, and my guess is Parady turned the tables on her and Lance. Tipped off the South African authorities that Lance was interested in mandrax, not manganese.'

'Manganese?' Claudia sat forward in her chair. 'The fossil cast found with Parady's skull was stained artificially, an orange-brown colour, to resemble the real fossil. Max Slocombe told us that manganese can stain bones during the process of fossilization. Parady's site must be in an area where there's manganese in the ground.'

'There are a number of those in southern Africa,' Rollo said, 'but yes, that could be a pointer to where Parady was working. Vaughn's cover in Africa was that he was prospecting for manganese. So there's your conflict of interests. Vaughn wanted the land as a convenient base for his drug-running operation. Parady was determined to protect his fossil site, and sabotaged Vaughn's plans.'

'So Vaughn killed him?'

'Arranged for his demise,' Rollo corrected. 'It's a possible scenario.'

Claudia frowned. 'But surely a professional hit man wouldn't dump the skull and the fossil cast on a rubbish tip, where someone might find them?'

Rollo didn't answer the question. He patted the file before him. 'I'll courier this lot to Fergus. It contains all known addresses of Lance and Runa Vaughn, here and abroad, plus a record of their suspected past activities. There's enough to suggest that Lance Vaughn had reason to want Parady dead. Fergus can take it from there.'

He met Claudia's anxious gaze, and smiled. 'I'll put in a covering letter to say that it's come to my ears that Parady and Vaughn coveted the same stretch of ground. I'll mention that I, like many others, would dearly love to see Vaughn indicted for murder, but that unfortunately protocol forbids my department to go after him. Fergus, of course, as he's directing the investigation into Parady's death, can do just that, with the full co-operation of the South African police.'

'You spoke about South African authorities,' Claudia said. 'Which ones? John wants names.'

Rollo chuckled. 'He'll find them in the dossier.'

He rose and walked with her to the door. 'Do warn Fergus and John that the folk in South Africa have their own imperatives, and must be treated with care. And anyone who goes near any Vaughn bolthole should be sure to take his snake-bite kit with him.'

He dropped a kiss on Claudia's cheek and patted her shoulder. 'Go well, my dear,' he said. 'Maggie will take you to lunch.'

XVIII

Lunch with Maggie was alfresco, bought from the local deli-catessen and eaten in Kensington Gardens. The talk was of old times. At two o'clock Maggie went back to her office, and Claudia took a taxi to the Alessandri Gallery.

It was situated in a neat little square, and it looked prosperous. Its bow window held only one painting, an acrylic of a black woman carrying a basket of fish along a wooden jetty. Her faded red skirt was kilted up to her knees, a yellow scarf was knotted round her breasts, and behind her,smudgy charcoal boats lay on an electric blue sea. Sun seemed to pour from the canvas. The price on a little velvet stand made Claudia blink. Evan Baldwin, it seemed, was doing very nicely.

She hesitated for a while in the entrance. Rollo had made a joke of protocol but Fergus would not. She'd already broken the rules by appealing to Rollo. She would break them again if she went through this door. Reason said go away. Instinct said go ahead. She went through the door.

At a black glass reception desk she bought a brochure. Its cover depicted the artist, dressed in faded jeans and a black straw hat. His face was blurred by shadow; a strange method of self-adver-tisement.

Beyond the desk was a foyer where several people were talking and sipping drinks. From the foyer, arches led to a number of display rooms. According to the catalogue, the one to the left showed pictures of Namibia, the one to the right featured Mozambique, and the one straight ahead, South Africa. Claudia chose the last.

The display had been mounted by experts – skilful placing, lighting in all the right places – but walking round the room, Claudia decided that the paintings needed no help. They were brilliant in technique, and in the energy and passion they exuded. Most of them already bore the red 'sold' sticker.

She halted to stare at a study of a buffalo, a great bulk bursting at speed from virulent green undergrowth. She leaned forward to examine the brushwork and felt someone touch her arm. Turning, she found herself facing a small man in a black satin caftan. He bowed over folded hands.

'My name is Dustin Bloom,' he said. 'Welcome to my gallery.'

'Claudia Hibberd,' she responded, and the man smiled. She had the feeling that he already knew her name.

He cut an extraordinary figure. His hair was combed upward in bright yellow spikes, like a dandelion. His features were delicate, nondescript. His eyes, which were ringed with black eyeliner, were bright blue and unblinking.

'You like the buffalo?' he said.

'Very much,' Claudia said. 'It's powerful. Challenging.'

The man's lips curled. 'They tell me a buffalo, if injured, may turn and stalk the hunter, and kill him. A vengeful beast. Are you familiar with Evan's work?'

'I've not seen much of it. Dr Max Slocombe, my godfather, has a very fine oil of a cheetah, and last week, when I went with a friend to visit Mrs Marian Baldwin, I saw Evan's portrait of his late father.'

Bloom's eyes narrowed, but he answered smoothly. 'The portrait was early work. Evan was only eighteen when he painted it, but he was devoted to his father, and the warmth of feeling comes through, despite certain technical faults.' A thin hand wafted towards the surrounding walls. 'Here we have the mature Baldwin. In my opinion he's the finest painter of wildlife in the world today.'

Claudia nodded. 'He seems to be at home in any medium. His sense of colour, and his handling of light, are remarkable. Where did he train?'

'The Slade. Also Paris and New York.'

'That must have cost money. Did he win bursaries or has he wealthy sponsors?'

Bloom's brows soared. 'No need, no need. Evan sells everything he produces. Always has.'

'With your help, I'm sure. So much depends on skilled presentation and marketing.' Claudia glanced again at the buffalo. 'Mr Baldwin knows Africa, that's plain. One can smell it in that picture, the dusty, herby earth and the acrid vegetation. Of course his father visited Africa, looking for fossils. Did he take Evan with him?'

'He did, and Evan's made his own journeys of recent years. He loves Africa.'

'He lives in Spain, so his mother said?'

Bloom's mouth tightened. 'He has a place in Spain.'

'And when he's in England?'

Bloom made no answer, and Claudia said ingenuously, 'Mrs Baldwin told us he was out of the country at the moment.'

Bloom's eyes seemed to grow smaller and brighter. 'You can't believe anything that old woman says. Evan doesn't live with her, hasn't done for years.'

Claudia thought of the Yamaha in the Baldwin garage but decided it would be unwise to mention it. Instead she said, 'So where does he stay when he's in England? I'd love to meet him, and so would my sorority.'

The dandelion head twisted to an odd angle and the thin fingers fluttered dismissively.

'There's little chance of that. I will mention it to him but I must tell you that Evan doesn't give interviews. He's an artist, a private person who doesn't care to bare his soul to strangers. Enjoy the exhibition, Mrs Hibberd. Should you wish to make a purchase, do pray speak to me, or to one of my assistants. So glad to have had this little chat with you.'

He wafted away and disappeared through a door in the rear wall. Claudia stood still, her mind racing.

Bloom was as dodgy as a fly in a sweet-shop.

He was ready to talk about Evan's art, but not about his whereabouts. Were they shacked up together? Surely that wasn't cause for secrecy these days? More likely Bloom was safeguarding his financial interests. Control of a top artist, the right to arrange his sales and take a handsome commission, was a prize to be defended against all comers.

Bloom obviously disliked Marian Baldwin. Was he bent on rescuing Evan from an over-protective mama?

But Mrs Baldwin had also been secretive about her son's activities. In that at least Baldwin's agent and his mother were at one. They both sought to protect him. Against what?

Was he dodging the tax man? A jealous husband? Or the police?

Was he just the sort of wimp who allowed other people to run his life?

The paintings in this room were not wimpish. She stared at the charging buffalo. 'You are marvellous,' she said aloud. 'I'm going to buy you. Where has that flouncy little Bloom gone?' She swung round in search of him, and cannoned into Evan Baldwin.

He looks like the buffalo, Claudia thought. Heavy head lowered, large eyes watchful and angry. Buffalo regardant and dangerous. But his voice, when it came, was surprisingly gentle.

'Dustin said you wanted to talk to me.'

Claudia managed a smile. 'Yes, Mr Baldwin. I'm an admirer of your work. I want to buy this picture.'

The anger faded from his eyes. He looked pleased. 'Good,' he said. 'I like this one. I got him right. He was so great, you know. A hunter with a fancy rifle was after him, one of those morons who'll pay thousands so they can nail a beautiful head to their crummy walls. The buff came for him like a steam train. The moron was a lousy shot, he just grazed the buff's shoulder. Then he jumped in his Jeep and lit out. I made my sketches while the buff was still snorting and stamping.'

He stood admiring his work, reliving the moment. Claudia decided he took after his mother in looks; medium height, sturdy build, and plenty of energy. He seemed to recall where he was, and turned to face her.

'You went to see my mother,' he said abruptly. 'Why?'

She knew she'd reached the point of no return. Lie, and there'd be no further speech with him. Tell the truth, and if he had something to hide he might well take flight as fast as the buffalo hunter.

She drew a long breath. 'I was with a friend who's gathering information about Martin Parady, the palaeoanthropologist, who was a student of your father's. Did you know him, I wonder?'

Evan gazed at her, his large eyes unblinking. She got the impression he'd expected the question but was unsure how to answer it. He said slowly, 'Parady used to come and see my dad, but that was years ago.'

'Did he ever talk to you about his work?'

'No. I wasn't into fossils.' Evan made a jerking movement of his shoulders, as if to throw off some memory. 'You want the picture. I'll call Dustin.'

'Wait.' Claudia put a hand on his arm. 'Stay, tell me about Africa. I can see you love it; it shows in your work.'

He glanced about the room. 'You don't just put paint on to canvas,' he said impatiently. 'You put what you feel, what the subject gives you. Africa gives me more than other places.'

'You've been there more than once.'

'Yeah. Sure. My dad took me on some of his digs, when I was a kid. After he . . . got ill . . . I went on my own. Africa's right for me. It's alive, you know?'

'Did you ever paint your father's digs? The fossil fields?' Her question had an extraordinary effect. Evan made a sweeping gesture, as if he was striking something away. He said loudly, 'No. Fossils are dead. I hate dead things. I paint life, not death.' He backed away from Claudia. 'I'll send Dustin to you.'

'Thank you,' Claudia said, but he wasn't listening. He put out a hand to caress the buffalo. 'Life,' he repeated, and moved away, shouldering through the crowd towards the rear door.

Dustin Bloom supervised the sale of the picture. He had lost his nervousness, or perhaps clothed it in a pretended calm. He chatted airily, and accepted Claudia's bank card with a flourish.

While the painting was being packed, Claudia walked quickly through the roomful of Mozambique art; pristine beaches, fishing boats, scenes in a crowded market-place. She looked at them through Evan's eyes, smelled the sea, felt the sun, experienced the pulse of the crowds.

Parcel in arms, she took a taxi to the station and caught the coach to Abbotsfell. As it neared the town, her mobile phone chirped. It was Thorneycroft. He enquired where she was, then said, 'Fergus and I are going back to the house. Something came up. We need to talk to you about it. See you later, love. 'Bye.'

They know, she thought. They know I've talked to Rollo. Fergus will kill me.

She spent the rest of the journey practising the story Rollo had composed for her protection. At Abbotsfell coach station she retrieved her car from the parking lot, and travelled to the Lowry house as if in a tumbril.

*

164

The two men were in the living-room, jackets and ties off, the table between them strewn with papers, beer cans and crumbs. The telephone, with its long extension cord, was in Fergus's lap. He set it down at his feet, and waved Claudia to a chair.

'We've had a communiqué from Rollo,' he said. 'Apparently he's been watching the Parady case because Parady clashed with a certain Lance Vaughn, who's suspected of running drugs into southern Africa. Rollo says that Parady tipped off the South African police about Vaughn's activities, which may have been the reason Parady was murdered.'

He paused, looking at Claudia. Her voice stuck in her throat and Thorneycroft came to her rescue. 'Lance and Runa Vaughn live in London, in one of those penthouses on the Thames estuary. They're out of town until tomorrow noon, but we'll be calling on them at 2 p.m. for a chat. How did your day go?'

Thorneycroft's expression was kind. Fergus was fiddling with the papers on the table and didn't look up. Claudia tried to begin her well-rehearsed speech, and failed.

'I went to see Rollo,' she said. 'And then I went to the Alessandri Gallery. I talked to the proprietor, and to Evan Baldwin. I know it was wrong, I shouldn't have done it, but I thought it would save time. I'm sorry, truly I am.'

Fergus looked up. 'It was wrong, Claudia. When someone is wanted for questioning, we can't have amateurs rushing in and muddying the water.'

'I know. I'm truly sorry.'

'Don't do it again.' Fergus lifted a fistful of papers. 'What Rollo has sent us is pure gold. He's told us enough about Lance Vaughn's exploits to put the man high on our list of suspects. Now tell us about your visit to the art gallery.'

Claudia launched into an account of her encounter with Dustin Bloom. 'He's a creep,' she said. 'He didn't want me to have sound or sight of Evan Baldwin. He seemed to be protecting Baldwin, just as his mother did. They're trying to cover up something. Yet Evan himself came and spoke to me.'

They made her repeat what he'd said to her. 'We discussed Africa,' she concluded. 'He loves the country and the wildlife. He's a conservationist, not a killer.' She saw cynicism in Thorneycroft's eye, and said earnestly, 'He's a wonderful artist, John. He's a creator, not a destroyer. He couldn't have had anything to do with Parady's murder. He scarcely remembers the man.'

'Yet when you asked if he'd painted fossils, he reacted somewhat violently.'

'Because they're dead things, and he paints life.'

'Or because he knows something about fossils – about one particular fossil – that he would rather forget.'

Fergus said, 'Your visit to Bloom's gallery clarified certain points for us, Clo. One, Marian Baldwin and Dustin Bloom both want to prevent us, the police, from questioning Evan. One wonders what he's done to merit such concern. Two, Evan seems unwilling to talk about Martin Parady, his father's star student. Three, he doesn't like to think about fossils. Four, he knows Africa well, and may have met Parady there, more recently than he cares to admit.'

'And five,' interpolated Thorneycroft, 'Dustin Bloom gets tetchy at the suggestion that someone sponsors Evan. Could it be that Evan's prosperity – and Bloom's – is tied to dirty money?'

Fergus looked at his watch. 'I have to get back to the shop. Tonight we'll rope Voysey in and make a plan about how to handle the Vaughns. I'll leave you to study Rollo's file.'

When he'd left, Claudia said again, 'I'm really sorry I jumped the gun.'

Thorneycroft grinned at her. 'What's in the parcel you hid in the hall?'

'I bought a picture. An investment. Is Fergus very angry with me?'

'Only as a matter of form. It suited Rollo's book to put us wise to Lance Vaughn. It suits our book to have been put wise.' He leaned back in his chair. 'We do need to move faster. Fergus and I have been over the facts of the case again and again, and got nowhere. There are so many unanswered questions.'

'What are they?' Claudia asked.

Thorneycroft enumerated. 'Who dumped the skull and the fossil cast on Abbotsfell tip, and why? What did Taft know that he refused to tell? Why did Taft hate to talk about happy family life? What's the connection between the Parady and Taft murders? Where did Parady go when he returned to England in April 2003? Who did he see, who did he talk to? Who killed him, and with what motive?' He paused, and added, 'Why has nothing been done for two years to locate the fossil site and develop it? Why is the Baldwin-Bloom camp so paranoid about Evan Baldwin's doings?'

Claudia said slowly, 'You've always held that two people were involved in the Parady murder – one who killed him and one who disposed of the bag on the rubbish tip. Which of the two mugged Levine, which of them shot Taft?'

'I don't know,' Thorneycroft admitted. 'I'm sure there were two people involved in the Parady murder. The killer was violent, obsessive, reckless, arrogant. Possibly insane. The person who dumped the bag was methodical, and had his reasons for not just throwing it into the Thames. The skull and cast were carefully packed, as if to preserve them.

'The person who mugged Levine was not methodical, he was reckless. He came close to being nabbed when Levine's friend happened on the scene. As for Taft's killer, I believe he worked alone. There was no accomplice. Taft knew the killer, trusted him. If we knew the reason for that trust, we'd know who was the killer.'

He picked up Rollo's report. 'I must do my homework. Go through this lot with me, will you? See if you can add anything from your meeting with Rollo.'

She moved to sit on the sofa beside him. 'I wish I could be with you when you question the Vaughns,' she said. 'I feel so involved in this case. Do you think I could ask Fergus. . . ?'

'No,' said Thorneycroft firmly. 'Don't push your luck.'

XIX

Fergus decided that he would go with Thorneycroft to conduct the interview with the Vaughns. Thorneycroft asked him how Voysey would feel about that.

'He's fine,' Fergus said. 'he'll be releasing the news today that the skull on the tip is Martin Parady's, and there'll be big pressure on us here, from the media and other interested parties. Voysey can handle that. And he accepts that we've handled the Parady investigation from the start, and are in a better position to corner Lance Vaughn than he is.'

The Vaughns' penthouse was in a luxury block that had replaced warehouses on the lower Thames estuary. A security guard admitted them to underground parking, a male clerk checked their identity at the reception desk, and a private elevator carried them up to the eleventh floor, where Fergus pressed an electronic buzzer.

Across the hall, the front door opened to reveal a woman in a white tracksuit. Her nuggety build suggested it should be worn with a black belt. She led them through an immense living-room, past a fitted bar with view windows that took in the Isle of Dogs, and through an archway to a television lounge.

'I will call the master,' she told them. 'He is speaking with South America. He will be here soon. Please to be comfortable.'

'Home,' murmured Fergus, 'was never like this.' His eyes roved round the art deco furnishings and fittings, and Thorneycroft knew he was thinking they might be bugged.

Thorneycroft moved to examine the full-length portrait that hung on an inner wall. Fergus joined him.

'Runa Vaughn,' he said, and tapped the initials 'E.B.' in a corner of the canvas. 'That must have earned him a nice fee.'

Runa Vaughn was undeniably a beautiful woman, but Baldwin had captured more than her surface appearance. There was self-satisfaction in the thrust of the full lips, and stupidity in the lustrous eyes.

'He got her right, I'd say,' Thorneycroft said, and a voice spoke behind him.

'He did indeed, Dr Thorneycroft. Runa was delighted.'

Lance Vaughn stood in a doorway to their left. He came towards them, smiling.

He was thick-set and muscular, his arms and legs rather short. Puffy lids veiled his eyes. The skin of his face was grey and pitted. Grey curls covered his skull and sprouted from the V-neck of a brilliantly patterned Hawaiian shirt. He wore dark red tailored slacks. A ruby ring glittered on his left hand, and he wore a watch that might do more than just tell the time. The total effect made Thorneycroft think of a Gabon adder: fat, colourful and deadly poisonous.

He led them to armchairs upholstered in pale mauve leather. 'I am always happy to accommodate the police,' he said. 'Can I offer you a drink, or tea, coffee?'

They refused the offer, and Fergus asked if Mrs Vaughn would be joining them. Vaughn nodded.

'She won't be long.' He smiled at Fergus. 'You told me, when we spoke on the phone, that you wanted to talk to us about Martin Parady. Why is that?'

'He was murdered,' Fergus said. 'His skull was deposited on the rubbish tip at Abbotsfell, in the Chilterns. We are anxious to inter-view everyone who may be able to shed light on the last few months of his life, and perhaps help us to establish the motive for his murder. You and your wife were acquainted with him, I under-stand.'

'Not well.'

'I'm reliably informed, sir, that you and your wife encountered Martin Parady while you were in southern Africa. A period lasting from August 2002 to April 2003.'

'That is correct.' Vaughn pressed his hands together, then spread them wide. 'Let's skip the fancy footwork, Chief Inspector. In the period you mentioned, I was in the north-western sector of South Africa, prospecting for manganese. Successfully, I might add.'

'During that time, did you meet with Martin Parady?'

Before Vaughn could reply, heels clattered on the tiles of the bar area, and Runa Vaughn appeared in the archway. She wore jeans, an emerald green shirt, and green leather half-boots. In one hand she carried a glass, in the other a cocktail shaker.

'That bloody ice-maker's useless,' she said. It was obvious she'd had too much to drink.

Vaughn bared his teeth at her. 'Runa, my dear, this is Chief Inspector Lowry, and Dr John Thorneycroft, who are enquiring into the death of Martin Parady. Sit down and listen to what they have to say to us.'

Her mouth dropped open. 'What you mean, death?'

'Martin is dead,' Vaughn answered. 'It was on the one o'clock news. It's a shock, but we must be brave.'

His voice carried warning. Runa sat down in the chair next to his, and stared at Fergus and Thorneycroft. Finding no comfort in them, she poured what looked like Martini from the shaker into her glass, and set about drinking it.

Fergus picked up the dropped thread. 'Did you and your wife meet with Martin Parady in South Africa?'

'Yes, two or three times – by chance, not intention.'

'Did you converse with him?'

Vaughn gave a grunt of laughter. 'Converse is a polite word. We argued, we quarrelled, our mood was one of mutual mistrust and dislike. Parady and I both coveted the same piece of earth, you see. He hoped to dig for fossils, I planned to mine manganese. Our aims clashed. Parady accused me of illegal activities. He complained about me to the South African authorities. Groundless complaints, but damaging.'

'In what way damaging?'

Lance blew out his lips, seeming to consider his answer. 'They took his part, and instructed me and my wife to leave the country at once.'

'Did you comply?'

'Of course. It would have been pointless to resist. African states don't relish entrepreneurs from Europe, they prefer to mine their own minerals. I've had considerable experience in the matter.'

'So I gather.' Fergus glanced at the notebook he held. 'You've experienced difficulties in Nigeria, Angola, Congo, Ivory Coast, and others. You've been instructed to leave various states in South America.'

'That is so. It's a natural hazard in my profession. One accepts such setbacks. One avoids anger; it wastes time and money.'

Runa gave a throaty laugh, and Fergus glanced at her, but she was busy refilling her glass. He turned back to her husband.

'Sir, where precisely were you conducting your search for manganese?'

Vaughn sighed. 'You must see that I can't answer that question. It would conflict not only with the interests of my company but with the instructions of the South African authorities. They have enjoined me to silence, and I don't wish to deepen their disapproval of me.'

'Can you tell us where Martin Parady was working?'

172

Vaughn merely gave Fergus a satiric look. He seemed to be enjoying himself. He'd spent years dodging difficult questions, and no doubt some of his interrogators had had nastier ways of getting answers than were permitted to the British police.

Thorneycroft spoke to Runa. 'Perhaps you know where Mr Parady worked, Mrs Vaughn?'

She stared at him mistily. 'No, I don't. When I talked to him about his work, he said silly stuff like he was chasing butterflies, or looking for the Garden of Eden.'

Thorneycroft smiled at her. 'Not helpful. I've been admiring that portrait of you. Evan Baldwin's a fine artist, and he had a beautiful subject to paint.'

She put up a hand to preen her hair. 'He said I was an interesting subject. He asked Lance over and over, could he paint me.'

'A compliment in itself,' Thorneycroft said. 'Baldwin can take his pick. He's a bit of a recluse, they tell me. Doesn't like mixing with the common crowd.'

'He mixed with me all right.' Runa smiled brilliantly at her husband. 'We had a fine time. In the morning, I'd pose for him, then after lunch we'd go swimming or sit in the sun. We'd have supper in his cottage – Evan would cook shrimps and stuff like that. We'd eat, drink and make merry. Evan's a good mixer, like I said.' She waved her empty glass. 'Better than Lance. Lance is a lousy mixer.'

Vaughn watched her, stony-faced. 'You're tired, my dear,' he said. 'You must rest before dinner.' He reached out and pressed a button. The nuggety woman came quietly through the inner door, walked to where Runa sat, and held out her hand. Runa struck it aside, but the woman persisted, and after a moment Runa got to her feet, still cuddling her glass and cocktail shaker. The woman steered her out of the room.

Vaughn cleared his throat. 'My apologies. My wife has a problem; she's an alcoholic. She has spells when she's totally free of it, but in times of stress, she lapses. I'm afraid this is one of those times. You must take what she says with a pinch of salt. She likes to see herself as a femme fatale, but I assure you, Evan Baldwin never dreamed of going to bed with her. His painting dominates his life. All his energy goes into his pictures. A dull dog, in fact.'

'When and where did Mr Baldwin paint the portrait of your wife?' Fergus asked.

'It was . . . let me see . . . January of 2003. I had business in Mozambique. Runa and I were there for two weeks, and Evan was there, painting. He did the portrait of Runa at my request. I tried to persuade him to come back to South Africa with us, we're building new offices in Johannesburg and I hoped Evan would do some murals there, but he wouldn't leave Mozambique. He wanted to complete a folio of work.'

'Do you know if Baldwin ever met up with Parady in Africa?'

'No, but it's unlikely. They were hundreds of miles apart, and both obsessed by their work. No time for fraternizing.'

'When did you return to England, Mr Vaughn?'

'Not until the middle of the year. We left South Africa in the first week of April, and went straight to Italy. I have a place in Umbria. We returned to London in June. If you want dates, you can check our passports.'

And they'll confirm your story, Thorneycroft thought. Vaughn was as slippery as Rollo had warned. He'd kept his lies to a minimum, raised the very questions he might have been expected to dodge, admitted frankly that he was unwelcome in Africa and at loggerheads with Parady. Finally, he could prove that he'd been out of England when Parady was murdered.

Fergus said doggedly, 'Did you communicate with Mr Parady after you left South Africa?'

'No. What point would there be?' Vaughn met Fergus's hard gaze. 'I was disappointed at the loss of my prospects in South Africa. I was angered by Parady's malicious intervention in my affairs, but I'm a businessman. I don't cry over spilt milk. I move on.'

Fergus turned over the pages of his notebook. 'Tell me, sir, were you acquainted with a man named William Taft?'

Vaughn looked blank. 'Who?'

'Dr William Taft, the police pathologist at Abbotsfell.'

'Yes, I read about him. He was shot, wasn't he? A dreadful thing, but I never met him, I'm of no help to you there.'

Fergus continued to ask questions, but could neither gain fresh insights nor dent Vaughn's self-confidence. At four o'clock he and Thorneycroft left the penthouse, Vaughn bidding them a cheerful goodbye at his front door.

As the lift bore them downward, Fergus said, 'I can see why Rollo wants to nail that one. Slimy customer.'

'The woman's his weak point,' Thorneycroft said. 'She hates his guts.'

'She enjoys her gilded cage,' Fergus answered. 'She won't leave him.'

There he erred, for when they drove out of the parking basement, they saw Runa Vaughn standing under a linden tree, a short way up the street. She waved. Fergus drew up level with her and she scrambled into the back seat.

'Drive around,' she commanded, 'I want to talk to you.'

Fergus cruised slowly along the riverside road. From the edge of his mouth he murmured, 'Just let her talk.'

Runa was craning round to stare through the rear window. Reassured by the empty street, she turned to face them. She was on some sort of high, her cheeks flushed and her eyes over-bright. She pointed a finger at Thorneycroft.

'You're not a cop. I've seen enough to know. You're just a doctor, right?'

'Right.' He smiled at her. 'How did you escape your jailer?'

She lifted a contemptuous shoulder. 'I do what I like. They

175

don't dare mess with me. Anything happens to me, there's stuff stashed away that'll make them sorry. I'm insured.' She leaned forward to rest her elbows on the back of Thorneycroft's seat. 'Lance is a bloody liar, making out he doesn't care what Parady did to him. That's crap; he was as mad as a hornet. He swore he'd fix Martin. It cost him plenty, losing the Mozambique deal.'

'What deal was that?' said Thorneycroft innocently, but she shook her head. He tried again. 'What did your husband mean by "fix"? Do you think he wanted to kill Parady?'

Surprisingly, Runa was affronted. 'Are you crazy? Lance doesn't kill people. We weren't even in England when the scumbag was killed.'

'When was that?' Thorneycroft said.

She squinted at him. 'The three o'clock news said April 2003. We were in Italy. How did it happen?'

'Someone smashed his skull.'

'Serve him right, the two-timing bastard. Whoever did it should get a medal.'

She was stupid, Thorneycroft decided, but not quite stupid enough to accuse her husband of murder. He switched tracks.

'Tell me about Evan Baldwin. Where did you meet him?'

'Johannesburg. Lance brought him to our hotel. He kept staring at me, he said he'd like to paint me, and Lance agreed.'

'Back there, you suggested you did more than pose for a portrait.'

Runa muttered something unintelligible, then said, 'I told you, we had some good times, but he didn't care about anything except painting.'

'He turned down the commission your husband offered him . . . to do the murals in the new office building.'

Runa scowled, and Thorneycroft said, 'Did your husband have a different job in mind? Did he want Evan to join his prospecting business? As a traveller, a courier, perhaps?'

She flung herself back in her seat. 'I don't know what the hell Lance wanted. I never asked and he never told me. All he ever does is give me orders.' She banged her fists on the seat cushions. 'He wanted me to find out what Martin was doing on that site, whether he had permission from the bigwigs, whether he had funds. Lance said, "Get it any way you can." He doesn't care how I feel. I hate him, I hate men, I hate them all, they're all pigs.'

Tears welled in her eyes and she pressed a fist against her mouth.

'Martin Parady could be very charming,' Thorneycroft said, and she nodded.

'Yeah. He was fun. He made me laugh. He made me think I mattered. But he was a liar like the rest.'

'Did he ever talk to you about his work?'

'No. I told you, when I asked him where he went, he gave me that garbage about butterflies, and the Garden of Eden. I knew he was digging for old bones. He liked them better than me. Then he and Lance quarrelled, and the next thing was, Lance and me had to get out of the country. Lance was furious. He wanted to clobber Martin, but Martin had cleared off to England. The swab didn't even say goodbye to me, and Lance wouldn't pay the hotel bill, I had to pay it myself. Scum, the both of them, but I'm going to get my own back on them, that's a promise.'

Sitting up, she rocked her body back and forth, smiling, savouring some inward plan.

'Parady's dead,' Thorneycroft said. 'You can't hurt him.'

'Oh yes I can,' she said. He saw a gloating malice in her face. 'I can pull him off his pedestal, can't I? Everyone thinks he's such a great scientist, a great hero, but I know different. He never paid back all the money I lent him. He told me about other women he'd dumped, he laughed about them. He was mean and cruel, and I'm going to see it all comes out. Wait till you read my article.'

'A press article?' Thorneycroft saw her complacent smile, and said urgently, 'Which paper did you go to?'

'*Mock Trial*,' she said.

Thorneycroft was alarmed. *Mock Trial* was the latest of the publications designed to pillory the rich and famous, and it was widely read.

'You can't do that,' he said.

Runa laughed. 'It's already done. You can read it next week.'

Fergus, who had so far remained silent, now stopped the car and turned to face Runa.

'Mrs Vaughn, I don't know how much you've been offered for this story of yours, but I assure you, it's not worth risking your life for. There's a murderer out there. He's already killed two people, and you're proposing to publish an exposé of one of his victims. Don't you see, if he reads what you've written, he'll wonder what else you know about Parady, how much Parady told you. He's going to wonder if it's safe to leave you alive.'

'I'm not scared of any of them, I told you, they can't touch me.'

'Don't be a fool. You may be safe from your husband's thugs, but what if this isn't one of them? What if it's someone beyond your husband's control?'

'Then you'd better do what you're paid for, Mr Policeman. You'd better catch him and lock him up, fast.'

'I advise you to stop publication of your article. Apart from putting you at grave risk, it will cause problems for a lot of inno-cent people.'

'I don't care.' Runa's face was set in glowering obstinacy. 'It'll make up for what I've gone through all these years. I want that money. It's my ticket out of here.'

'A ticket to a wooden box and six feet of earth. You may not live to enjoy a penny of the money.'

For answer Runa flung open the rear door of the car and slid out on to the pavement. She headed away at a brisk trot, towards a neighbouring taxi rank. Fergus made as if to turn the car, but Thorneycroft stopped him.

'It's no use, mate, she's made up her mind. If you try to stop publication, *Mock Trial* will cry freedom of the press and publish anyway.'

'And what about the other people who are going to suffer because of that silly cow's avarice? If she's written about Parady finding a fossil site, it'll start the feeding frenzy Slocombe's warned about. Not only will the vultures wreck Parady's site, they'll destroy any chance we have of finding out what really happened between Vaughn and Parady.' Fergus gunned the car away from the kerb. 'How do I get on to the ring road? I have to get back to Abbotsfell, fast. Voysey must follow up on the Vaughns and Baldwin. They're our best prospects yet.'

'The Vaughns, yes. They have a grudge motive, and the means to hire a hit man. But why Baldwin?'

'He had a fling with Runa Vaughn, yet Vaughn condoned it. He actually wanted Baldwin to do the murals in his new building. It could be Baldwin was already on Vaughn's team. Maybe that's where he got the cash for his expensive training and his world-wide travels.'

'There's no proof of that.'

'Someone funded Evan at the start of his career, and if he accepted dirty money once, he'd be hooked, wouldn't he?'

'Doesn't make him a killer.'

'No, but perhaps an accomplice, who took on the job of disposing of Parady's skull and the fossil cast.'

'And dumped them on the Abbotsfell tip? Why?'

'Maybe Evan can explain that to us. He was in Africa at the same time as the Vaughns and Parady. He was involved with the Vaughns. He knew Parady from his youth. Voysey must get him to come down to Abbotsfell to confirm the identity of Claudia's reconstruction. He has to answer a lot of questions.'

A road sign loomed, and Thorneycroft said, 'Take the next left and we'll avoid the city. What are you going to do about

179

Slocombe's problem? It's essential to protect Parady's site.'

'All I can do is warn the ministries about Runa Vaughn's article. Maybe they can alert kingpins in South Africa. It's outside my bailiwick.'

'Not really. There's an overwhelming likelihood that Parady's murder is linked to the fossil. You have the right to approach the South African police for relevant information.'

'I do, and given time I could send a couple of men out there, but as things stand, *Mock Trial* will spill the beans on Monday, and the shit will hit the fan.'

'What if an acknowledged expert were to go to South Africa, with the backing of the top brass in his profession? What if Slocombe went, and talked to the South African authorities and the big names among the African fossil-hunters? And what if I went along to ride shotgun?'

'Who do you imagine would pay for that little jaunt?'

'I'll pay my own way, and I'll lay odds Slocombe will, too.'

'Slocombe's a potential suspect.'

'But you have no proof of his guilt. Maybe it exists, out there.'

'What can you hope to find in a couple of days?'

'Proof at least that the cast was taken from a genuine fossil, and that a new species, a vitally important one, has been discovered.'

As Fergus looked sceptical, Thorneycroft said, 'The fossil is at the heart of the case, Fergus.'

'Maybe so, but we don't know where Parady found the thing.'

'He found it in an area where there's manganese, where there's a protected plant with leaves like pink butterflies, a plant that smells like liquorice and is used medicinally. The Garden of Eden, Runa said. Those people who deported Vaughn know where he was prospecting, which means they know where Parady was working. I suspect that Rollo knows they know, which is why he sent us that file. He gave us a name, what's more. A man called Simeon Vilakazi. Maybe he'll take us into his confidence.'

Fergus hesitated, then shrugged. 'Talk to Slocombe,' he said, 'after we've met with Evan Baldwin.'

Claudia had hung Evan Baldwin's painting of the buffalo on a vacant hook in the Lowrys' hallway. Thorneycroft studied it with interest.

'Great, isn't it?' Claudia said, and Thorneycroft nodded.

'Marvellous.' He was thinking that Baldwin's pictures were the common factor in the case. Max Slocombe owned more than one; Lance Vaughn had commissioned Baldwin to do a portrait of his wife. Dustin Bloom and Marian Baldwin were protective of his skill, perhaps because they profited from it?

Baldwin himself was an enigma. A recluse, Bloom claimed, yet when Voysey requested that he come to Abbotsfell to identify the reconstruction of the Parady skull, he'd raised no objections.

He arrived on Friday morning, driving a silver Mercedes sports car. Fergus brought him up to the top floor, where Voysey and Kelly were waiting. Baldwin shook hands, and said, 'Well, where is the model?'

Fergus unveiled the head and Evan stared at it intently. After a while he said, 'It's Martin Parady. A good likeness; it's captured his chutzpah.'

Watching the young man, Thorneycroft felt that he had his own share of that quality. He came to the table and took his place with no sign of nervousness.

Fergus thanked him for coming, and launched into his preamble. 'The model you have just identified as Martin Parady was built on a skull discovered two weeks ago, among material from the Abbotsfell rubbish tip. Your identification confirms that made by Dr Inez Parady, Martin's daughter, and Dr Max Slocombe, a colleague who knew him well. How did you come to know him, Mr Baldwin?'

Evan answered calmly. 'My father was a palaeoanthropologist,

181

and taught Martin. He came to our house sometimes. I read in the papers, yesterday, that he'd been murdered.'

'What did you feel about that?'

'I was shocked, of course.'

'When last did you see Mr Parady?'

'Years ago.'

'Did he stop calling at your home, then?'

'Yes. My dad died, and I left home to study art. Martin had his career; he spent most of his time abroad, I think.'

'Did you follow his career?'

'No. I have my own; that's enough to worry about.'

'According to Mr Bloom, you trained at the Slade, also in Paris and America. How was that funded?'

'I had scholarships, I did odd jobs like most students do, and I sold my work.'

'Did you have a sponsor?'

'No.' Evan's eyelids flickered. 'I had commissions to paint specific subjects.'

'Did Mr Lance Vaughn offer you such commissions?'

'Occasionally. He bought several of my pictures.'

'Over what space of time?'

'Over about seven years. Lance buys as an investment. He doesn't have any feeling for art.'

'So you have known Mr Vaughn for some seven years?'

'I told you, yes. What's the point of these questions?'

Fergus ignored the remark. 'Did Mr Vaughn commission you to paint his wife Runa?'

'Yes.'

'When was that?'

'In September 2002. In Mozambique. I was building a portfolio of pictures. Lance and Runa turned up at my hotel in Maputo. Lance had business there. He asked me to do the portrait, and I did. They liked it and bought it.'

'During that time, did you become intimate with Mrs Vaughn?'

Evan's face reddened but he answered directly. 'We slept together a couple of times. It didn't mean anything to me. I knew Lance's tricks.'

'What tricks, Mr Baldwin?'

'Lance uses Runa to persuade men to do what he wants.'

'What precisely did he want you to do?'

'Two things. Find out where Martin Parady was working, and help Lance decorate his new building in Joburg.' Evan sniffed. 'I don't play Lance's games. I don't like him. He's a good customer but that's all.'

Fergus nodded. 'Did you at any time between September 2002 and April 2003 see or communicate with Martin Parady?'

'No.' Evan folded his arms. 'He was in South Africa. I never went there. I stayed in Mozambique.'

'Lance Vaughn returned to South Africa, did he not?'

'Yes. He said he was prospecting for manganese.'

'Did he say where?'

'No. He didn't discuss his business with me.'

'Did he tell you that he'd clashed with Martin Parady?'

For the first time, Evan looked uneasy. He mumbled, 'Runa said once they were like two dogs with one bone.'

'A fossilized bone, perhaps?'

Evan grimaced. 'I don't know anything about fossils.'

'Your father was an expert, wasn't he? Didn't you learn from him?'

'He took me on some of his trips. I hated it. Digging for bits of dead things, dead a million years. Let them lie, I say. Leave them in the ground where they belong.'

Voysey leaned forward. 'That didn't happen to Martin Parady's bones, sir. After he was dead and buried, someone dug up his head and knocked out his teeth.'

'I don't know anything about that.'

'You say you read of his death in the newspapers.'

'I glanced at the headlines, that's all. I hardly knew the man. I haven't seen him for years. I can't help you find who killed him.'

Voysey consulted his notes. 'Does the name William Taft mean anything to you, sir?'

'No. Who is he?'

'Dr Taft was the Abbotsfell pathologist,' Voysey said. 'He conducted the post-mortem examination of Martin Parady's skull. Last Wednesday night, Dr Taft was shot dead.'

Evan gripped the arms of his chair and rose clumsily to his feet. He seemed to have difficulty in finding words.

'I don't know what you're on about,' he blurted. 'I don't like these questions. Why are you pestering me? I have an exhibition on, in London, and I need to be there. I've told you all I know. I hope you'll leave me in peace now.'

Voysey rose to block his path. 'Just a couple more questions, if you don't mind, sir. When did you leave Mozambique?'

Evan breathed deeply, and when he spoke it was with his earlier calm. 'In late April of 2003,' he answered. 'I came back to England for my father's memorial service. I stayed about three weeks, then I went home to Spain.'

'Can you produce proof of that? Your passport, for instance?'

'The passport I had then has lapsed. My new one only shows this year's journeys. But my agent and my bank will vouch for what I've told you.'

'Thank you. We'll be in touch with them.'

When Fergus had shepherded Evan away, Voysey looked challengingly at Thorneycroft.

'What did you make of him, then?'

'He started well,' Thorneycroft answered. 'He was frank about his relations with the Vaughns.'

'I dunno. All that about Vaughn buying his pictures, that could be an easy way of paying for illegal activities. Vaughn's into dirty deals. Baldwin travels round the world, doing his pictures. He could be Vaughn's agent, gather info, carry messages or even drugs. Vaughn pays for it by buying pictures. Hard to prove there's anything crooked about it.'

'I watched Baldwin's body language,' Thorneycroft said. 'He wasn't fazed by questions about Lance, or about having it off with Runa Vaughn. But when you asked about Parady, and fossils, he showed anxiety, and when you asked if he knew Taft, he entirely lost his cool.'

'So?'

'So it's possible that Lance Vaughn did arrange a hit on Martin Parady, and that some time later, Evan Baldwin obliged Lance by disposing of the skull and the cast.'

'An accessory after the fact?'

'I don't know. He may not even have been aware of what was in the kit-bag. He reacted far more strongly when you asked him about William Taft.'

'He said he didn't know Taft.'

'I think he lied,' Thorneycroft said. 'I think he knew Taft, and I think he's been to Abbotsfell before now.'

'Not driving that fancy Merc,' Voysey said. 'Too easily recognized.'

Kelly spoke after a long silence. 'He could have used his bike. Nothing special about a Yamaha, and he could have ridden it right up to the window of Taft's car, couldn't he?'

That evening, with Fergus's consent, Thorneycroft phoned Rollo McLeod and Max Slocombe.

'Now what?' Rollo said.

'We need a facilitator,' Thorneycroft told him. 'I want to go to South Africa. We have to protect Martin Parady's find.'

'Rubbish. That can only be done by the South African government.'

'You have strings you can pull.'

Rollo made no answer, and Thorneycroft said sharply, 'Do you know where the fossil site is?'

'I'm not at liberty to discuss that. Why do you want to know? It's none of your business.'

'I intend to go to South Africa, with Max Slocombe. He has real clout with the palaeos. If there's a valuable fossil lying around in the dust, Slocombe can identify it and invoke world support for its protection.'

'And your rôle in this touching drama?'

'Parady's murder and Taft's murder are tied to the fossil. We suspect that Lance Vaughn and Evan Baldwin were implicated in Parady's murder, but we need confirmation from people in South Africa. If we can discover why Parady was killed, we'll be able to establish who killed him, how, when and where.'

There was a pause, then Rollo sighed. 'Very well. I'll talk around. You can travel as my courier, taking important documents to Simeon Vilakazi. From there on it's up to you.'

'Great. Thanks, Rollo.'

'You'll have the documents tomorrow,' Rollo said, and the line went dead.

Thorneycroft called Max Slocombe and told him about Runa Vaughn's agreement with *Mock Trial*. Slocombe was appalled.

'The woman must be stopped,' he said. 'If she mentions Parady, fossils, the Garden of Eden and liquorice plants in the same breath, there are plenty of people who'll put things together and head for that northern escarpment. Who must I talk to? Home Office, Foreign Office? I know the Prime minister . . .'

'All too slow,' Thorneycroft said. '*Mock Trial* will publish her article on Monday. My plan is to fly to South Africa as soon as possible. I'd like you to accompany me, to identify Parady's site, look at his find, and convince whoever's in charge that they have to be ready to fend off a flood of treasure-seekers.'

'When do we leave?'

'It's for our own account, Max, there's no funding.'

'Tch, money's no consideration. If we can locate that fossil, and it's what Parady claimed it was, the funds will flow like balm in Gilead. When do we leave?'

'The day after tomorrow. I've fixed the bookings to Johannesburg. I've got some semi-official backing. Once we're out there we'll link up with a man who can tell us where the site is.'

'I'm a poor walker, John. My leg . . .'

'Don't worry. My facilitator knows his job. We'll get there. You understand this is a matter of strictest confidence.'

'Of course. You have my word. And thank you. I can't say how much this chance means to me.'

Slocombe's voice was trembling. He sounded on the brink of tears.

XXI

For the next few days, Thorneycroft felt he inhabited two worlds; the world of the present in which he sought a double murderer, and the world of a million years past where he stumbled in ignorance, searching for his own beginnings.

With Slocombe he took the daytime flight to Johannesburg, reaching the city sprawl as the surrounding veld changed from dusty green to crimson. They found, as they entered the airport buildings, that Rollo had more than fulfilled his promise of help.

Simeon Vilakazi was there in person to meet them, and whisked them through luggage and passport routines with VIP speed. He was a man one might not notice in a crowd: slender-bodied, quietly spoken, wearing spectacles. But he moved with the grace of an athlete, and the eyes behind the hornrims were cool and appraising.

He had made reservations, he informed them, at a small hotel in the suburbs. 'It's quiet; you won't be troubled by the press or anyone else,' he said. 'You have a suite with a private lounge. We can confer there, if you wish, unless you prefer to wait until tomorrow?'

'Tonight,' Thorneycroft said. 'Can we have drinks and dinner in the suite? There's a lot to discuss, if you can spare the time.'

Vilakazi drove them to the hotel. He was, he explained, in

charge of environmental affairs for a part of Limpopo Province. He had known Mr McLeod for many years, and had worked with him on 'several projects'. Mr McLeod had briefed him very fully on the matter of the death of Martin Parady – a great tragedy that so brilliant a man should be lost to his profession and the world. Dr Thorneycroft and Dr Slocombe were very welcome, both valued for their special skills.

Vilakazi glanced at Thorneycroft, who was in the front passenger seat. 'You believe that Martin was murdered because of the fossil site?'

In that one sentence, thought Thorneycroft, he's said that he and Parady were on first-name terms, and that he knows why Slocombe and I are here. He remembered Rollo's warning, that the people in this country had their own prerogatives, which must be respected. He spent the rest of the journey telling Vilakazi about the meeting with Inez Parady, and the letters she'd received from her father.

'Inez told us her father claimed to have discovered a fossil of great importance. She believes he went to England in April 2003 because he felt his work was threatened by a criminal named Lance Vaughn. Parady got Vaughn and his wife deported from this country, but of course you know that.'

Vilakazi nodded sombrely. 'Vaughn's an evil man. It's possible he had Martin killed.'

'We're working on that, but the immediate problem is that Vaughn's wife Runa has sold a story to a rag called *Mock Trial*. The story's about Parady, and it may give hints about the location of the fossil site.'

'And movement in the water,' said Vilakazi, 'brings the crocodiles in.'

Their suite at the hotel provided five-star comfort. Slocombe dispensed drinks from a well-stocked bar. Thorneycroft handed Vilakazi the sealed envelope Rollo had given him. Settled in an armchair, Vilakazi studied his companions over the rim of his glass.

'What is it you want of me?' he asked.

Thorneycroft opened his briefcase and extracted Levine's photographs of the fossil cast.

'This object was found in the bag that contained Martin Parady's skull,' he said. 'That information has not been released to the media, but if by any chance Runa Vaughn knows of it, she may have mentioned it in her article. Dr Slocombe thinks it represents a new hominid species, one more highly evolved than Homo erectus, possibly the immediate predecessor of modern man. A species that left Africa some 150,000 years ago, and entirely replaced the erectus populations of Asia and Europe. In short, the species Martin found is the emerging Homo sapiens.'

Vilakazi folded his hands round his glass. 'Please go on.'

'Inez Parady,' continued Thorneycroft, 'couldn't identify her father's site, but the letters suggest it is in a valley where there is manganese in the soil, where a protected plant with medicinal properties grows, a plant with butterfly-like leaves. Runa Vaughn, who had an affair with Parady, told us he wouldn't say where he was working, but he mentioned "looking for butterflies" and "the Garden of Eden". He was actually telling the truth. In his mind, his fossil site was Eden, the home of Eve – Mitochondrial Eve whose genes were the source of the new species.'

'All this is guesswork, isn't it?' Vilakazi took a pull at his whisky. 'You don't know the location of the site.'

'No, we don't. But Runa Vaughn may know it, and I believe you know it. Parady and Vaughn were fighting for the same strip of territory, and I am sure your authorities must know where that lay. Parady had to have permission to hunt for fossils, and Vaughn to prospect for manganese. One man was deported, and the other is dead, but the site still exists, and in three or four more days, it will be under threat because of Runa Vaughn's article in *Mock Trial*.

'We need your help, Mr Vilakazi. We can discover where the site is by applying to your government, and your police force, but by that time it will be too late to safeguard the fossils buried there.'

Thorneycroft got to his feet and recharged glasses. Back in his chair, he said, 'My interest lies in trying to track down a murderer. That is the particular concern of the British Police Force. However, we are very conscious that we can't allow our interests to intrude on those of South Africa, and we're aware that you have your own priorities. We appreciate that you may have plans for Parady's site.'

Thorneycroft paused, but Vilakazi neither moved nor spoke. Slocombe broke the silence.

'Mr Vilakazi, I must tell you that my whole interest is in what Martin Parady may have found. And I confess that I am burning to go where he went, see what he saw. It puzzles me that though you must know where he was working, and what he found, the facts have been kept secret for nearly two years. I know there must be good reasons for that, but . . . can you not take us into your confidence? We can be trusted to respect whatever you choose to tell us.'

Vilakazi looked from one face to the other. At last he said slowly, 'I will speak to you in confidence. I will tell you about Martin's site. It is not news, it has long been known to the people of my father's village. The legends told us that old bones lay in the hillside behind our houses. Long ago, there were people who had actually seen these bones, but in the great-grandfathers' time God closed up the cave where they lay. It remained closed for a hundred years or so.

'Then in the year 2000 part of the ceiling of the cave fell down, and the mouth of the cave was opened again. We are told it was water that wore away the dolomite rock, and caused a sink-hole.

'Martin Parady found it. He came to the elders of the village and asked for permission to go into the cave. At first they refused him.

191

The valley where the cave is is the burial place of our ancestors. It is sacred to the local people, who are not all Christians, but ancestor-worshippers.'

Vilakazi stared into the liquid in his glass, as if into a crystal ball.

'There is another reason Martin was refused,' he said. 'In the past, whenever fossil bones were found, they were removed by white people, taken away to the big cities. Some were taken out of the country, others were put into museums, and people from all over the world came to see them. The glory of owning the fossils, and the money from the tourists who came, went to the people in the big cities. Nothing came to the poor people who owned the ground where the fossils were found. They do not want the same thing to happen this time.

'When Martin was told this, he understood. He said that if he was allowed to work in the cave, he would promise to persuade the authorities to build a safe place for the fossils there, close to the village. He would find trained people to examine the fossils and classify them, but then they would be returned to the safe place. Martin said it would take a lot of money, but he knew it could be raised.'

'You believed in his promises?' Thorneycroft said, and Vilakazi nodded.

'Martin didn't lie about his work,' he said. 'He was allowed to go into the cave and work there. He found old bones, the head in your photos. Then Vaughn came, wanting to dig for manganese. The two of them quarrelled. We threw Vaughn out, and Martin left also, but it wasn't for fear of Vaughn. A lion isn't afraid of a carrion crow. Martin went to England to raise money to start work on the dig, and to build the safe place. He had already spoken to the top palaeoanthropologists in this country, and they agreed with what he wanted to do.

'We waited for him to come back, but he never did; there was no word of him. At last we knew he must be dead. Nothing but death would have kept him away. For two years there have been arguments, delays in our plans. We have not been able to move forward.'

Slocombe said urgently, 'You have to move now, Mr Vilakazi. You have to protect the fossil site. The authorities can do that, and if you want someone to restart what Parady began, will I fit the bill? I have some influence. I can raise money, and find trained scientists to staff the project. I can talk to people here and abroad.'

Vilakazi still hesitated, and Slocombe laid a hand on the arm of his chair. 'We owe it to Martin Parady. He found the fossil skull. It will always be his find, but now it must be properly examined and the facts recorded and presented worldwide. I will see these things are accomplished, you have my word, but on one condition. I have to see the skull and the site it came from. I have to know that they truly exist.'

'There would have to be written agreements,' Vilakazi said.

'Of course. We can discuss that with all the interested parties.'

Vilakazi got up from his chair. 'I must make a phone call.'

'Use the phone in my room,' Thorneycroft said, and Vilakazi departed, closing the door after him.

Slocombe stared after him, both hands raised heavenwards. 'My God, John, it's true, it's happening. Parady's fossil exists. You realize what this means? It confirms his belief that modern man evolved in Africa. His dream – and mine, come to that – is realized.'

'A pity he didn't live to enjoy the glory . . . and the material gain.'

'Martin wouldn't have cared about that. He lived to know he could prove his theory right. That's more to a scientist than anything else. Not many of us are privileged to establish a great truth. And I've lived to be involved, God be praised.' He smiled hugely and hauled himself to his feet. 'Can we have dinner up here? There are so many questions I have to ask Vilakazi.'

Thorneycroft went to the house phone and asked for room service.

Vilakazi appeared, wreathed in smiles. 'I will take you to the village tomorrow,' he announced. 'It is cleared with the department. They will arrange a 4x4 for us. The roads are very bad.'

Over dinner, Slocombe and Vilakazi talked without pause. Thorneycroft was silent. His mind was not on the mysteries of evolution and fossil-hunting, but on his image of Martin Parady.

Vilakazi, the man on the spot, did not think that Vaughn had posed a threat to Parady. Parady had hurried to England not to escape from Vaughn's thuggery but to start a crusade. He had not been killed because he was a quarrelsome womanizer, nor because someone hoped to steal his discovery from him.

His death was rooted in something far more profound; in that sphere where conjecture becomes ideas, and ideas theories, and theories truths with which to measure the universe.

After the meal, while the other two men argued and planned, he went to his room to put through a call to Fergus. In agreed code, he reported that Rollo's documents were safely delivered, that they had been well received by Simeon Vilakazi, and that tomorrow they would visit the place of Parady's fossil.

That message conveyed, he spoke to Claudia for a long time, about things unconnected with evolution or murder.

They left Johannesburg early the next morning, Simeon driving the Jeep, Slocombe beside him, and Thorneycroft in the rear seat.

For the first hour they followed the motorways north and west, but after that they turned on to B roads. The country was prosperous, cornland and grassland punctuated by dark stretches of fruit and timber trees. In some places they skirted industrial and mining areas.

Later the terrain became hillier and poorer. They saw thin cattle with wide-curved horns, scattered groups of mudbrick houses, and shacks of corrugated iron. About eleven they reached a wide valley cupped in a ring of rocky cliffs. In the centre of the valley lay a village where the houses looked sturdier, and there was a store, a police post, and a small church.

Vilakazi turned off the road and drew up next to the church. In the thin shade of a kirkia tree, an old man stood waiting. He came to meet the car, and Vilakazi performed introductions.

'My father, Hosea Vilakazi,' he said. 'He is the verger of this church, and the chief elder of the village.' The old man shook hands, and at once engaged his son in an altercation in their own tongue. Simeon spoke with humility, but with urgency, and after some minutes Hosea turned to Thorneycroft.

'My English is not good,' he said. 'My son says I must trust you, that you will not lie to us.' He glanced at Slocombe, held up a forearm and tapped it with gnarled fingers. 'He says you know about bones. Old bones. You were friend for Martin. I will show you the skull.'

He walked ahead of them into the church, which was little more than a shed fashioned from wood, and cement blocks. An altar of varnished pine stood at the east end, and rough benches served as seating.

Hosea signed to the visitors to sit down, and moving to the rear of the altar, he produced from under it a battered metal box. Returning, he set the box down on the bench in front of Thorneycroft, unlocked it, and lifted out an object wrapped in a piece of blanket. He peeled back the blanket.

The skull confronted them across more than 100,000 years. Its surface gleamed a dark golden brown in the uncertain light of the church. There could be no doubt that it was the origin of Parady's plaster cast.

Thorneycroft stared at it in fascinated awe, but Slocombe drew a sobbing breath and stretched out trembling hands. Hosea hesitated a moment, then lifted the skull into Slocombe's grasp. Slocombe held it tenderly, turning it this way and that, then setting it down in its woollen bed.

Thorneycroft found his voice.

'Max? Is it what you hoped?'

Slocombe nodded, his gaze still riveted on the skull. 'I think so. Yes. Yes. The cranium is long, room for a big brain. The jaw is parabolic, not squared, and the teeth are adapted to eat meat as well as leaves. The foramen is large, suggesting a spinal cord strong enough in the thoracic area to enhance breathing. It's not quite modern man, but it looks closer than Homo erectus . . . The face is flatter, you see, and there's a proper nose instead of the snouty look. But I'm just speculating. Guessing, hoping. Yet I feel sure.' He ran his hands over his face. 'God, I have so many questions. There's so much to do.'

Thorneycroft spoke quietly to Simeon. 'Who else knows about this? Have you shown it to the authorities?'

'To three only,' Simeon answered, 'on their promise of silence. But they're very impatient now.'

Slocombe gave a dry chuckle, imagining their impatience.

'The time for silence is past,' Thorneycroft said. 'The news will break in a few days . . .'

Hosea Vilakazi said sharply, 'It is not for you or my son to decide what must be done. My people will not allow the bones to be stolen from them.'

Slocombe said quickly, 'You are right, sir. Your people have a right to keep them, but it's hard to be the keeper of such an important thing as this. I can help you, I have friends who can find money to build a place for the bones, and bring men and women to look after them. But I must know exactly what Martin found. I have to see the place where he found the bones. Without that, I can't persuade others to believe what I tell them.'

Again, Hosea fell into discussion with his son. He fixed

Thorneycroft with a piercing stare. 'You can be lying to me. So many have lied to us, cheated us. Why must I trust you?' Simeon made as if to speak, and the old man lifted a hand. 'I know you believe we must move on, but what if you are wrong? What if I throw away this great chance for my people? Martin said we must keep it secret until the right time. How can I know if that time has come?' He shook his head, and his gaze swept the walls of the church, the makeshift benches and patched roof.

'God opened the place of the bones,' he said. 'He sent us Martin. I think He has sent you.'

Folding the skull in its wrapping, he settled it in its box and carried it to the altar. There he stood with head bent, hands folded in prayer.

Slocombe spoke urgently to Simeon. 'This precious thing can't remain here; it must be securely housed, and the cave must be guarded. In a few days, your village could be under siege.'

Simeon met Slocombe's eyes. 'It was brought here in a security van and it will go back the same way, to safekeeping. Martin left money for this, and he left a letter saying that the fossils must not be taken away from this village. He planned to raise money to build a proper place for the bones to rest, a place to attract tourists and to spark development throughout the area.'

'Will your government back such an enterprise?'

'One day, but not now. All the money is going to Maropeng. It's a R347 million project to create a theme park that will trace the history of earth from its beginnings; the story of our evolution, the proof of our place in the universe. It's a great project, but we can't wait for the time when it's up and running. We have to protect our fossils and make sure they aren't carried off to other places. My father is trusting you to help us in this work.'

'I'll help you all I can,' Slocombe said, 'but you must remember that I'm a foreigner in your country. There are experts here who have a far greater right than I have to decide what must be done

197

with Martin's find. Your father said three other people know about the fossil skull. Are they palaeoanthropologists?'

'No. My father wouldn't break his word to Martin, but I persuaded him to speak to people who can act to protect the cave and the fossils in it. They're on standby, if we need them.'

Slocombe nodded. 'Good. One thing I can do is raise money. I can launch an international fund, a Martin Parady Trust, that will provide whatever funds you need to develop this site as you wish. That is a promise.'

Hosea had left the altar and was carrying the box to the door of the church. Two men stood there, one of them armed with an assault rifle. Hosea handed the box to the second man, and the two moved away.

Hosea beckoned to his visitors.

'Come,' he said. 'I will take you to the cave.'

XXII

They set out in the Jeep. A rough track took them past the outskirts of the village and through a band of natural bush into a valley hemmed on three sides by jagged cliffs. There were no shacks on its slopes. A few thin cows grazed, watched by a small boy. Here and there the winter grass was starred with patches of dark green and rose pink vegetation, the liquorice plant of Inez Parady's description. From the head of the valley a stream flowed.

No one spoke. This is a sacred place, Thorneycroft thought, the burial place of the ancestors of the people, and before that of creatures long extinct. A place stretching back beyond history, beyond man, to the creation of earth and to an eternal God.

Simeon parked the Jeep on a shelf of level ground near the foot of the cliff, and lifted two battery lamps from the back. One he retained, the other he gave to his father. The party picked its way over turf strewn with rocks.

'There was a lime quarry here once,' Simeon said, 'but after the first rockfall, it became too dangerous to work it.' He led the way up a path that climbed to a narrow cleft in the rock face. Shrubs and creepers almost blocked it. 'We can get through if we crawl,' he said. 'It scratches, but at least it keeps the bats out.'

They crawled past the entanglement, Thorneycroft helping Slocombe, and found themselves in the mouth of a tunnel that angled downward into pitch darkness. Simeon and Hosea switched on their lamps, and first Thorneycroft and then Slocombe edged down a steep incline, into a cavern whose lime-encrusted walls glittered with points of red, yellow and blue fire.

Thorneycroft stared about him. The cave was far bigger than he'd expected, and its roof was in places quite low, in places lofty. To his left, the floor of the cave sloped to a pool of black water, the source perhaps of the stream they'd passed. To his right, the ground was higher, and drier, and showed the work of man.

The rock appeared to have been swept, and the loose earth and pebbles carried to one end of the cave, where large sieves had been placed. Next to the sieves were trays and boxes, neatly stacked. A pile of larger rocks lay beyond them, against the rock wall.

Directly ahead of him, illuminated by the two lamps, was a small cleared space and a gently rising shelf of rock, which was covered by a tarpaulin. Hosea stepped forward and lifted the tarpaulin, and Slocombe pressed past him and fell on his knees before the rock shelf. Thorneycroft moved to peer over his shoulder.

The lamplight fell on ridges and whorls of stone. There were no fossils visible – not so much as a chip of bone, or a loose pebble was to be seen – but Slocombe was looking up at him with unmistakable joy.

'The spinal column. It's exposed here, just a fraction.' He touched a smooth protuberance, and twisted round to address Hosea. 'The skull was separate, was it?'

'Yes,' the old man said.

Slocombe returned to his examination of the shelf, and the rock face behind and above it. At last he reached up a hand, and Thorneycroft helped him to his feet.

'Mr Vilakazi,' he said to Hosea, 'how did Martin find this place?'

Hosea shrugged. 'He came one day, he talked to me in my

house, he asked many questions. He asked if we dug lime here, if there was . . .' He glanced at his son for a word.

'Manganese,' Simeon supplied, and the old man nodded.

'Yes. That. He knew about the plants that grow here. Then he asked about old bones. I told him there were none, but he laughed and pointed to the stone by my door. It has a shell in it. Martin said it was very old. I asked him what he wanted, and he said he was looking for the first man or woman. We talked for a long time. One day I brought him up here.'

Hosea paused, looking about him. 'I have lived here all my life, but Martin told me things I did not know about these rocks, and what is in them. At first I did not believe him, but my son told me that it is true, and that Martin was a man who could bring the bones out of the rock, so that people would come and give us money to pay for houses and water tanks and a school for the children.

'So I said, "He can come". He worked here many weeks, and he found the skull. It was in five pieces, but he mended it, and he made the copy of it. When that was done, he began to work in the shelf, there. He took away loose sand and stones, very slowly, until it was as you see it. Then the man Vaughn arrived.'

'Did Vaughn speak to you?' Thorneycroft asked.

'No. Never. The sangoma in the village said Vaughn was a poisonous snake and we must have nothing to do with him. My son spoke to Martin about him, and he was sent away, out of the country. Then very soon Martin went away himself, to England. He never came back to us.'

Slocombe, who had taken a lamp and directed its beam at the roof of the cave, said, 'There are other fossils up there. They'll help us to date the rock strata.' He returned to his study of the rock shelf.

Thorneycroft looked at Simeon. 'Did Martin talk to you about his find?'

201

'He said he'd found Adam,' Simeon answered, and Thorneycroft felt a shiver go down his spine. That creatures had been trapped in the rock, like flies in amber, and a 100,000 years later brought to light again, was a concept to paralyze the mind. He felt a longing to be out in the open air, and he turned towards the tunnel, but Slocombe was before him, calling to Hosea that they couldn't stand about here, they had to talk, there was work to do, people to be consulted, they must hurry hurry hurry.

Returning to Hosea's house, they drank tea as dark as sin, ate samp and beans and the picnic the hotel had packed, and talked. It was late afternoon before they had laid a plan that met Slocombe's approval and Hosea's consent.

The sun was dipping when they said goodbye to the old man and set out for Johannesburg. Slocombe and Simeon, in the front seats of the Jeep, talked without cease, but behind them Thorneycroft sat quiet, thinking about Martin Parady, who had made the find of the century and paid for it with his life.

Over a hurried dinner, Slocombe could talk of nothing but the fossil. 'There's a chance we'll find most of the skeleton,' he said. 'That would be the ultimate prize. Hands, feet, they'd tell us so much. Simeon's promised to see the skull's stowed in the bank in the nearest town, until we can make proper arrangements. I have to speak to my colleagues here; we'll need all the pull we can muster. The cave must be guarded. I shall be up all night, making lists of people who must be involved.'

Thorneycroft cut across the flow.

'You're a religious man,' he said. 'If that fossil proves that modern man evolved 100,000 or so years ago, what happens to the Bible story? Did the earth and mankind come to being in seven days, or after myriads of evolutionary years?'

Slocombe chuckled. 'And how did the universe come about? By blind chance, or by God's will? I believe the creation of earth and mankind was indeed a miracle, but one brought about in God's time, not ours. Read Psalm 90. It says plainly that 1,000 years, in God's sight, are like a day gone by, or a watch in the night. We're finite beings. We can't envisage eternity, or timelessness. Genesis explains the creation in terms we can understand. It describes how the light came, the sky was formed, the lands and seas divided, and how the planet was clothed with plant and animal life. And over that same vast space of years, Homo sapiens evolved, by God's plan, and in God's time.'

Slocombe turned his brandy glass in his hands. 'I'm a scientist, and I also believe in God. I accept the theories of scientists, and the dogma of religious bodies. Both breeds scrabble for evidence to support their beliefs, but we can't test Christ's godhead in a laboratory, we can't reproduce the Big Bang in a test tube. In the end, we all have to seek hypotheses that go beyond the provable facts. We all have to reach for the truth by faith alone.'

He tilted his head back, studying Thorneycroft. 'I've been self-ish, exulting in the triumph of my journey, but what about yours? Have you gained anything from it, anything relating to your investigation, I mean?'

'Yes,' Thorneycroft said. 'I've learned why Parady was murdered.'

'Indeed?'

'Yes. From the start of the case, I've seen Parady as a conniving bastard who broke faith with everyone who loved him, who exploited others to achieve fame and fortune for himself. I've believed he was murdered for his faults. Now I realize I was mistaken. He was murdered for his virtues.'

'Which were?'

'He had immense skill and energy, and he poured it all into his work. Whatever else he did, he never betrayed his profession. He held to the Out of Africa theory of modern man's evolution, and he devoted himself to proving it right. He didn't give a damn for

fame or fortune. As you yourself said, his satisfaction lay in proving a theory, establishing a scientific truth. He didn't go back to
England because he was scared of Vaughn. He went back to show
the cast of the fossil to people who would recognize it for what it
was, and what it meant to the world. That's what got him killed.
Do you agree?'

Slocombe's eyes, at once bright and sad, were fixed on
Thorneycroft. 'Yes. I agree. And do you know who killed him?'

Thorneycroft set down his empty glass. 'I have a theory,' he
said. 'Now I must scrabble for the facts to prove it.'

The release of the news of Martin Parady's murder brought the
results Fergus had feared. Media interest rose to fever pitch, and
queries poured in from scientific bodies around the world. There
was also a larger than usual response from poison-pen writers,
most of whose efforts were consigned to the rubbish bin.

Voysey brought one offering to Fergus on Monday morning.
'Came in the mail,' he said. 'Forensic found no prints on it.'

The cutting in the plain envelope showed Claudia's smiling face,
but the sender had drawn a scarlet line across her throat, and
printed the words 'YOU NEXT' across the caption.

Fergus got to his feet. 'Ask Mrs Hibberd to come down,' he said.

Claudia arrived, looking anxious. 'Not John?' she said, 'not the
plane?'

'No, nothing like that, but unpleasant.' Putting a hand on her
shoulder, Fergus showed her the cutting. 'This sort of thing
happens in a lot of our cases, Clo. The freaks send us hate mail.
It's usually bluff, but we have to take every precaution. Inspector
Voysey will arrange an armed guard for you during the day, and I
will ask Molly Field to sleep at the house. She's an excellent shot.'

He saw her begin to protest and said firmly, 'No argument. Until
this case is settled, you will receive police protection, not only

because it's your right, but because you're important to us as an expert, and a key witness.'

'You won't tell John, will you? I don't want him worried.'

'I won't tell him.'

Voysey saw her back to her workroom, and Fergus made a number of phone calls. Rollo's secretary told him that Lance and Runa Vaughn were down with flu and hadn't left their penthouse for three days, and Dustin Bloom said that Evan Baldwin was 'utterly tied up in his exhibition' and hadn't stirred from the gallery.

But the Vaughns and Evan Baldwin had lackeys who could post a letter from them, in any part of the country.

The letter was postmarked Watford, which was all too close to Abbotsfell.

Fergus longed to be able to keep these people under twenty-four-hour surveillance, but he didn't have the evidence to justify such a move or the personnel to implement it.

He fumbled for a handkerchief and wiped sweat off his face.

XXIII

Thorneycroft took an early-morning flight to England on Tuesday morning, leaving Slocombe and Vilakazi to plan the defence and development of Parady's site.

Arriving at Heathrow in the late evening, he picked up his car and drove to his apartment off Victoria Street. There he dumped his suitcase, flung open windows, and put through a call to Fergus.

Fergus was surprised to hear his voice. 'You're back early. What happened? Did you check on Vaughn and Parady? Did they clash?'

'Yes. It was no contest. Parady won; the Vaughns were deported.'

'Motive for murder. What about Evan Baldwin?'

'It seems he was never in South Africa. We found Parady's site. Rollo's contact, Simeon Vilakazi, took us to the village and his father showed us the cave where the fossils are. We've seen the skull Parady found, and Slocombe believes there are other parts of the skeleton to be recovered. He says that Parady has proved that the Out of Africa theory of evolution is correct.'

'How in hell does that help us?'

'The Vilakazis confirmed that Parady returned to England to enlist support for his discovery. I think his first move would have been to visit the man who was his teacher and mentor. Adrian Baldwin.'

'Yes! Now that is interesting, because Voysey's established that Evan Baldwin was in England in April 2003, the same time Parady was here. Baldwin knew Parady. He could have arranged to meet him, killed him.'

'Why?'

'Because Vaughn told him to. Vaughn pays, Baldwin obeys.'

'There are too many gaps, Fergus. Why would Baldwin bury the body, then dig up the head and dump it on Abbotsfell tip? Where does the fossil cast fit in? I agree that Evan was an accessory after the fact, he dumped the bag on the tip, but that doesn't make him the killer. And who killed Taft?'

'Perhaps Vaughn arranged that hit. We have enough to bring Baldwin in for questioning. He lied during the first interview, you said so.'

'Yes, but . . .'

'We'll bring him in tomorrow. Right now, Voysey and I have an appointment with Bedver Smythe. He wants to set dates for the resumed inquest on Parady, and the inquest on Taft. Are you coming back here tonight?'

'No, I'll sleep over. Is Claudia there?'

'She went out with Policewoman Corbett for a meal. I'll give her your love. Oh, and while you were away, someone called Maurice Topman phoned – said he was leaving for Ireland, but he'd fax some stuff to you. He wouldn't say what.'

'Great. I'll see you tomorrow.'

Thorneycroft hurried to his study where the fax machine stood. The receiving tray was full of paper. He retrieved it and sat down to read Morrie's report.

John old chommie, you set me a rare puzzle, trying to find out about Ellie Nicholls' goings-on. I asked around my theatre mates, but those that weren't dead were short on memory. All I could get from them was that she was a good dancer and good for a laugh, which doesn't help you much.

But then I heard that she was pally with a girl named Sue Phelps who was a nurse at Paddington Hospital, and after a bit of bribery and corruption I got Ms Phelps's address. She lives in a basement pad in Maida Vale, with a cat named Goofy and about a thousand photographs.

We had a nice chat over tea with a slug of rum and it turned out Ms Phelps knew all about Ellie and her good friend Mortimer Taft. Ellie had a son born at Paddington H. christened William. When Ellie finally married Mortimer they took Will off to Bath as their legit son.

Well, I thought that would be what you wanted to hear and I was ready to leave, but after the second tea-and-it, Ms Phelps revealed that Will was Ellie's second child. Before she met Mortimer she had a daughter by a male nurse at Pad Hosp, and it seems he was the real love of her life, because when Taft wasn't in town, Ryan Brady was the man who came around. He couldn't marry Ellie because he was a Catholic and married to a woman in Knebworth. The daughter's name was Miranda and she was a tartar to Ellie, but good with her dad, and William adored her, never let her out of his sight.

Ms Phelps showed me a photo of Ellie with Miranda and William. Looked happy, all of them, but it seems Mortimer wouldn't have Miranda within a yard of him, and when he married Ellie he took William with them, but Miranda was sent to live with Brady and his wife. That went okay for almost seven years, then Ryan got himself killed. He was a biker, owned a Harley-Davidson, and a heavy truck collected him and killed him outright.

Mrs Brady refused to keep Miranda, said she was sick of her tempers, so the kid went into care, and then to a children's home. She did all right, got her A levels and trained as a masseuse in Cambridge.

She married one of the professors there, name of Adrian Baldwin.

After she married, Miranda broke with her old pals, Ms Phelps included. But a few years later, while Ms Phelps was still working at Pad Hosp, a young doctor turned up, said he was William Taft, Miranda's half-brother, and wanted to get in touch with her. Phelps told him what she told me, and warned him, he'd not get far with Mrs Baldwin, Marian as she called herself, because she did not want anything to do with her old life.

Willam said he'd give it a go, and Phelps asked him to let her know how he got on, but she never heard from him. End of story.

That's all I can tell you, mate. Don't forget you owe me a crate of beer when I get back from Ireland. Amstel's my preference. Good luck with your chase, you nosey chancer.

Love,

Morrie

Thorneycroft grabbed the telephone. Fergus's mobile number didn't respond. Probably Bedver Smythe banned mobiles in his presence. Thorneycroft rang the Abbotsfell station and was connected with Voysey.

'There've been developments,' Thorneycroft said. 'Maurice Topman sent me a report. He's hit pay-dirt. A reliable witness told him that Ellie Nicholls who married Mortimer Taft had an illegitimate daughter, Miranda, two years before she met Taft. The father was a married man named Ryan Brady.'

'Wait,' Voysey said. 'I'll record, for the Chief.'

The recorder was switched on and Thorneycroft continued.

'When Mortimer married Ellie, he accepted William as his son, but wouldn't take Miranda. William loved her and he loved the girl's father. Being torn away from them at the age of five was traumatic. It conditioned his life.

'The girl was fostered by Brady and his wife. William lost touch with her, but as an adult he traced her. She was now married to Professor Adrian Baldwin, and calling herself Marian.'

Thorneycroft paused, and Voysey said excitedly, 'That's the link we've been looking for. William and Marian are half-brother and -sister. All one happy family.'

'Not happy,' Thorneycroft said. 'William tried to make it so, but Marian would have none of him. However, my guess is that he kept tabs on her son, met him whenever possible, and fostered his career. I think the £100,000 he withdrew from his investments went into some sort of trust for Evan Baldwin. Paid for his training, launched him as a painter.

'Martin Parady came to the Baldwins' house. Adrian was his patron. Again I'm guessing, but I think he fathered Evan. You remember that there was a rumour that while he was at Cambridge, Parady had an affair with a professor's wife? Max Slocombe and Professor Brink both told me the story was idle gossip. But what if Parady did knock up Marian and then desert her, what if Adrian Baldwin married her and gave the child his name? Wouldn't Slocombe and Brink, as his closest friends, do all they could to quash the scandal?'

'Yeah, that's right. So Evan had two motives to kill Parady: one was Parady cheated on his mother, and two, Vaughn would pay him good money to do the job.'

'I'm not sure Evan knows that Parady sired him,' Thorneycroft said. 'He shows no animosity against Parady.'

'He's our man,' Voysey insisted. 'He's lied to us; he swore he never met Taft, said he'd never been to Abbotsfell. I reckon he threw that bag on the tip. And Taft knew it, Taft knew Evan was in Abbotsfell about the time the bag was dumped. Taft saw Evan with the bag. That's what he remembered, and wouldn't tell us.'

'That's speculation. I don't think Baldwin's the killer.'

'It's a possible explanation, isn't it? When Taft learned that the murder victim was Martin Parady, he saw the connection between the Baldwins and Parady. He guessed Evan killed Parady, and he warned Marian that her boy was in big trouble. So what did she do, she warned Evan, and he decided he'd have to shut Taft's mouth. When we questioned him about Taft, he was downright flaky, you have to admit.'

'That could be because he loved Taft. Taft was his benefactor.'

'Evan Baldwin's a cold bugger that doesn't know the meaning of love. This is great stuff, John. I'll tell the Chief. He'll be back in ten minutes, and we can pull Baldwin in for further questioning. That's if he doesn't bolt. I'll get the London lads to check on him.'

'I'm in London,' Thorneycroft said. 'I'll go. Save time. I'll call you.' He picked up Maurice's report, folded it into his pocket, and ran down to his car.

The Alessandri Gallery was closed for the night, but the windows on the upper floor were lit. Thorneycroft pressed the door button marked Bloom and gave his name to a voice box. The door clicked and he entered the building.

Lights guided him through a tiled hall and up carpeted stairs. He stepped into a living-room where much of the furniture was made of glass. A figure in a blue caftan rose from a cushioned dais and swam towards him.

'Dr Thorneycroft. What a pleasant surprise.' Dustin Bloom's regard was glassy, his smile too fixed for comfort. Drink or cocaine, Thorneycroft wondered, and brushed the outstretched hand.

'I'm sorry to disturb you,' he said. 'I'm looking for Evan Baldwin. Is he here?'

'I fear not.' Bloom's eyes wandered over Thorneycroft as if trying to assess his weight. 'Evan should paint you. You are a tiger, beautiful but dangerous.'

'Where is Evan, do you know?'

Bloom waved thin fingers. 'Gone. He drove off an hour ago, in a great rush.'

'Did he have luggage with him?'

'I didn't notice.'

'Did he say where he was going?'

'No, and I didn't ask. Would you like a drnk? Whisky, gin, what's your choice?'

'Nothing, thanks.' Thorneycroft stepped closer to Bloom. 'I have to talk to Evan. It's extremely urgent. Is he planning to leave the country?'

Bloom stared. 'God, no. His exhibition doesn't end until Sunday.'

'Has he gone to visit his mother?'

'He may have, but I do urge you not to try to storm that citadel. Mummy Baldwin might pour boiling oil on you. She's a jealous bitch, I know from experience.'

'Perhaps,' said Thorneycroft baldly, 'she thinks your interest in her son is purely commercial.'

Bloom stiffened, and the smile faded from his face. 'You're right about me,' he said softly. 'I'm gay, I'm greedy, and I do drugs. But you're wrong about Evan. He's straight, he's a great painter and a true friend. When he's in England he spends time with me because he knows that helps me. He never lets me down. He never lets anyone down. You have the wrong picture of him, if you think otherwise. Now I'd like you to get the hell out of here.'

Thorneycroft left the gallery with a coldness in his mind. Bloom was right. Evan Baldwin did not fit the profile of the killer. It was likely he was an accessory to the murder of Parady. He'd dumped the kit-bag and its gruesome contents on Abbotsfell tip. He'd lied about his acquaintance with William Taft. He'd taken Vaughn's money for his paintings and slept with Vaughn's wife, but there was nothing to suggest he was the violent psychotic who'd crushed

Parady's skull and blown out Taft's brains.

Reaching his car, Thorneycroft stood still. Something was nagging at his memory. The Yamaha in the Baldwins' garage was licensed to Evan. He'd linked it in his mind to the photograph in Marian Baldwin's lounge, the picture of a man astride a bike, with a blonde leaning against him. Not a Yamaha bike. Something much more splendid. He strained to recall the details of the photo. A Harley-Davidson, of a date long past. The rider not Evan. The blonde not his girlfriend.

Thorneycroft climbed into the Rover and called Fergus. The line was engaged. He tried again and got through. Fergus sounded anxious. 'I've been trying to reach you,' he said. 'Voysey's brought me up to speed. Where are you?'

'At the Alessandri Gallery. According to Bloom, Evan left here an hour ago. He may have headed for his mother's house in Simnell.'

'Yes. I've organized for the local plods to go round there and watch the house until back-up gets there.'

'Armed back-up and a trained negotiator?'

'Armed, but the only negotiator in Cambridge is working on a bank hold-up, seven hostages taken.'

Thorneycroft swore. 'By now Baldwin's already in the house. I'll get there as fast as I can. If the back-up hasn't arrived, I'll try to negotiate. Tell them they're dealing with a psycho.'

'You think Baldwin's likely to kill his own mother?'

'She's the one who rides the Yamaha, Fergus. I think she's likely to kill him.'

When Thorneycroft reached the ring road, a traffic cop on a motorbike flagged him down.

'Chief Inspector Lowry fixed for me to escort you to Simnell,' he said. 'Follow me.'

They travelled at speed, siren whining, but at the outskirts of

Simnell the speed-cop turned away, and Thorneycroft drove quietly through the sleeping village. He left the Rover at the mouth of the Baldwins' lane, and went forward on foot.

The house showed lights in the front rooms and over the front door. Evan Baldwin's Mercedes was parked on the verge by the main gate, and as Thorneycroft approached, a uniformed police-man stepped from the shadows and addressed him.

'Dr Thorneycroft? Sergeant Hubble, sir.'

Thorneycroft nodded, scanning the façade of the house. 'Is Baldwin inside?'

'Yes. We got here too late to stop him. She's been yelling at him non-stop.'

They could hear her, a voice that pierced the silence of the night, rising at times to a shriek. Thorneycroft considered Hubble: middle-aged and corpulent, but sensible-looking.

'How many of you are here?' he asked.

'Just me and Constable Pritchard, sir. He's round the back. The Cambridge detail's on the way, another quarter of an hour, they reckon. Pritchard's got the radio in the car; he'll give us warning. I got up close to the house and took a look through that middle window – the curtain's not quite closed. Mrs Baldwin's got a gun on him. He's sitting on the sofa, over to the left, and she's walk-ing up and down. Sounds like she's preaching at him. I heard her say he must repent of his sins. She's a right nutter, if you ask me, specially lately.'

'Has she shown this sort of behaviour before?'

'Well, after her husband died, she had kind of a breakdown. Real attached to him, she was, and couldn't seem to accept he'd gone. Blamed everyone from here to Land's End for his death, though we all knew he was a very sick man.'

At this moment, a man's voice sounded inside the house, and the woman's shriek rose to drown it.

'At least he's still alive,' Hubble said, and Thorneycroft nodded.

'Yes, but he shouldn't argue with her.' He came to a decision. Reaching for his mobile phone, he said, 'I'm going to move in closer, and try to speak to her.'

Hubble looked alarmed. 'Might just tip her over the edge.'

'She's already over it. She could pull the trigger any moment.'

'I doubt she'll answer you.'

Thorneycroft smiled grimly. 'Few women can ignore a ringing phone,' he said. 'If I can persuade her to let me into the house, I may be able to keep her talking until back-up comes. You get round to Pritchard, and tell him to put Cambridge and Abbotsfell in the picture. Then come back here and wait for the cavalry to arrive. I hope they're quiet about it.'

Hubble circled away, and Thorneycroft trod softly over the lawn towards the front door. He could hear Marian Baldwin clearly now, the phrases repeated over and over in a monotonous diatribe. He crouched in the shadow of the front porch, and called up the Baldwins' number from the mobile's memory bank. He punched it in, and heard the phone begin to ring inside the house. It rang for some time, then stopped. Thorneycroft tried a second time, and the phone was answered at once.

'What do you want?' The voice was savage with rage.

Thorneycroft spoke quietly. 'Mrs Adrian Baldwin?'

He heard a long-drawn breath, then she answered. 'Adrian Baldwin is dead.'

'Men like him never die,' Thorneycroft said. 'Their work lives after them.'

There was silence, then she said, 'Who are you?'

'John Thorneycroft, and I have a message for you, from an old friend of Adrian's. Max Slocombe. You remember Max?'

'I remember Max.' She sounded wary. Thorneycroft waited, and eventually she spoke. 'What message?'

'Max and I have been to South Africa,' he said. 'We went to test a claim about a fossil find. It could confirm the theory of the

215

evolution of modern man. We learned—'

She cut him short. 'One theory only. One theory. Multi-national, Adrian said. Multi-national. Max didn't believe him. Max was against, always against.'

'He's changed his mind.' Thorneycroft prayed that he sounded sincere. 'His message to you is that Adrian was right and Martin Parady was wrong.'

She was silent, and it was more frightening than her speech. Suddenly she chuckled.

'Max said that? Changed his stupid mind! What made him change his stupid mind?'

'Martin Parady found a fossil in Africa,' Thorneycroft said. 'He thought he'd found a new species that proved him right. But Max has examined the fossil, and he says Parady was mistaken.'

He heard her muttering to herself and he wondered how much of the palaeo jargon she recalled; how much his words meant to her.

Waiting, he strained his ears for the sound of motor engines, some sign that the back-up was near, but there was nothing.

Marian Baldwin spoke suddenly, her voice sharp. 'I know who you are. You're a policeman.'

'I'm a doctor.' Thorneycroft kept his voice quiet and steady. 'I've come here because I want to talk to you. I want to help restore your husband's reputation. Please let me in.'

She gave a long sigh. 'There's a panel beside the door. Press the top button.'

He did as she bid, and stepped into the hall. A door to his left led to a formal lounge, not the room where he and Claudia had met Marian Baldwin. On the far side of the room, Evan Baldwin sat on a sofa. His mother stood behind him, and held a handgun pressed to his head. She beckoned, and Thorneycroft stepped forward slowly, hands held clear of his body. She signed to him to sit next to her son.

He sat, and felt the muzzle of the gun brush the nape of his neck. Marian moved round to face him and he saw that the time for reason was past.

The pleasant countrywoman of his first visit had disappeared. Her face was swollen and flushed, her eyes red-veined, and her mouth moved continuously, twisting and jerking. She leaned towards him.

'Why didn't Max come himself?'

'He's still in Africa. He said I must be sure to tell you that Parady was wrong and Adrian was right.'

Her face contorted. 'What good is that now? Adrian's dead. The shock killed him. That liar and cheat killed him.'

'Tell us about it. Evan and I need to know the truth from you. We'll listen quietly, if you'll tell us what happened.'

She backed away, frowning. 'I don't remember. I don't want to remember.' She rubbed her free hand over her mouth and he saw that under her anger lay grief and a gnawing fear.

'It's all right,' he said. 'Everything is all right. Martin is gone; he'll never trouble you again. Tell us what happened and then it will be finished for good.'

She blinked, as if she was focusing on an inner vision. 'He came here,' she said. 'It was late. Adrian had had a bad day and I was tired. Tired from looking after him. Then Martin came.'

'Unannounced?'

'Yes. Just a knock on the door and there he was. I told him over and over I didn't want him in the house but he never took any notice. He came, and Adrian let him come.'

'That night, he came to show Adrian something, did he?'

'Yes. A plaster head. He showed it to Adrian. He said he'd found fossils in a cave. A new species, he said. Adrian looked at the thing and it upset him, he was pale and shaking. I tried to take it away from him but he wouldn't let me. He was talking to Martin, asking him questions. They talked and talked as if I wasn't there.'

'I could see it was bad for Adrian. I was frightened for him. I said to Martin, "Get away from here, you're making Adrian ill. He can't be ill, he's giving an important lecture next week." Martin said, "That's why I've come. He can't make the lecture, he can't make a fool of himself. He understands that I've come as a friend."

'I tried to push Martin away and Adrian told me not to. Adrian took Martin's side. I hated Martin. I hated him. I picked up a candlestick and I hit him. He fell down. Adrian tried to get out of his chair, but he couldn't. He couldn't move or talk; he couldn't breathe.'

Marian broke off, her voice dropping to a mumble. She seemed to have forgotten where she was. Thorneycroft moved forward a trifle, and at once she stiffened and levelled the gun at his chest. He sat still.

'Did you take him to hospital?' he said.

'Yes, but he died. Two days later, he died.' She rocked from side to side. 'It was Martin's fault. Martin killed him.'

'Martin's fault,' agreed Thorneyfcroft. 'So what did you do with him?'

Her mouth closed tightly. Thorneycroft smiled at her.

'Is it a secret? Let me guess. You put him in the flower-bed, in the trench you'd dug for the sweet peas. And that was the end of that.'

She watched him, head lowered. The room was quiet. Nothing moved in the garden outside, but far down the road a dog barked, the high, loud barking of a watchdog disturbed.

'Not the end,' Marian said. 'He wouldn't go away. He watched me. I couldn't get away from him. I had to get rid of him, once and for all.'

'So you dug him up.'

'Yes. I was going to finish him, you see, but this fool stopped me.' She swung to face Evan. 'I told him to put the bag somewhere safe. He agreed. I thought it was over but it wasn't.'

218

She swung the gun towards Evan. 'You should have destroyed him,' she said. 'But you left him for the police to find. You cheated me. You took his side.'

'No.' Evan spoke for the first time, and with fury. 'I protected you. I lied to protect you. But you killed Uncle Will; you shot him like a dog.'

'He was a dog.' She was screaming again, and her feet began to stamp and shuffle. 'He was the lucky dog; he got everything. My mother took him and left me with nothing.'

'Will loved you,' Evan shouted. 'He always loved you, and you killed him.'

Evan was rising to his feet, and Marian sprang forward, levelling the gun. Thorneycroft launched himself at her, knocking her arm sideways, grappling her to the ground. The gun went off and Evan screamed. Thorneycroft had Marian pinned, but she fought him like a wolverine and the gun went off a second time. There was an explosion that seemed to be inside his own head, and he spun into blackness.

There were too many people in the room. He tried to sit up and an arm pressed him back. A male voice said, 'Lie still, take your time.'

Stun grenade, he thought, and turned his head. A man was bending over Evan, cutting away his trouser leg. Leg wound was better than dead. He looked for the woman and saw her between two men, on the far side of the room. Handcuffed, thank God. So was he. Standard stungun procedure.

He sat up and said, 'I'm OK. Get me up.'

Hands heaved him to his feet and lowered him into a chair. He put his hands to his head. No blood. The fuzziness eased and he took deep breaths. A man in a jumpsuit watched him.

'Mrs Baldwin killed Martin Parady and William Taft,' Thorneycroft told him.

The man had a blackened face and a white smile. 'She's under arrest,' he said. 'We've informed Abbotsfell that we'll be taking her to the psychiatric ward, under guard.'

'What about her son, Evan Baldwin?'

'Also to hospital, under guard. Your chief's request.'

'I'll follow them,' Thorneycroft said.

His identity and probity confirmed, he was uncuffed and allowed to telephone Fergus. Mrs Baldwin was loaded into a police car, and Evan into an ambulance, and Thorneycroft joined the procession into Cambridge.

Evan was admitted to theatre for treatment to his leg wound. Mrs Baldwin was heavily sedated, and a policewoman was stationed to watch her. Thorneycroft was given a bed for what was left of the night, but didn't sleep.

Fergus and Voysey arrived at the hospital at eight o'clock next morning to arrest Marian Baldwin. The resident psychiatrist had already examined her and pronounced her mentally ill.

'The magistrate will refer her to a mental institution for observation,' Fergus said, 'and there's a good chance she'll be found unfit to plead. Best thing, in the circumstances.'

On that, there was common agreement, but dealing with Evan Baldwin was less straightforward.

'He's an accessory after the fact of Parady's murder,' Voysey insisted. 'He withheld information, he obstructed the course of justice. The law has to take its course.'

'The law requires us to question him,' Fergus said.

Voysey wasn't mollified. 'His own mother admits he disposed of a murdered man's skull.'

'She also attempted to shoot him dead. We'll listen to what he has to say.'

Cautioned, Evan said he did not require the presence of his lawyer.

'I should have spoken earlier,' he said, 'but at first I didn't realize . . . and later, I couldn't because she is my mother. I didn't know what to do . . .'

'Start at the beginning,' Fergus said.

Evan looked as if he wasn't sure when that was. He said slowly, 'She's always been bolshie. She's had a lot to bear, but she loved my dad and she hated Martin Parady. That's always been the way of it.'

'Do you know why she hated Parady?' Thorneycroft asked.

Evan regarded him steadily. 'No, I don't.'

You know, Thorneycroft thought, but you're never going to say. Adrian was and always will be your father.

'Martin should never have come to our house,' Evan went on, 'but he and my dad were close. It was their work. Fossils. They lived in a different world. I'm sure that when Martin came that last time, it was because he wanted to share his discovery with my father, and warn him that the Out of Africa theory was going to be proved beyond doubt. My mother didn't understand that. She just saw that what Martin said was bad for my dad, and she lost her temper and lashed out at Martin. Seeing her do that killed my father.'

'Do you know where she disposed of Parady's body?'

Evan shook his head dumbly, and Fergus said, 'It was probably somewhere on the property. We'll start the search tomorrow. Do you know when and why she exhumed the head?'

Evan eased himself higher on his pillows. 'A year after my father died,' he said, 'I came back to England from Australia. My mother was having a clear-out – she'd thrown away a lot of junk – and when I walked into the house she was sitting in the kitchen. The skull, and the plaster cast, were on the table. She told me someone had sent them to my father. I believed her. People do send queer things to palaeoanthropologists.

'Mother said it was rubbish and she hated it – I must get rid of it for her. I said I would. I packed the things in a bag from the attic. I wiped everything clean and wrapped it carefully, because I felt kind of guilty, throwing out what someone else might value.

'A couple of days later, I went to Abbotsfell to see Uncle Will. I thought I'd show the things to him, see what he advised, but on the way I decided my mother wouldn't like that. She never wanted me to take Will's advice. So when I got to his house, I just let him think it was my gear in the bag. When I left him, I chucked the bag on to a truck that was taking stuff up to the tip.

'I forgot all about it. But then there was the storm, and the bag turned up, and there was talk that it could be a case of murder. I was worried, and scared. Not that I suspected my mother. I never thought she could do such a thing, but I did think someone else could have sent the skull to my dad, palming off a victim's head on us. So I just kept quiet.

'It was only when they said the skull was Martin Parady's that I thought my mother could be involved. I still couldn't talk because . . . well . . . she's my mother. I kept hoping you'd find some solution, one that let her out.'

Evan halted, swallowing tears. 'If I'd spoken, Uncle Will would be alive. When he was shot, I knew she'd done it. She kept phoning me, telling me I must come to Simnell, we must talk. I never went. I couldn't stand to be near her, and yet I . . . I couldn't turn her in. Until last night. She phoned me and I could tell she was crazy. I knew I had to talk to her, persuade her to see a doctor or something. I drove out to Simnell.

'As soon as I walked into the house, she pulled a gun on me. She called me a fool, a traitor, she said I loved Uncle Will more than I loved her. I just sat still and waited for her to kill me.' He looked at Thorneycroft. 'If you hadn't come, I'd be dead.'

The tears overflowed. He put an arm across his eyes and wept.

Fergus and Voysey stayed long enough to lay formal charges

against Marian and Evan Baldwin, and then set out for Abbotsfell, to begin the much greater task of building cases that would stand up in court.

Thorneycroft returned to his flat in London, to collect his baggage and make two phone calls.

The first was to Max Slocombe, who was shocked to hear of Marian's situation, but whose main concern was for Evan.

'There's no vice in him,' he maintained. 'He's not violent, he's not a liar.'

Thorneycroft agreed. 'His story was weird, but I think it was the truth.'

'So what will become of him? He can't go to jail.'

'With a good defence lawyer, he'll probably get off lightly. He knows his delays may have cost William Taft his life. That's punishment enough, in my view.'

Thorneycroft cut short Slocombe's rhapsodies about the way events were shaping in South Africa, and phoned Claudia.

'Are you all right, love?' he said. 'Fergus told me you had hate mail.'

'I'm fine.' Her voice wavered, and rose. 'You had no right to go into that madwoman's house. She might have killed you.'

'She's in custody. She'll be cared for. It's all over now, I promise.'

Claudia gulped. 'She seemed such a pleasant woman. How could she have been so violent?'

'Paranoid insanity,' Thorneycroft said. The real answer was much more profound; the twists of fate that built resentment into an all-consuming rage that demanded blood.

'Are you still there?' Claudia said. 'How was Africa?'

'Amazing. Wonderful. A journey across a a hundred thousand years in a few hours. It made me understand what people mean when they say "time out of mind".'

'Tell me about it.'

'The moment I see you. This afternoon.'

'What will you do now?'

'Help Fergus as long as he needs me, but I still have a few days' leave left. I thought of going to France. I wondered. . . ?'

He hesitated, afraid to speak.

'John,' Claudia said, 'if you still want to marry me, why in hell don't you say so?'

Thorneycroft said so.